PRAISE FOR J. R. WARD AND HER BLACK DAGGER BROTHERHOOD SERIES

'Frighteningly ad

Publishers Wee

'J. R. Ward is the undisputed queen of
her genre . . . Long live the queen'

Steve Berry, *New York Times* bestselling author

'J. R. Ward is a master!'

Gena Showalter, *New York Times* bestselling author

'Ward brings on the big feels'

Booklist

'Fearless storytelling. A league all of her own'

Kristen Ashley, *New York Times* bestselling author

'J. R. Ward is one of the finest writers
out there—in any genre'

Sarah J. Maas, #1 *New York Times* bestselling author

'Ward is a master of her craft'

New York Journal of Books

J. R. Ward lives in the South with her incredibly supportive husband and her beloved golden retriever. After graduating from law school, she began working in health care in Boston and spent many years as chief of staff for one of the premier academic medical centres in the nation.

Visit J. R. Ward online:

www.jrward.com
www.facebook.com/JRWardBooks
@jrward1

By J. R. Ward

The Black Dagger Brotherhood series:
Dark Lover
Lover Eternal
Lover Awakened
Lover Revealed
Lover Unbound
Lover Enshrined
Lover Avenged
Lover Mine
Lover Unleashed
Lover Reborn
Lover at Last
The King
The Shadows
The Beast
The Chosen
The Thief
The Savior
The Sinner
Lover Unveiled
Lover Arisen
Lassiter
Darius
The Beloved

The Black Dagger Brotherhood:
An Insider's Guide

The Black Dagger Brotherhood:
Prison Camp
The Jackal
The Wolf
The Viper

The Black Dagger Brotherhood World:
Dearest Ivie*
Prisoner of Night*
Where Winter Finds You
A Warm Heart in Winter
A Bloom in Winter

The Black Dagger Legacy series:
Blood Kiss
Blood Vow
Blood Fury
Blood Truth

The Lair of the Wolven series:
Claimed
Forever
Mine

Novels of the Fallen Angels:
Covet
Crave
Envy
Rapture
Possession
Immortal

The Bourbon Kings series:
The Bourbon Kings
The Angels' Share
Devil's Cut

Firefighters Series:
The Wedding From Hell:
The Rehearsal Dinner*
The Wedding From Hell:
The Reception*
Consumed

*ebook novella

A
BLOOM
IN
WINTER

THE BLACK DAGGER BROTHERHOOD SERIES

J. R. WARD

PIATKUS

PIATKUS

First published in the US in 2024 by Gallery Books,
An imprint of Simon & Schuster, LLC
Published in Great Britain in 2024 by Piatkus

1 3 5 7 9 10 8 6 4 2

A CIP catalogue record for this book
is available from the British Library.

ISBN 978-0-349-43068-3

Printed and bound in Great Britain by Clays Ltd, Elcograf S.p.A.

Papers used by Piatkus are from well-managed forests
and other responsible sources.

MIX
Paper | Supporting
responsible forestry
FSC® C104740

Piatkus
An imprint of
Little, Brown Book Group
Carmelite House
50 Victoria Embankment
London EC4Y 0DZ

An Hachette UK Company
www.hachette.co.uk

www.littlebrown.co.uk

To the pair of you.
True love blooms eternal,
no matter the season.

GLOSSARY OF TERMS
AND PROPER NOUNS

ahstrux nohtrum (n.) Private guard with license to kill who is granted his or her position by the King.

ahvenge (v.) Act of mortal retribution, carried out typically by a male loved one.

Black Dagger Brotherhood (pr. n.) Highly trained vampire warriors who protect their species against the Lessening Society. As a result of selective breeding within the race, Brothers possess immense physical and mental strength, as well as rapid healing capabilities. They are not siblings for the most part, and are inducted into the Brotherhood upon nomination by the Brothers. Aggressive, self-reliant, and secretive by nature, they are the subjects of legend and objects of reverence within the vampire world.

They may be killed only by the most serious of wounds, e.g., a gunshot or stab to the heart, etc.

blood slave (n.) Male or female vampire who has been subjugated to serve the blood needs of another. The practice of keeping blood slaves has been outlawed.

the Chosen (pr. n.) Female vampires who had been bred to serve the Scribe Virgin. In the past, they were spiritually rather than temporally focused, but that changed with the ascendance of the final Primale, who freed them from the Sanctuary. With the Scribe Virgin removing herself from her role, they are completely autonomous and learning to live on earth. They do continue to meet the blood needs of unmated members of the Brotherhood, as well as Brothers who cannot feed from their *shellans* or injured fighters.

chrih (n.) Symbol of honorable death in the Old Language.

cohntehst (n.) Conflict between two males competing for the right to be a female's mate.

Dhunhd (pr. n.) Hell.

doggen (n.) Member of the servant class within the vampire world. *Doggen* have old, conservative traditions about service to their superiors, following a formal code of dress and behavior. They are able to go out during the day, but they age relatively quickly. Life expectancy is approximately five hundred years.

ehros (n.) A Chosen trained in the matter of sexual arts.

exhile dhoble (n.) The evil or cursed twin, the one born second.

the Fade (pr. n.) Non-temporal realm where the dead reunite with their loved ones and pass eternity.

First Family (pr. n.) The King and Queen of the vampires, and any children they may have.

ghardian (n.) Custodian of an individual. There are varying degrees of *ghardians*, with the most powerful being that of a *sehcluded* female.

glymera (n.) The social core of the aristocracy, roughly equivalent to Regency England's *ton*.

hellren (n.) Male vampire who has been mated to a female. Males may take more than one female as mate.

hyslop (n. or v.) Term referring to a lapse in judgment, typically resulting in the compromise of the mechanical operations of a vehicle or otherwise motorized conveyance of some kind. For example, leaving one's keys in one's car as it is parked outside the family home overnight, whereupon said vehicle is stolen.

leahdyre (n.) A person of power and influence.

leelan (adj. or n.) A term of endearment loosely translated as "dearest one."

Lessening Society (pr. n.) Order of slayers convened first by the Omega, and now by his son, for the purpose of eradicating the vampire species.

lesser (n.) De-souled human who targets vampires for extermination as a member of the Lessening Society. *Lessers* must be stabbed through the chest in order to be killed; otherwise they are ageless. They do not eat or drink and are impotent. Over time, their hair, skin, and irises lose pigmentation until they are blond, blushless, and pale eyed. They smell like baby powder. Now inducted into the society by the Omega's son, they no longer keep jars for their hearts, as they did in the past. Women now may be inducted.

lewlhen (n.) Gift.

lheage (n.) A term of respect used by a sexual submissive to refer to their dominant.

Lhenihan (pr. n.) A mythic beast renowned for its sexual prowess. In modern slang, refers to a male of preternatural size and sexual stamina.

lys (n.) Torture tool used to remove the eyes.

mahmen (n.) Mother. Used both as an identifier and a term of affection.

mhis (n.) The masking of a given physical environment; the creation of a field of illusion.

nalla (n., f.) or *nallum* (n., m.) Beloved.

needing period (n.) Female vampire's time of fertility, generally lasting for two days and accompanied by intense sexual cravings. Occurs approximately five years after a female's transition and then once a decade thereafter. All males respond to some degree if they are around a female in her need. It can be a dangerous time, with conflicts and fights breaking out between competing males, particularly if the female is not mated.

newling (n.) A virgin.

the Omega (pr. n.) Malevolent, mystical figure who previously targeted the vampires for extinction out of resentment directed toward the Scribe Virgin. Existed in a non-temporal realm and had extensive powers, though not the power of creation. Now eradicated, and replaced by his son, Lash.

phearsom (adj.) Term referring to the potency of a male's sexual organs. Literal translation something close to "worthy of entering a female."

Princeps (pr. n.) Highest level of the vampire aristocracy, second only to members of the First Family or the Scribe Virgin's Chosen. Must be born to the title; it may not be conferred. Have been outlawed by royal decree, but underground factions do exist.

pyrocant (n.) Refers to a critical weakness in an individual. The weakness can be internal, such as an addiction, or external, such as a lover.

rahlman (n.) Savior.

rythe (n.) Ritual manner of asserting honor granted by one who has offended another. If accepted, the offended chooses a weapon and strikes the offender, who presents him- or herself without defenses.

the Scribe Virgin (pr. n.) Mystical force who previously was counselor to the King as well as the keeper of vampire archives and the dispenser of privileges. Existed in a non-temporal realm and had extensive powers, but stepped down and gave her station to another. Capable of a single act of creation, which she expended to bring the vampires into existence.

sehclusion (n.) Status conferred by the King upon a female of the aristocracy as a result of a petition by the female's family. Places the female under the sole direction of her *ghardian*, typically the eldest male in her household. Her *ghardian* then has the legal right to determine all manner of her life, restricting at will any and all interactions she has with the world.

shellan (n.) Female vampire who has been mated to a male. Females generally do not take more than one mate due to the highly territorial nature of bonded males.

symphath (n.) Subspecies within the vampire race characterized by the ability and desire to manipulate emotions in others (for the purposes of an energy exchange), among other traits. Historically, they have been discriminated against and, during certain eras, hunted by vampires.

talhman (n.) The evil side of an individual. A dark stain on the soul that requires expression if it is not properly expunged.

the Tomb (pr. n.) Sacred vault of the Black Dagger Brotherhood. Used as a ceremonial site and, previously, the storage facility for the jars of *lessers*. Ceremonies performed there include inductions, funerals, and disciplinary actions against Brothers. No one may enter except for members of the Brotherhood, the Scribe Virgin's successor, or candidates for induction.

trahyner (n.) Word used between males of mutual respect and affection. Translated loosely as "beloved friend."

transition (n.) Critical moment in a vampire's life

xiv   GLOSSARY OF TERMS AND PROPER NOUNS

when he or she transforms into an adult. Thereafter, he or she must drink the blood of the opposite sex to survive and is unable to withstand sunlight. Occurs generally in the mid-twenties. Some vampires do not survive their transitions, males in particular. Prior to their transitions, vampires are physically weak, sexually unaware and unresponsive, and unable to dematerialize.

vampire (n.) Member of a species separate from that of *Homo sapiens*. Vampires must drink the blood of the opposite sex to survive. Human blood will keep them alive, though the strength does not last long. Following their transitions, which occur in their mid-twenties, they are unable to go out into sunlight and must feed from the vein regularly. Vampires cannot "convert" humans through a bite or transfer of blood, though they are in rare cases able to breed with the other species. Vampires can dematerialize at will, though they must be able to calm themselves and concentrate to do so and may not carry anything heavy with them. They are able to strip the memories of humans, provided such memories are short-term. Some vampires are able to read minds. Life expectancy is upward of a thousand years, or in some cases, even longer.

wahlker (n.) An individual who has died and returned to the living from the Fade. They are accorded great respect and are revered for their travails.

whard (n.) Equivalent of a godfather or godmother to an individual.

PROLOGUE

Thirty-three years ago . . .
Bloomin' Buds Flower Shop
Connelly, New York

E very night."

Frowning, Milly Trumble put her purse down by the cash register and rubbed her sunburned shoulder. "Every night?"

Her best friend, Judy Descartes, nodded and stepped back to inspect the bouquet of red roses she was arranging on the counter. At the age of fifty-two, the woman had a cap of gray hair, an apron with ivy appliqué on it, and the direct manner of someone who'd raised four boys in a three-bedroom house with a husband who worked for the fire department.

"Yup, he started right after you flew out. He comes five minutes before closing and buys one white flower. Other than that, everything was business as usual—"

"One flower?"

"Yup, and he pays with a ten-dollar bill and leaves the change." Judy put her hand out. "Could you pass me the baby's breath?"

Milly glanced around at the shelves full of windowsill plants, scented candles, and cards for all occasions. Then she checked on the glass-fronted walk-in that was stocked with buckets of roses in different colors, as well as carnations and various other blooms. Nothing was out of place, and there were receipts overflowing the in-basket, all ready for her to go through.

"Will you stop." Judy blew a wisp of hair out of her face. "Did you think I was gonna burn the place down in the last week?"

"Of course not."

Judy waved a hand toward the pile of baby's breath. "Hello?"

"Sorry." She moved the tangle of tiny white sprays closer to her business partner. "Here."

"Did you really come right from the airport? I figured you'd go home and get a good sleep first."

"I wanted to make sure everything was okay."

Which was true. But this was also her first vacation since the divorce two years ago, and the idea of walking into that dark, empty house made her stomach hurt. Plus the time away hadn't been worth it. She'd gotten a sunburn, sand in every shoe she had, and all she'd done was worry about the shop.

And of course, she'd missed Roger. Who was on a honeymoon with the new Mrs. Trumble.

"Did you miss me?" she blurted as she patted at her hair. She'd gotten it cut and dyed it blond before she'd left.

She hated the way it looked.

"Of course I did." Judy speared the baby's breath into the arrangement, the tiny buds like fireflies against a red night. "And before you go and start counting peonies, yes, the flowers came in for the Clancy wedding bouquets and that ridiculous planner of theirs has already been in. Twice. That event is going to be ridiculous. We didn't do 'planners' in our day. I don't know what's wrong with these girls now. Everyone thinks they're a Hollywood star."

"Sometimes it's more about the pictures and the ceremony than the guy they're standing next to." Milly tilted to the side and frowned at the bouquet. "Hold up, that section on the left needs more—"

"I know, I'm working on it—"

Bing!

Judy lifted her wrist and tapped her watch. "Right on time."

Milly turned to the shop door—and time slowed to a crawl. The man who entered her and Judy's pastel paradise was dressed in black—was that leather? the whole outfit?—and standing tall and wide as the building itself. He was positively enormous, with shoulders that seemed to press on the walls of the shop, and a tightly shorn head of dark hair that nearly brushed the ceiling. But the holy-crap wasn't just about his size. His face was harsh in the ways of winter, the bones showing in hard cuts as if he didn't eat enough, his stare black as the pits of Hell, his expression harsh and aggressive.

Milly jumped as she felt a hand touch her arm.

"Relax, will ya," Judy hissed. "And stop it. You don't have to call the police."

"I wasn't going to—"

"Then why's your phone in your hand?" In a louder voice, Judy said, "Nice to see you again."

She squeezed out from behind the counter and approached the man like one of those circus wranglers who got into the ring with tigers.

"Would you like to enter the walk-in? I know you prefer to take your time picking."

Judy went over and opened the glass door, standing to the side like an usher. And even though the giant man hardly seemed the type to take direction from anybody, he put his hands into his—leather!—pants, lowered his head, and went forward.

Ordinarily, Milly couldn't stand that fridge being open for anything other than a quick pass through as you might as well burn money leaking all the cold out, but like she was saying anything?

When he was inside, Judy let things ease shut and came back behind the register. As she punched another sprig of baby's breath into the roses, she said, "Stop staring."

"I'm not," Milly shot over as she kept . . . well, staring.

Inside the glass box, the man was a living shadow that blocked the view of the flowers, the moon not so much eclipsing the sun, but devouring it and leaving nothing on the plate, no crumbs or scraps.

Or that should be petals or leaves, right?

Oh, whatever. She was terrible with metaphors. That's why she handled the accounting.

"How long does he take in there?" she whispered as she studied his profile. "I think his eyes are closed."

"He stands there for a while. Then he picks something out, gives me that ten-dollar bill even though I tell him I'll just charge him two dollars, and leaves."

Milly glanced at the cash register. "And he's never tried to . . . ?"

"Good God, you're suspicious."

"You didn't think the same thing the first time he walked in here?"

"Shh, he's coming out."

Milly grabbed for her purse and resolved that she'd hit him with it if he started anything. Although that would be like taking a flyswatter into a brass knuckle boxing match. But whatever.

He'd chosen a white rose, she noted. And a good one, one that had just started to unfurl from its tight curl.

"Nice bloom you got," Judy said. "Milly will take care of you."

When Milly didn't move, Judy glared and took over, wiping her hands on her apron and then ringing things up with a series of beeps. The register's drawer shot forth like the ten-year-old machine was sticking its tongue out, and the money changed hands.

"You sure about this?" Judy held the bill up. "I keep telling you it's only—"

"Keep the change." The man didn't meet Judy's stare as he turned away. "Thank you."

"Guess we'll see you tomorrow," Judy murmured as she put the tenner in the drawer and closed things up.

"No," he said over his shoulder.

"No?"

As he paused, those hooded eyes lingered on the fragile white petals of the rose. That big hand could have crushed the stem, fisted the bloom, and thrown it all to the ground so those huge boots could destroy the delicate bud. Instead, he held what he'd purchased with care.

"I've got no one to buy flowers for anymore." That dark stare skipped to Milly and dipped down to her purse. Then he scanned the shop. "Habit sometimes is all we have, though."

The nod he gave them was almost courtly, and then he walked out.

As the *bing!* of the door faded, Milly looked at Judy—and then, as it had always been between the two of them, they came to the same conclusion at the same time: They both hustled for the exit, and leaned out to see around the appliquéd sign on the glass.

No one was there. Not on the sidewalks. Not getting into a car parked in the angled spaces. Not walking in the glow of the town square's peach-colored gaslights.

Milly looked back and forth. "What—where'd he go?"

Connelly was a ghost town this late. Heck, seven fifty-seven p.m. might as well be after midnight. Even the diner was shut down, and so were the lawyer's office, the shoe shop, the dressmaker's, and the bank. The pharmacy was still open for another hour, but its glow was far off, on the next corner.

No car driving away. No purr of a departing motorcycle. Not even a pedaling bike disappearing down the road.

Also no big man, in black leather and massive boots, striding off heavily enough to crack the pavement.

"It's like he up and disappeared," Judy breathed.

"Oh, no. He lost his flower."

Milly hopped out into the cold. The white rose had been dropped about ten feet from the door, and she picked up the stem. The petals were bruised from where they'd hit the sidewalk's rough cement.

"It's starting to snow," Judy said as she looked up at the sky. "You're really not in the Bahamas anymore."

Milly took a moment to glance around at the tiny downtown that was as familiar as her own reflection. She'd been born and raised here, and she was going to die here, too. Alone. Because Roger had a new Mrs., like he'd traded in an old car for the newer model.

"First snow of the season," she said as she tracked the flakes that were spinning down from the sky.

"Come inside, Milly. You'll catch pneumonia."

Heading back into the warmth of their little shop, the chill stayed with her as she pictured the man in black leather. It felt a little strange to feel compassion for a stranger, especially one who looked like that. But she was sad for him. Whoever he was.

Then again, she was the other side of his no-go coin: She had no one to buy her flowers anymore. And living in this town, where all the men her age were either married or relatives, she wasn't going to find one.

She put the bloom to her nose and breathed in. The sense that life had passed her by already made her feel eighty years old.

The man had had the same air about him.

"I got chicken cacciatore leftovers tonight," Judy said brusquely. "Too much for me and Joe to eat by ourselves now that we're empty nesters."

Milly looked at her best friend. Judy was back

behind the counter, pushing at the roses like she didn't approve of her efforts.

"You don't have to do that."

"Of course I don't. But I did miss you." Judy bent down and brought something out from under the counter. "Here. For your rose."

The little vase was just the right size, and Milly blinked a couple of times. Good thing she had to turn away to the sink and fill it up.

"That sounds great," she said roughly as she tucked the stem into the narrow neck. "Thanks—"

"Roger's going to regret this whole thing," Judy announced. "And when he comes back to you, you need to make him grovel."

"He's not coming back. He's married."

Judy emphasized her words with a red rose. "He still loves you. Mark my words."

"Well, I can't love him anymore. Not after this."

―――――

As Apex dematerialized away from the town square, he traveled through the cold night in a scatter of molecules, as any vampire could do, did do, often did. When he re-formed, it was in the parking lot behind the Willow Hills Sanatorium, and as he looked up at the building's back elevation, he saw none of the stained brick, the decaying mortar, or the broken windows.

His memories were like a movie being projected onto the rear flank, the images eclipsing that which actually existed, taking over reality like a tax collector.

Instead of the central core and the two wings that seemed to stretch out for miles on either side, he saw an SUV screeching out from the lot, with Mayhem behind the wheel and Kane half dead from his burns in the back. Apex was in the rear as well, having tossed the latter in with him, and he'd been in charge of returning fire against the flank of prison guards who got right on their ass in their own vehicles.

Somewhere down the road, there had been an explosion. A crash.

And it was after that, when they'd surfaced from the wreck, that his life had changed forever.

Wolves had surrounded them . . . except they hadn't been wolves. They'd been wolven, a mystical subspecies in the vampire world, two entities existing in one body.

Shifters.

He'd seen Callum for the first time that night, both in that lupine form . . . and in his humanlike one, the male's hair white and flowing over his torso, his eyes a gleaming light blue, his body powerfully built as predators always were. The meeting had been unforgettable for so many reasons, not in the least because the guy had been buck-ass-naked after he'd shifted— because, hello, it wasn't like Levi's could spontaneously manifest themselves.

The wolven had been utterly unapologetic for the nudity. As any animal would be.

And he had been . . . heartbreakingly beautiful in the moonlight.

Coming back to the present, Apex became aware of a sting on his hand. Inspecting the sensation, he found a drop of blood on his forefinger.

Guess there had been one errant thorn on that rose. Go fucking figure.

Sucking the wound closed, he walked over to the rear entrance, put in the code, and went up a short stack of stairs. He paused at the second reinforced door. He knew what he was going to find on the other side, and hesitated. But come on, like anything was going to change if he waited out here? Came back another night? Never went inside again?

The male who mattered the most to him would still be gone. He needed to get used to it.

Opening the heavy steel door and stepping over the threshold, he regarded what had been the prison camp warden's private quarters as if he had never seen them before. The open space was kitted out like the war room it had been, with munitions mounted at the ready on the blank walls, uniforms and supplies organized neatly, and the table with a map of the facility's layout unfurled and kept flat by a couple of Coke cans at the corners.

These private accommodations were the crown jewel of whoever'd been running the place, and now that the liberation had occurred? Guess that hadn't really changed.

And fuck him, he couldn't help himself. Even though it made him feel like he'd been stabbed in the chest, he took a long, slow, deep breath in through his nose.

Callum's scent lingered in the air, the heady spice bobbing under the fragrance of the other blooms that Apex had brought to the wolven. The cedar-ish cologne-that-wasn't-cologne wasn't fresh, though.

It was already fading.

"You're pathetic," he said. "Fucking insane and *pathetic*."

In the center of the room, the empty bedding platform was surrounded by all the white flowers he'd brought in offering to a male who'd been so badly traumatized, he hadn't even known Apex was there. The roses and peonies and carnations stood up in the little glass beakers he'd stolen from the prison camp's drug processing rooms, and there was no reason to keep adding water now.

He pictured the wolven lying there, that white hair flowing over the pillows, that pale blue stare trained up at the ceiling like Callum had been waiting for some kind of rescue from above.

Like a zombie, Apex went across until the steel toes of his boots touched the mattress edge. As he looked down at the imprint of the body that had lain there for the last week, the contours in the memory foam were like the outline of the victim at a homicide scene.

More memories, now. Of the siege to overthrow the head of the guards and her crew of for-hire guns. The Black Dagger Brotherhood had come at just the right time, and they were in control now. It was a good thing. The prisoners who had survived were getting proper medical care and attention, and the drug shit had been shut down.

But not everyone had been okay.

"You were only here to help us," he whispered. "It's not fair."

Sitting down on the edge of the platform, he splayed his hand out on the sheet, pushing his palm toward the depression. He stopped just short of touching the indent.

"I tried to save you," he whispered. "But I was too late."

Casualties were to be expected in any fight . . . gunshot wounds, soft tissue injuries of all kinds, broken bones. Deaths.

That last one wasn't always the worst outcome. Sometimes living through what happened to you was harder.

Or rather . . . what was done to you.

That was the brutal lesson Apex had had to relive—and watching Callum lie in a comatose stupor had carved the truism into the soul: Though that wolven had breathed and had a heartbeat, what had made him who he was, that snark, that sass, that sexy taunt, was gone. All that had been left was the husk.

It made Apex want to kill that bitch all over again. She'd taken something that had been beautiful, used and abused it, ordered her own guards to rape the male—and had intended to keep Callum tied down, like some kind of toy to play with when she was bored.

And feed from at her leisure.

God, if he could just make her know the pain she had caused.

His vengeance made him believe in *Dhunhd*. But all Apex had been able to do was deal with the aftermath.

In a lame attempt to make a difference, he'd washed Callum's battered body gently. Had put food to the wolven's mouth and fed him. Made sure there was water. He'd sat next to this bed, his head propped on his knees, his eyes going sandpaper from lack of sleep . . . as if he could just will the recovery by devotion alone. The only time he'd moved aside was when Nadya had come to tend the wounds at Callum's wrists and ankles, and make sure that certain . . . internal injuries . . . were healing.

And Apex had only left the private quarters to bring food back for them and then to go to that flower shop, every night right before it closed, to buy another flower. He hadn't been able to tell the male how he'd felt before, and each of the blooms had been the words that he wished he'd spoken when he'd had the chance.

He'd also hoped that the delicate fragrances might lead Callum back from wherever he was in that head of his.

Wasn't smell supposed to be one of those senses that could reach through to a person, even when they weren't completely conscious?

Except it hadn't made any difference. The only thing he'd accomplished was giving the wolven a reliable schedule so that when Callum had decided it was time to go, he'd known when the coast would be clear to leave.

Even though there hadn't seemed to be any change in his condition, a recovery had been happening, all those meals that had been fed, all those drinks that had been soda-strawed into those lax lips, being used for exactly what they'd been for: Callum had been getting stronger. He'd just kept that to himself—and tonight, he'd waited for Apex to go down and gather First Meal provisions.

The eggs and bacon, toast and coffee, were stone-cold over there on the table, next to the map.

When Apex had come back, he hadn't believed what he was looking at when he saw the empty bed. And then the assassin in him had done a quick sweep of the room and cataloged which guns had been taken. Which knives. As well as the combat pants, the fleece, the jacket. The boots and knapsack.

"So you haven't found him, either—"

Spinning around, Apex ripped a forty caliber autoloader out from under his arm and pointed it at the male vampire who had come to stand behind him.

Whoever it was put his hands up. "Easy there. It's me. You know who I am."

Blink. Blink—

All at once, the handsome, patrician features came into focus. Kane, the former aristocrat, was looking like he'd inadvertently bumped into a wasp's nest— and had left his Raid can back in the car. He was also dressed like the soldier he now was, and maybe that was the confusion.

Nah. Apex was just losing his mind. That was the problem.

The gun lowered on its own. And as he reholstered it, he nodded at the empty bed. "Callum's really gone."

Kane's arms returned to his sides. "So you didn't find him in the building? On the grounds?"

"No reason to look. We're not going to find him."

Kane glanced around the private quarters, like he was expecting the wolven to jump out from behind a folding chair or maybe the table with the cold food on it.

"He couldn't have gone far."

"Bullshit." Apex shrugged and got to his feet. "He's in better shape than he let on. I should have known. I watched those bruises heal over the last week with my own damned eyes."

The flowers around the bed seemed stupid now. No more Bloomin' Buds Flower Shop for him. No doubt that woman, and her paranoid, sunburned friend, were going to be glad to see the last of him.

"He'll be back," Kane said.

Apex focused on that indentation on the mattress. "No, he won't."

"But he didn't say goodbye. So he'll be back."

Apex took one last look around. Then he did a subconscious check of his weapons: two guns under the arms, both forty calibers. A knife on his belt. A chain in the chest pocket of his leather jacket, and a set of brass knuckles on the other side.

"So you're leaving, too, then?" Kane murmured.

"I only stayed because of him." He shrugged again. "Sorry, I'm no great savior, ready to roll up the sleeves and help around here. But you already know this, don't you."

Kane's eyes narrowed. "What I know is everything you showed me when you stayed by *my* side."

Great. The last thing he needed was a reminder that this was his second trip through the park with a male who didn't love him back. Oh, wait. Kane had been burned, instead of sexually assaulted by multiple people.

Guess Fate, that fucking asshole, had decided to change things up, after all.

To keep from seeming like a total SOB, he muttered, "Take care of yourself, Kane. You have my number—"

"And I'll call you when Callum returns."

"Yeah, you do that. Sure."

Funny, he couldn't remember the first time he'd met Kane, but he was not going to forget this moment as they parted for good. He went over, stuck out his palm, and lied:

"See you later."

The reality was, Kane wasn't going to be calling him, Callum wasn't coming back—and there was absolutely no reason Apex was going to cross paths with this male he'd once thought he was in love with. Hell, the fact that the pair of them had met at all had been an impossibility. An aristocrat and an assassin? Nope. Destiny had a fucked-up sense of humor, though. Kane had been falsely accused of his crime and that was how he had ended up in the *glymera*'s hellhole. And Apex had belonged in the prison: He'd killed all the people he'd been accused of early-graving.

Kane glanced down at what was being extended out to him. "We're staying here, Nadya and I. The Brotherhood's going to use this facility long-term to take care of what's left of the prison population and transition them . . ."

The male kept talking and Apex just checked out. He didn't have any energy to spare for the happy endings of other people—

When his hand was taken by a firm grip, he came back to the present. "Take care of yourself."

Hadn't he already said that? Whatever, he only wanted to get the fuck out of here.

"That sounds like a permanent kind of goodbye," Kane said softly.

You bet your ass it is.

Apex pulled his hand away and turned for the door he'd come through—

"I never thanked you."

Frowning, Apex glanced over his shoulder. "For what?"

"All those hours you spent by my bedside. You were a good friend."

Staring across at the male, who was now so much more than just a vampire, Apex thought back to the old location of the prison camp—and everything that had happened there. He hadn't looked too far into his feelings then, especially when it came to Kane. He'd known he wouldn't like what he found.

Friendship had not been it, for him.

Yet what he'd thought had been love had just been training ground for the real thing: Callum had been the true love he had never wanted or needed.

"No problem."

When he found himself in the parking lot once again, he pivoted and looked back at the abandoned sanatorium. He'd never thought about getting his freedom before. For the century he'd been held captive, he'd been too busy fighting for survival, and not really all that interested in life anyway. Besides, if you were into killing things, what better place to be? A lawless, hidden prison ruled by a succession of freelance dictators after the aristocracy forgot about the damn place—

and all the people they had falsely put in with real killers and degenerates.

Liberation had never been in his future. Him falling in love with a wolven? Also not something he'd ever seen coming. But him once again alone in the world? Not tied to anyone or anything?

Apex turned away, closed his eyes, and concentrated on calming himself.

It's my fucking theme song, he thought as he dematerialized off into the bitterly cold night.

CHAPTER ONE

Thirty-three years later . . .
(Present day)

Snowplowing was like vacuuming. Except with heavy equipment.

As bands of flakes lashed against the truck's windshield, the bright shock of the headlights was reflected back into the cab. Which was not what you wanted when it was a whiteout to begin with, but who the hell cared. On this thousand-acre estate, in the way-up-north part of upstate New York, what was the worst thing that could happen?

You ran shit off into the pine trees and walked home—

No, not home, Callum corrected in his head. He didn't have one of those.

Reaching for the dash, he turned the heater down,

then resettled in the seat. He'd been out for a good hour, and he had no interest in speeding the job up. The mile-long lane into the historic Adirondack great camp had been carved out of the forest back when construction on the big house had begun in the late 1800s, and in the winter, clearing the drive was a nightly thing. So, yeah, no reason to rush. There was also a meditative quality to the work, the way ahead mostly obscured, the piles on the sides growing higher and higher as he went all the way to the gate and came back.

Also, time had no meaning for him anymore.

He'd been employed at Camp Ghreylke as an off-season groundskeeper since September, and the isolation was the main reason he'd taken the position. Nobody fucked with him up here. He just cashed his checks, ate, slept, and didn't think about what might be coming next.

He was choosy about the plow, though. Mounted on the front of the Ford Super Duty was a head that had more rust, scrapes, and dings than a beater from the twenty-twenties, but like all things that had been made in the good ol' days, it was tougher and better than the new shiny red one that sported the property's official logo.

That flimsy fucking thing, with its gold leaf and that crest, could stay in the maintenance garage. It had left streaks in the center of the plow field, had the wrong curve so a constant splash of snow was kicked up over the hood, and the angle was not steep enough for the side outflow to be high enough.

And who knew he'd have an opinion on any of that—

The streak came from the left.

The predator in him was the only reason he saw the flash of movement through the blizzard. Then again, his wolven side was always with him, even if he hadn't shifted, so his eyes automatically tracked whatever it was through the snowfall.

As he felt his nostrils flare, a growl percolated up over the sound of the engine and the heater.

For a split second, everything inside of him came to life, his thigh muscles twitching, his skin pricking, his jaw burning, as the other half of him demanded to be let out. The contrast to his usual numb detachment was like a flare of light in the darkness, but he let it slide.

It had been a long, long time since anything had made him feel alive, and he preferred shit that way.

He just kept plowing forward in a slow, relentless

path, one hand on the wheel, boot lolling on the accelerator, stare fixated out into the storm.

The next crossing was a minute later. And there were two of them.

Callum hit the brake, even as he didn't know why. There were all kinds of four-legged things on the estate. What the hell did he care—

Three more.

The coyotes shot across the lane, hopping off the ridge he'd created on the right, flowing like water across what he'd cleared, jumping up and over the pile on the left.

Drumming the steering wheel, he opened his mouth to stretch his jaw. His teeth were tingling, especially the canines in the front and the large molars in the back. He could feel the rib bones of the prey breaking down as he gnawed on them, and taste the warm, fresh meat.

Then again, it was in the nature of predators to hunt and bring down—

Even more of the rangy little fuckers ran in front of him.

Callum was out of the cab before he was aware of deciding to move, the cold slapping at his cheeks and making his bare hands curl up. But the sounds from deeper in the pines were what got his attention.

The hunting pack was chattering with excitement, the vocalizations piercing through the falling snow. They'd found their next meal, and he knew they were circling the deer—or whatever it was—but taking their time with the attack because the torture of delay was part of the ritual of dominance.

His nostrils flared and he imagined the scent of the fear.

The prey drive that echoed in the center of his chest was familiar and all the easier to ignore because he'd been shutting it down for how long now? Yet it was hard not to remember that he'd once been a part of what the coyotes were: a community of hunters that went out to bring food back, that protected a territory, that were tied by blood and common interest to a clan—

The scream that threaded through the wind was an all-wrong that snapped him into focus For a second, he could have sworn he'd misheard it.

Like the coyotes, the sound came again.

Cranking his head to the side, he thought . . . nah, it couldn't be. He couldn't believe that female who'd been staying in the big house for the last couple of nights was out in weather like this—

When the desperate yell was repeated for a third time, Callum started running. Getting over the waist-high mound was just a one-two punch of his feet, but on the far side, he got into trouble. The snow was almost up to his mid-thighs, and it was like moving through poured cement as he dragged himself along.

Another pair of male forest dogs bolted by him.

They were whip lean and fully mature, and as his presence registered, they veered wildly away from him, recognizing an apex predator and not wanting to fuck with—

His surge of aggression was so great, Callum was powerless to fight the shift.

His wolven self exploded out of his molecular makeup, his jeans and his flannel shirt shredding under the force of the change, his limbs retracting before reconstituting in an entirely different form, paws extruding from his feet and hands, a lupine muzzle extending from his face, fur clothing his bare skin.

And now . . .

He ran.

CHAPTER TWO

H ey, I was glad to hear from you. Why's that
such an insult?"

When Apex didn't respond, the other
vampire in the Chevy Suburban's passenger seat
looked over. And kept fucking talking. Like Mayhem
had been doing for the last two fucking hours on the
Northway in a blizzard.

Why was air free? Maybe if it cost money, the
male would ration the shit.

"I mean, I've missed our little yappy-yaps like
this." Mr. Chatty leaned across the console. "I know
you have, too. Fireside talks. Yup, they're my love language. Uh-huh. Yeeeeeeah."

Annnnnd the fucker was sporting a mullet. Because . . . of course he was.

"So. How 'bout them Yankees?"

When Apex didn't reply, cue the tapping: The male turned his thighs into a drum set, his forefingers sticks on the muscles under those jeans, the tippity-tappity-ratta-tat-a-lum-a-lim-a-ding-bat the kind of thing that made Apex question his choices in life.

He should have driven the luggage and equipment up himself, and had the guy ghost to the coordinates.

On that note, Apex eyed the shoulder of the highway. If the weather weren't shit, he'd pull over and tell the twitchy bastard to go on ahead, for the love of God. As it was? He wasn't interested in bottoming for the succession of semis that were behind them.

"—or are you a Red Sox man, like some people we know? Huh? Helllllllllllllllllllllllllo."

Fuck, he had to say something. "I don't like basketball."

Mayhem's head cranked in his direction, and those super pale peepers popped. "Okay, that would be baseball. But we can argue about the Golden State Warriors and the Lakers if you want."

"I don't like football."

When the male just kept staring, Apex was forced to glance across the interior. Over the last thirty years since the prison had been liberated, nothing much had changed in the guy. He was still lean, in a bare-knuckle fighter kind of way. He was still brilliant, and hiding his IQ under a bushel of smartass. He was still—well, yeah, he'd grown his white-blond-and-deep-black hair out into that *Lethal Weapon* mullet.

Probably because he didn't make time to go to the barber and had whacked off the shit around his face with a pair of safety scissors.

"What," Apex muttered as the windshield wipers slapped back and forth.

Mayhem slowly shook his head. Like he was contemplating something that violated the laws of physics and wasn't sure whether it was going to wipe out the planet. "I'm just curious how they let you drive a car, s'all."

"Huh?" Before there could be a follow-up, Apex leaned into the windshield and focused through the sweeping wipers and the waves of flakes that ebbed and flowed in the headlights. "Fucking finally."

The exit sign was the beacon he had been praying for.

As they drifted onto the ramp, Mayhem muttered, "And here I thought we would be driving north forever. Or maybe this trip's just *feeling* like eternity."

The SUV handled the unplowed decline like a champ. The stop sign at the bottom? Not so much. They sailed right through the no-go with a set of locked winter treads—a reminder that four-wheel drive did not mean four-wheel stop. Fortunately, no one else was out at midnight in the blizzard, so as they came to a halt in the middle of the plowed county road, it wasn't a problem.

"When are you going to tell me what we're doing?" Mayhem pushed a hand into his wool peacoat and offered something. "Life Saver?"

Apex put his head down on the steering wheel. "Okay, I'm not that and neither are you. Don't get ahead of yourself—"

"The candy? And fuck that, even if you'd throw a drowning male a rock, I'm always ready to save someone."

Lifting his head, Apex thought all about the ways stones could be used with the right follow-through. Then he waved off the offer of the colorful little tube and put the engine in reverse.

"I already told you, it's just an IT job."

"Yeah, but doing what?" A whiff of cherry drifted

over as the male crunched on one of the disks. "Sure, the pay's good. That's all I know, though."

The K-turn was fun what with snow blowing all around, the onslaught alternating between a pixelated wall of flakes, a blank wash of no-see-shit, and a black void with a potential drop-off at the shoulder.

"When we get there"—Apex straightened the wheel and headed them forward—"I'll give you more details."

Apex had to give the guy some credit. The computer specialist was still rolling with the information void, which could have been his personality or maybe was due to the fact that he didn't have any better alternatives when it came to work or people who wanted his company. Some things didn't change, after all. Mayhem had been the only person in that fucking prison who had just wandered in and decided to stay awhile. He'd literally blown fifty years in that hellhole just . . . because.

The fucker was quirky to the point of stupidity. He also had a skill set that was mighty handy when you were wiring a drafty old Adirondack mansion like it was the White House.

"Can we at least start with where the 'there' is?" Mayhem said.

"Here."

"How existential—"

"No, we're here."

Apex banged the turn signal, even though there was no one around to care, and piloted them into a break in the pine trees. Someone had been doing the plowing, so it was easy to get to the grand entrance to the property.

"Holy shit," Mayhem remarked, "what is this place? A ranch that mines human kings and gold bars, right outta the dirt?"

The guy might have had questionable taste in haircuts, but he had a point. The wrought iron gate was all kinds of filigree and fancy with a golden monogram in the center, and looming, spear-topped poles on the top that looked like they'd been made to display decapitated heads. The setup did not belong in the Adirondack Park.

But no one was asking Apex's opinion on the shit. Most especially not the male he worked for.

"Do you know a code or are we hitting the gas and just plowing through this gate?" Mayhem put his palms together. "*Pleaaaase*. For my birthday? Can we bust it open?"

Apex pulled up to a screen mounted on a pile of

rock, put the window down, and stretched his arm out into the blizzard. As he entered a six-digit sequence and the two halves split down the middle to open, his passenger cursed.

"You are *such* a snooze."

He hit the gas when there was enough room to pass. "We are not here to vandalize the place."

"So is now the time when you tell me what we *are* doing?"

"Almost."

On the far side, the lane continued onward, and the snow persisted even in the dense forest, the fluffy pine boughs not slowing down the fall. He kept the speed steady, even though everything was plowed and the road ahead was clear.

Just as they came up to a curve, he had the strangest premonition. Later, he would wonder how he knew— except had he really? At the moment he started to turn the wheel to the left, he only had a sense that something was coming, something important, that was—

The red taillights of a vehicle that was stopped in the center of the lane were glowing like a pair of evil eyes.

"Looks like the plow guy gave up," Mayhem murmured. "Hey, maybe I can—"

"No."

"You don't know what I'm going to—"

"You're not plowing anything."

"That's not what your mama said last night."

Don't kill him, Apex told himself. *At least not before he syncs the sensors up with the monitoring program.*

Opening the door—because either he got out of the SUV or "shotgun" was going to move out of the vernacular and into the locked-and-loaded-at-his-passenger zip code—he stepped free of the warmth and took his parka with him. As he walked toward the parked truck's ass, he pulled on his Patagonia and tried to shield his face from the onslaught. The blizzard was going balls wild, the snow slicing into his eyes, going up his nose, trying to get into his mouth—

Meanwhile, that strange feeling that had kindled just under his skin . . . got louder and louder, until it was practically screaming.

Walking down what turned out to be a Ford, he noted the driver's side door sported the same crest that was on that gate.

There was no one in the cab.

Open the door, some voice from somewhere said in his head.

"What we got?" Mayhem said off in the distance. "Ghost plower?"

Apex watched as his hand reached forward and landed on the latch. Freeing the catch, he pulled the panel open, and—

The scent tackled him like something physical.

And even though he knew exactly who it was, he leaned forward, squeezed his eyes shut, and breathed in through his nose. Just to be sure.

As he was exhaling, Mayhem came up to him. "I said, what we got?"

At that moment, a pack of dogs started howling, somewhere in the forest. Like they were bringing something down.

So they could eat it.

CHAPTER THREE

Mahrci, blooded daughter of Whestmorel the Elder, had come out in the storm only to make sure the feeding station for the deer, which she'd set up and maintained for the last couple of nights, had a fresh load of grain on it. Worried about the herd, she'd put a fifty-pound bag of feed on her shoulder and hoofed it out from the barn, the snowshoes keeping her on top of the three-foot accumulation while she got sandblasted by flakes.

There was no way one of the ATVs could have made it through, and dematerializing with the kind of weight she was carrying was impossible.

Plus, in a weird way, she'd liked the feel of the

storm battering her. She'd been locked in the octagon of her own mind since she'd come up here, so it was good to fight against something physical.

Yeah, until everything had gotten away from her.

The first of the coyotes had snuck up on her just after she'd unlocked the snowshoes and brushed off the platform she'd built in the wood shop. She'd seen the animal out of the corner of her eye as she'd started to cut a pour hole in the burlap—

She'd been so surprised, the Swiss Army knife she was using slipped.

And went right through her glove, into the meat of her palm.

The blood had come quick, pooling inside the ski mitten before dropping into the snow. Even with the blizzard whipping everything around, the scent had been a copper rush in her nose, and a calling card she didn't need.

Another coyote had ghosted out of the slashing snowfall. And another. And more.

Until they had surrounded her.

No mystery there: The predators had been smelling exactly what she was.

Instantly, because fear was the penultimate fuel

source of the body, her heart rate had tripled, which increased the bleeding—and meant she couldn't calm herself and dematerialize.

She'd tried, though, to close her eyes and concentrate, but she'd been terrified about being snuck up on and attacked from behind.

There'd been no way to get herself back to the big house.

And then the boldest of them had come for her, shooting forward and nipping at the back of her ankle. Even through the snow pants, she'd felt the bite, and a scream had ripped from her throat.

Not that there was anyone who'd come for her. That groundskeeper was a ghost, and the estate was otherwise empty—which was why she'd come here.

The next attack was triangulated, three of the coyotes lunging forward at once, their jaws snapping at her, their whip-thin bodies fast and strong.

So now she was screaming even more as she clambered up onto the platform. Wheeling around at her attackers, she kept the knife in front of her—not that she was going to be very effective with the three-inch blade.

More coyotes came out of the blizzard.

Mahrci panted and tried not to focus on how wet

her glove was, how much blood was staining the snow, how light-headed she was getting—

"Heeeeeeeeeeeelp!" she called out for no reason.

Was this how she was going to die? Out in a god-damn snowstorm, at her father's pretentious summer retreat, in the dead of winter?

And now she knew why it wasn't "the living" of winter.

She jabbed the tiny little blade at the snarling jaws that popped up over the lip of the platform and disappeared. With every jump, they got a little higher, and she had the sense she was being toyed with: The platform was just four feet off the ground. They could get at her if they wanted—

"Fuck you!" she hollered as she stabbed at air.

She kept cursing and thrusting with the blade. After everything she'd been through, *this* was the way she went out? After all the shock, all the indecision, all the panic and confusion—and then what she'd done just before she'd left Caldwell?

Her death came by being torn apart by feral border collies?

"I hate you!" she yelled as her eyes flooded with tears that had nothing to do with the cold, the snow, the wind.

Or even the coyotes.

Meanwhile, the predators were not impressed with her defense. They had clearly done this before, circling their prey, closing in that circumference, their bright, greedy eyes locked on their meal, those open jaws chattering as they chuffed and howled in excitement, in the storm, in the snow.

Her tears burned as they froze to her cheeks—

The final attack was like a lightning strike, four of them coming forward on the compass points and jumping right up onto the platform like it was nothing to them. Because it *was* nothing to them.

Suddenly, there were teeth everywhere, going for her ankles and calves, her lower body, her arms. She stabbed what she could, knowing she had to stay on her feet, but they anticipated her every move—and she was lost in this knife fight between their sharp canines and the camping blade that she'd taken with her on a whim—

The bite locked on her Achilles tendon, and pain lanced through her whole body. Howling, she twisted around and tried to go after the mottled flank with her "weapon," but her balance tilted and she started to fall.

Pinwheeling her arms, she couldn't catch herself, especially as the coyote yanked back and took her foot out from under her. The world spun as she lurched off the platform, and there was plenty of snow to receive her, the pack zeroing in instantly as she hit it.

Mahrci landed badly on her arm, and lost her breath. Trying to stay conscious, she flopped onto her back and fumbled with the knife. As she looked up, all she saw were the bared teeth in those muzzles, the rapt eyes, the greedy, licking tongues that were tasting her flesh already. With a weak hand, she waved the blade around, and she gasped for air to reinflate her lungs.

She screamed one last time, into the darkness, into the blizzard—

No, wait. That sound was *not* coming from her.

The coyote who was closest to her face, the one who was the most aggressive and had attacked first, was suddenly gone. Yanked backwards into the storm.

And then—he somehow went flying over her? Like . . . airborne?

The pack wheeled around, those deadly muzzles swinging away from her.

That was when she heard the growling. Deep and low: A bigger, far more dangerous beast altogether.

The snow was falling in such heavy sheets it was hard to see, but something was looming—and then it was attacking.

Another coyote was dragged out of sight, and the yelping was loud enough to carry over the wind.

All at once the whole lot of them growled at something she could not see—and surged in unison out of view.

Mahrci didn't understand what was happening, but funny how your survival instinct kicked in and didn't ask a lot of questions. She needed to get off the fucking ground. That was the only thing that mattered.

Dragging herself back to the platform, she grabbed on to the rough boards and hauled her body upward.

As the wind relented for a moment, what she saw . . . made no sense.

A tremendous white wolf was attacking the coyotes, tearing into them, ripping their throats open, clawing at them. Blood, tufts of mottled fur, and flying chunks of snow kicked up by the fight marked what became a battlefield.

Except it was no contest.

That wolf dominated the lesser predators, the clap of its jaws like lightning cracking across the sky, its eyes glowing with vengeance that pierced through the lashing snow.

Mahrci looked around. The clearing where she'd put the feeding station was about thirty feet in diameter. If she made a run for it, she might be able to reach one of the pines and climb up—

Two shots sounded out. *Pop! Pop!*

The wolf raised its head to the sounds, and just as it did, one of the coyotes got him good, launching at his rear flank and biting him on the back leg.

Bad move. The wolf spun around and . . .

The carnage was immediate—and a reminder that she was about to be out of the fire, into the firing pan. Iron pan. Fire—*fuck it.* As soon as that wolf was done eating her initial attackers? It was going to have her as the entrée.

Except that had been a gun. And animals didn't shoot.

"Help! I'm over here!" she called out.

Two figures stepped free of the ring of pine trees, and she recognized the one on the left.

"Praise Fates," she whispered as she started to sag.

The next thing she knew, her eyes were rolling back and she was out cold. Her last thought, as she lost consciousness . . .

What the hell was her father's head of security doing here?

———

To get to the coyote attack, Apex had re-formed every fifty yards through the dense pines, triangulating the sounds of the high-pitched, excited barking and the occasional scream. On the last leg, he started to smell all the blood, but he was too distracted to bother parsing out how much was vampire and what part was coyote.

The shit was fresh, there was a lot of it, and that was all that mattered.

He already had his gun up as he became corporeal for the final time, and he pulled the trigger at the sky once, twice, as he tried to make sense of the scene: There was a female vampire up on some kind of rickety platform, and a dogfight in the snow below her. Not that it was much of a fight.

The wolf was winning. Or . . . wolven, as was the case.

Dear God, was it possible? How . . . was this possible?

"Callum," he whispered in a voice that broke.

"Shoot them," came a hiss at his ear. "Come on, we gotta get in there and save her."

Mayhem's voice broke through the stupor, and Apex cuffed off a couple more bullets. But not directly into the melee. Besides, it was all but over as the wolven—

The boldest coyote, the one who'd tried to score a direct bite on the rear leg of the inevitable victor, was tackled and savaged, the smaller animal dominated as its throat was ripped open, more blood staining the white wolf's muzzle red, the white snow pink.

That ended it. What was left of the pack ran off, scattering across the drifts.

And the wolf looked up from its prey with a growl.

As that ice-blue stare locked on Apex, its snarl eased a little.

"Shoot it!" the female gasped from the platform. "You're next!"

No, he thought as his eyes burned. *I'm not next.*

He'd have to choose me to kill me, and he's never going to do even that.

"He's not going to hurt us," Apex choked out.

The wolf lowered its head, and with its eyes still on Apex, it picked up the carcass. Then the predator trotted off, disappearing into the storm, leaving a trail of blood behind.

As Apex reholstered his gun under his arm, he did his best to hide the fact that his hands were shaking. Meanwhile, Mayhem jumped forward to the female, who was slumping in her gray-and-red parka and ski pants. Things were said between the pair of them, but there was no tracking any of that and not because of the wind.

All that white fur blended perfectly into the snow. Then again, that male was a ghost no matter what form he was in.

Forcing himself to engage, Apex went over to where Mayhem was all but praying on his knees. "How badly are you—"

He stopped as the dark-haired female looked up at him. For a split second, he didn't trust what he was seeing. What the hell was his boss's daughter doing here?

Shit, this just got complicated, he thought as she stayed mute.

"We need to get you back to the house," he said with exhaustion. "Can you walk?"

Mahrci, a.k.a Mahricelle, blooded daughter of Whestmorel the Elder, looked away from him. Snow was gathering in her messy hair and flakes clung to her face where her fear tears had streaked down her cheeks. She was too pale, and shaking as if she were naked in the cold.

"I can carry her," Mayhem said roughly. "You take that gun back out."

Had he put it away, Apex thought numbly.

As he rearmed himself, the other male leaned down and spoke in a quiet way that went against everything he was as a vampire. Mayhem was a marching band that had bad rhythm and horns that hadn't been tuned right. Suddenly, he was something out of an ASMR channel?

"Our SUV is just out on the lane," the guy said gently. "We can drive you in that way, okay?"

After a moment, Mahrci nodded and put her blood-dripping glove out. "I cut myself."

"It's all right." Mayhem took her arm and positioned it over his shoulders. "We'll deal with it when we're home."

Annnnd now he's a candy striper, Apex thought.

There was some more quiet conversation, and then the female gasped as Mayhem carefully picked her up in a cradle.

"You go first," Apex ordered.

"Where's your gun?" Mayhem demanded.

"Right here. I got this."

Bullshit, he had anything. As he trudged in the wake of Mayhem the Good Samaritan and the teeth-chattering, bleeding, in-shock daughter of his fucking employer, Apex's mind was sucked back thirty years into the past. To that prison in the sanatorium. And the private quarters of that head of the guards.

So that he was once again standing over that empty bed with the white flowers in the little beakers.

Every blink brought him another image of Callum—but at least not all of them were from the end of things. Some of the mental pictures were from the beginning, from that crazy escape from Willow Hills, where the wolven had stood with members of his clan, and those predators had changed from one form into another.

Apex had never seen anything like it. There had been none of that ancient movie shit, no *American Werewolf in London* rough cuts, no *The Howling* cracks and snaps.

Smooth, like water, as if every cell were two things at the same time, and as a train changed tracks without a hitch given proper rerouting, so too did the wolven switch between one incarnation and the other.

Yet—as unforgettable as Callum was—Apex wasn't sure he would have recognized the wolven just now if he hadn't first scented the male in that truck cab.

"It's okay, you're going to be okay . . ."

The reassuring words were coming out of Mayhem's mouth, drifting back over his shoulder on clouds of breath that dissipated in the storm. Yet the syllables fed into Apex's brain as something he himself had spoken—because he had. At the end, at that bedding platform . . . he had said those exact words, over and over, to Callum as the male lay on his back like a corpse, his bruises and internal injuries healing as his soul and spirit had remained mortally injured—

"Apex'll get the door. Won't he. *Apex.*"

As his name was repeated sharply, he jumped to attention. How the hell had the SUV come up so fast?

"Yeah, I got it."

Heading over and opening the rear door, he glanced back at the brand-new truck with that nasty old plow on its front grille.

After all these years, he'd thought Callum surely would have died by now. Or disappeared out west. Down south. Anywhere but here, so close to where everything had happened.

Mayhem brushed by him to put the female in one of the captain's seats. After he belted her in, there was an awkward back-out, and then the guy got in on the other side, next to her.

As Apex shut them in together, he looked at the

truck again. It had been left running, and he hadn't shut the door properly so the interior light was on.

The fact that he could see the driver's seat so clearly, yet no one was in it, made him think about the way the wolven had been haunting him all these years, a vacancy that was perpetual, every seat, every sofa, all the rooms he had ever walked into and the halls he'd gone down, the yards he'd entered and the cars he'd traveled by . . .

Always empty because Callum wasn't there.

"Apex?"

At the sound of his name, he jerked to attention and discovered he'd put himself in the SUV. And as he looked up into the rear view mirror, Mayhem was staring at him like the guy was considering whether Apex could remember how to drive.

"I got this," Apex muttered as he put things in drive.

Bullshit.

CHAPTER FOUR

The Audience House
1075 Cedar Post Road
Caldwell, New York

The Black Dagger Brother Tohrment, son of Hharm, waved his freshly made cherry Danish back and forth. Around his mouthful, he said, "No, no. It's fine, what can I help with?"

As the commanding officer of the Black Dagger Brotherhood, he was used to people asking him questions. Usually they were about shifts out in the field. Munitions. Assignments for guarding Wrath here at the Audience House.

At least it was no longer about the TV remote when Lassiter made everybody and his uncle watch *Growing Pains*.

Because, sure, by all means, let's watch a seventy-year-old sitcom about—

"Sire?"

Tohr came back to attention. "Sorry. Have a seat."

Saxton, the King's solicitor, did not join him at the table in the kitchen nook. The dapper male continued standing there against a backdrop of *doggen* preparing pastries with his perfect, precise posture. Dressed formally as always, tonight he was in a tweed suit with a hunter's red waistcoat and a coordinating ascot. With his blond hair swooped off his high forehead, he was like something from an earlier century, the Old Country ways and that aristocratic accent the kind of thing that took a brother back.

"I do not wish to intrude on your repast," he hedged.

"Not at all." Tohr wiped his mouth with a damask napkin and motioned to the seat across from him. "Come on, talk to me."

The kitchen was super busy, *doggen* bustling around between the island in the center of the homey space, and the professional-grade oven that was seeing a raft's worth of pastries and muffins going in and out of its heat. All the goodies were going to be eaten, too. The Audience House had a full registry tonight, twenty civilians coming in to see the King, with Tohr on sentry duty along with Phury, Zsadist, and Rhage. The registration process of the first three appointments was already started with some of Saxton's paralegals working the males and females up, and the other brothers were waiting in the King's room—

Tohr frowned as the solicitor stayed where he was, a file folder of paperwork in his hands, his eyes moving over to the pair of cooks. Who had been in the household for as long as anyone could remember.

But the solicitor looked worried.

Tohr got to his feet. "Hey, let's go to your office."

The visible relief on that F. Scott Fitzgerald face was the second red flag, and Tohr wasn't surprised that there were no words exchanged as they entered the steel-reinforced core of the farmhouse. From this bomb-shelter-worthy hall, there were a number of access points into the rooms that the citizens cycled through as they registered, were presented to the King, and then were assigned follow-ups to their issues or ceremonies as needed. Saxton had been the one to design the workflow, Tohr had drawn up the building design with the Jackal, and this new system, which was an improvement on the way things had been done, had been implemented as they'd begun to use this facility about thirty years ago.

Plus now it was actually Wrath the civvies were seeing, and not Rahvyn pretending to be the King.

Things had finally fallen back into place after three decades of being upside down in the worst possible way.

"Allow me," Tohr said as he got to the second door in.

After he opened things, the King's solicitor bowed a little and walked through.

"So what have we got?" Tohr closed them in together. "What's up with that paperwork?"

In contrast with Saxton's sartorial distinction, the male's office was strictly utilitarian, with a nothing-special desk that had two laptops set on it, an extra monitor, and papers set in orderly piles at right angles. There was no decoration on the walls, not even an extra chair for a visitor, and the shelving was lined with a complete set of the Old Laws. No photos, no knickknacks, no clutter, no nonsense. Here, it was business and business only, and Tohr had always liked that about the guy.

"This was left in the waiting room at the end of last night." Saxton held the file out. "I'm not sure what to make of it."

Tohr took what was offered, opened the folder, and frowned as he got an eyeful of columns of numbers. "What is this?"

"Financial tables, I think. Given that all of them have a decimal point followed by two digits."

"I see that." Tohr kept leafing through, in search of a name . . . any kind of identifier. "There are no headers, though. So are these bank account balances? Some kind of financial modeling?"

"I don't know." Saxton crossed his arms over his chest. "I haven't been able to decipher any of it. You'll note there's a four-digit number on the upper right of each one?"

"Uh-huh."

"Maybe that's an ID? Anyway, the lot of them were found in the waiting room at closing."

"Okay." Tohr shut the file. "So we can reach out to the civilians who came through, see which of them left it behind, and give it back. No big deal."

It was hard to understand why the solicitor was being so cagey—

"I already made the inquiries." Saxton cleared his throat. "Each one of them denied bringing it in. And John Matthew, Qhuinn, and Butch, who were on guard, have never seen it before. I sent them some photos."

Annnnnnd there it was, Tohr thought grimly. *The fly in the ointment.*

"So who the hell left it in our waiting room?"

"That's what I'm concerned about."

"Have you looked at the monitoring footage?"

"I'm going to ask V for it, but I wanted to check in with you first." Saxton picked up a business-sized envelope. "This is what the pages came in. There's nothing on the front, and the flap was sealed."

Tohr took the envelope, but didn't give a shit about it. "Did anything happen that was out of the ordinary?"

"No. We had three matings and two young for Wrath to bless. There was a property dispute, but it was only over a television—nothing like the number of zeroes on those figures. And then there was a death to certify, a name to register, and the planning committee for the Winter Festival."

"Maybe it's tied to expenses for that?"

"The female and male who came as representatives were the first people I went to. They denied it was theirs."

Tohr glanced up. "And V hasn't seen this yet."

"I'm going to him next. Maybe he can decipher the figures."

Reopening the folder, Tohr took his time on a second trip through the pages. Twelve entries, with a total at the bottom. Then, broken down, fifty-two entries, with the same sum. Same format for each of the twenty or so pages, but the figures were different, as was the four-digit sequence in the upper right.

"Maybe these are dues," Tohr said. "Or . . . contributions. To the festival."

But why wouldn't the organizers claim the paperwork?

He went to the last page and frowned. "I don't get this, though. What are all these other numbers here? It's nearly a solid block."

Saxton cleared his throat again. And then didn't speak.

"What," Tohr demanded, in the brusque tone of voice he used when dealing with new recruits—or when two of his brothers were arguing.

So not the kind of way he ever spoke to Saxton.

The solicitor put his palms forward. "I have no opinion—"

"You're a lawyer. That's your job." More gently, Tohr tacked on, "I'm asking you what you think."

The reply came out in a rush. "No one comes in here without authorization, and everybody knows we have monitoring cameras all over the place. Why would someone leave these papers and then lie about it? It doesn't make sense."

Tohr nodded and tucked the folder under his arm. "I'll take it from here."

Saxton glanced at the neat piles on his desk.

"You didn't do anything wrong," Tohr said. "This is not on you, and of course I'll let you know everything I find out."

The male flushed. "I worry, you know. About everything that happens here. Loose strings, things that feel messy? I cannot abide by them."

"Understood." Putting a hand on the solicitor's shoulder, Tohr nodded. "And that's why you're so good at your job—"

His phone vibrated in his pocket, and he held up his forefinger as he took it out. "'Scuse me."

When he got a look at who it was, he frowned. "Hey, Hollywood, what's—"

Rhage's words came hard and fast. And when the report was finished, Tohr cursed under his breath. "I'll be right there. Yeah, I know the address."

As he ended the call, Saxton said, "Is everything okay?"

"No, it's not." Tohr gave the folder back to the solicitor and headed for the door. "You need to take that to V, right now. I'll check in when I can."

CHAPTER FIVE

The Adirondack great camp was a sprawling, cedar-shingled throwback to the cusp of the twentieth century, when a class of humans with railroad, coal, and banking wealth built wilderness retreats away from the hot lock of Manhattan's summer swelter. With log post supports on its wraparound porch, chimneys at the peaks of its roof, and diamond-paned windows, the structure was both grand and charming in its blanket of snow, the tendrils of smoke and all the yellow light glowing out of that old-fashioned bubbled glass a halo of homeyness.

The plowed lane passed an outbuilding and circled up to the front entrance, and Apex stopped the SUV in front of the porch steps. He'd barely hit the brakes when Mayhem opened his door and jumped out.

While the male shot around to the other side, Apex glanced over his shoulder. "Your father doesn't know you're here, does he."

Mahrci stared down at her bloody glove. "No, he doesn't."

"So you called off the mating." When she didn't reply, he shrugged. "Why else would you run up here?"

The door beside the female opened and Mayhem leaned in. His eyes had a focus that Apex had never seen before—not that he was all that close with the guy—and when Mahrci insisted that she could get out herself, the guy looked like she'd volunteered to walk into a volcano carrying a gas can.

But she got out and even managed to stand. For a second or two.

As she listed to the side, Mayhem was ready to be her fetch-and-carry again, scooping her into his arms before she face-planted on the shoveled walkway.

"Ah, the romance," Apex muttered to himself.

Sure enough, Mayhem carried her up onto the porch as if he were holding a treasure in his arms, and at the door, she did the duty on the latch, opening things for them. They disappeared inside, leaving the entrance wide, just like the rear car door.

"Thanks." Apex cursed and curled his hands on the steering wheel and squeezed. "And don't worry about all the Antarctica around here."

Except he didn't really feel the cold leaching into the SUV, either.

Nah, all he could think about was heading back out the lane and seeing if that truck was still there. And if it was, he was inclined to just put shit in park and wait it out.

The wolven would return for it, sooner or later.

Pride was what stopped him.

In the last couple of decades, Apex had made no secret where he was in Caldwell—and he'd stayed in touch with Lucan, who was part of that wolven clan on the mountain. If Callum was here, on this estate? He was a matter of mere miles from his home territory, and it was difficult to believe that the subject of the prison, the breakout, and where everybody had ended up hadn't been broached at least once.

If only because Lucan was a nosy sonofabitch and he'd want to test the waters.

Everyone in the prison had known about Apex sitting by that bed for all those nights. The nursing routine had been the kind of about-face that people couldn't sync with his reputation—

A set of headlights blared through the blizzard and the hair on the back of his neck stood up.

Turning in his seat, he watched out the side window as the truck with the beat-to-crap plow turned in to one of the outbuildings and stopped.

As the motion-activated security lights flared, Apex's hand grabbed for the latch before he could think about what he was doing, and the next thing he knew, he was cutting across the distance, marking a fresh-cut trail of boot punches over the pristine snowpack. As those headlights were killed, the truck's driver's door opened on the other side of the vehicle.

He picked up his pace—

In the bright light of the exterior lanterns, he caught sight of that white hair . . . just a hint showing above the top of the cab.

Now he slowed down. Then stopped about ten feet away. He opened his mouth to say something, but he had no voice and told himself it was because he was swallowing too many flakes.

Thirty years disappeared like they'd never been.

Shoving his hands into his leathers, he took them out again. Finally, over the din of the wind and the thundering in his chest, he said, "You know I'm here."

There was the sound of the door shutting . . . and then the wolven walked down the side of the truck. His profile was like a knee in the gut. None of his features had changed, even though his hair was much shorter now, a brush cut standing those platinum waves straight up: His cheeks and jaw were still carved from a good base of bone, the nose straight, the lips full, the eyes deeply set.

The bare shoulders were a surprise.

The pecs were . . . a shock.

And when the male rounded the back bumper, the full-naked was an overwhelm that just shut everything down.

Except come on, all those clothes that Callum had undoubtedly been wearing before he'd shifted had been destroyed on the change. Unless he'd ditched the wardrobe first and decided not . . . to . . .

. . . put it all back on.

"Put what back on?"

Apex blinked a couple of times as that voice went in one ear and hit his brain with a Cuisinart blade. But then he caught up to the conversation.

Shit, he must have said that out loud. "Hell—" He cleared his throat. "—o."

Callum's pale blue eyes were steady in the way a wolf's were, unblinking, fixated—and unbothered by all the nudity. The male showed no embarrassment at the fact that his rather . . . impressive . . . attributes were out in the breeze.

The cold breeze. Which wasn't diminishing things in the slightest, not that Apex was looking directly.

"This is a surprise," Callum said.

"Yeah. It is."

"What are you doing here?"

"I work for Whestmorel."

Callum nodded over his shoulder at the truck. "I'm the groundskeeper here."

"I'm doing some logistics for him. A special project, you might call it."

Well, look at all this compatibility going on. Who needed horoscopes when you could just covet your co-worker . . .

In the silence that followed, the storm's gusts blew around them, the swirling snow completing the embrace that Apex was sure only he wanted.

"You saved her life." When there was no response, he couldn't bear the awkwardness. "Mahrci's."

Like there was any question who had nearly been Purina Coyote Chow? Fuck.

"Are you okay?" he heard himself say.

"Of course, why wouldn't I be." Callum nodded at the main house. "You staying the night?"

His heart skipped a beat. Even though it had no reason to. "I am."

"We lose power with storms like this. If it goes out, I'll make sure to start the generator so you don't have to come get me."

There was a brisk nod, and then some kind of generic see-ya or something.

Callum walked off, moving with that fluidity that was more lupine than human.

"You're bleeding," Apex said loudly. "Your ankle."

A dismissive hand was raised over the shoulder as the wolven disappeared through a side door. Ten seconds later, the second story of the six-bayed garage lit up, light streaming out of the row of windows.

Apex stayed where he was, his head tilted back, the snow falling in his eyes and stinging, as he watched the male close heavy drapes one by one, down the line.

Until not even a glow showed from that which had blazed with such light.

CHAPTER SIX

Callum closed the last drape before the collapse happened. He hadn't expected to go down to his knees, but without warning, there he was on the floor. Like he was praying.

Except he wasn't.

He didn't believe in higher powers that listened to mortals anymore. And while he was on the subject of not believing . . . how was Apex here?

"You came back to Connelly," he reminded himself in a hoarse voice. "You chose to return."

So how could he be surprised he ran into the male?

Lowering his head, he rubbed his eyes. "I thought he'd be gone by now, that's why."

His hand braced against the carpet as he sagged to the side, and then he just fucked the effort right off and let himself fall over onto his back. As he lay there, he stared up at the exposed beams overhead. They were a nice honey color, their rough cut flanks full of the character that came from hand-tooling. He imagined they were just as they had been when this outbuilding had been constructed around 1911, after the initial one had burned down. With the windows low to the floor and the roof's overhang, there'd been no fading to the wood because the sun couldn't reach that high up into the peaked roof.

The walls were finished with boards of the same honey hue, the flooring as well. If he'd had any soul left, he'd have appreciated the pine-scented, open quarters very much. With the galley kitchen and bathroom having been done over recently, it was the perfect meeting between the built-to-last past and the mod cons of the present.

Abruptly, he imagined Apex walking in. The vampire's presence would suck in all the air molecules and ruin the brittle order of the place, messing up the bed Callum had made earlier, pitching the clothes in the old-fashioned wardrobe around, breaking all the dishes and glasses in the cupboard. He'd even tear the mirrored medicine cabinet out of the bathroom wall, and smash the claw-footed porcelain tub and the sink.

Hell, that male would bring down the structure. Until it was unrecognizable.

Even as he didn't touch a damn thing.

Cranking his head to the side, Callum narrowed his eyes on the duffle and the suitcase he'd pushed under the bed. When he'd unpacked them, he'd expected to stay until the weather turned warm, and the buds came out on the bushes and trees.

He wasn't going to make it to spring. Not if Apex was going to be in the big house.

"I need to leave now."

His torso rose on his hips, as if he were coming awake in a crypt like something that was dead and shouldn't have been able to move. Like he was the human stereotype of a vampire. And going with that flow, it was ironic that between him and Apex, he was the one who wasn't really alive—

The sound of heavy boots coming up the stairs was not a surprise, and he told himself to get vertical. Put some clothes on. Pull himself together—

Oh, for fuck's sake. He hadn't closed the damn door.

At least he could close his eyes.

"I'm fine," Callum said without bothering to keep the edge out of his voice.

There was a pause. "You're fine? Is that why you're on the floor, staining that rug red with blood?"

Apex's voice was a deep, low rasp, the kind of thing that had, years and years ago, made a wolven think about things that were best done without clothes on.

"I don't need—" Callum jumped as he popped his lids and found the vampire standing over him. "Do you have *any* concept of personal space."

"Not in a medical emergency I don't."

Lifting his leg, Callum pointed to his ankle— which, okay, fine, was dripping a little. "You call *this* a medical emergency? I'd hate to see you with a real problem."

He regretted the comeback as soon as it hit the airwaves. Of course, the male had already dealt with that. When Callum's body had been in bad shape.

But who needed to bring that up.

"Where are you going?" Callum demanded as the guy turned around and headed to the bathroom.

As the vampire barged into the loo, he threw the light switch—and there was altogether way too much to see. Down below, in the snowstorm, it had been easier not to focus on the male.

Now clarity was coming at him. Like a freight train.

Apex was more muscular than before, and his face had filled out in a way that made his raw beauty even more bold and striking. His dark hair was cut in a classic high-and-tight, like he was in the military, and snowflakes were melting in a lazy way on top. He was dressed in black leather, and all that hide over all that physical power was another reason to look away. But come on, like that vampire was ever going to go dad bod? And yes, there were weapons on him, a hunting knife holstered at his waist on one side, that gun he'd shot off at the sky under his arm. There was probably more, hidden away, but well within reach—

Snow was also melting on the collar and the shoulders of the jacket, and for a split second, he imagined himself getting up, going across . . . running his hands over the leather and clearing off the cold flakes . . .

If his life had taken a different course all those years ago, he would have done that. And it would have been natural because Apex would have been living here, too. And they would have been happy, buying each other flowers even in the winter—

Nice frickin' fantasy. Which was a total waste of neuropathways. One, you didn't get a do-over in life. And two, happily ever afters were fiction.

"I'm fine," Callum called out as he looked at his ankle properly.

Just a couple of puncture wounds. No big deal. He'd had them before.

After Apex got the water running in the sink, the vampire started going through that medicine cabinet and then the cupboards.

"What are you looking for in there," Callum muttered. "A black hole?"

"Why don't you have a first aid kit in here?"

FFS, he barely kept food in the kitchen. And Mr. Medicine wanted a transplant team?

When Apex finally came out, he had two smaller towels with him. One was damp and sudsy. Guess the dry one was for ... well, drying off—

Nope. The thing was put across Callum's hips.

Oh, right. Guess he was naked.

"Dog bites are dangerous." Apex knelt down. "You have to keep after them."

Callum hissed as the warm towel with the suds brushed against the teeth marks on his ankle.

Apex's eyes flipped up. "Sorry."

It didn't hurt, but Callum was not interested in explaining that he'd jumped for another reason: No one had touched him in any way in a very, very long time. Matter of fact, it had probably been Apex himself, back in . . .

The strangled sound that rose up Callum's throat, that came up from the past, was just barely caught and held—and like a wild animal, it tried to get free.

"You don't have to do this," he said roughly.

The vampire stopped with the cleaning. But didn't look up. "How can I not."

"You don't start."

"Too late for that, isn't it."

Rubbing his eyes, Callum tried to find a change of subject, something else to say. Words failed. Then again, he never allowed himself to think about the past or the vampire who had both kept him alive . . . and driven him away from that old, crumbling sanatorium—

Goddamn it, the soft stroking on his ankle made him want to scream.

Apex was just so gentle with the soapy corner of the hand towel, the blood turning things rose-colored in a bad way—and what do you know. Suddenly, between one blink and the next, they weren't here, in this pine-scented outbuilding, on this rich male's estate. The calendar was set back to another lifetime, and they were in a different place.

He was coming around from a coma, his body's pain signals overwhelming so much of his brain . . . except for one thing: Awareness of how this fierce vampire took care of him.

Callum moved his foot out of reach. "That's enough. It's good."

Apex sat back on his heels, and the silence that crashed down had Callum looking at the open doorway and wondering which one of them was going to use it first.

"Do you have any Polysporin? Neosporin?" Apex asked.

"Yeah."

"Where?"

"I'll deal with it later." When the male didn't move, he tacked on, "You can go—"

"I'd wondered if you were dead," the vampire said. "All these years. When I didn't hear anything about you."

Callum held out his arms. Turned this way and that on his hips. "Still alive."

In the sense that he had a pulse and lungs that went in and out.

"Have you been back to Deer Mountain a lot?"

He shook his head. "No."

Apex glanced away. Then nodded as if coming to some kind of conclusion. "Here."

The hand towel with its diffused bloodstains was held out, and Callum took it because he figured it was the quickest way to get the male to depart.

"Mayhem's with me." Apex got to his feet. "If you want to avoid him also, you'll need to give a pass to the big house for that reason, too."

"I never go over there." He thought of the generators. "Unless I'm required to."

"Okay—"

"When are you leaving?" Callum blurted.

The laugh that came back at him had an edge. "When my job's done. That okay with you?"

The male didn't wait for a reply. He just went back over to the stairs, his powerful body moving like he was stalking something. When he hesitated on the threshold, Callum kept his mouth shut so he didn't press for details. Like, was this a kitchen installation that was going to take months? A roof repair that would last a week? A boundary line assessment of some kind that could be done in twenty-four hours?

If it was that last one, he could make that work. With the others? He was seriously thinking of handing in his resignation now.

Apex looked back over his shoulder, those unforgettable, jet-black eyes narrowing. And then he just descended the steps without another word.

When the door at the bottom was opened and then closed softly, Callum let his head drop.

I'm sorry, he mouthed, even though he didn't know what exactly he was apologizing for. Fate was a cunt, for sure, but that was hardly something he was responsible for.

Looking at the hand towel, he ran his thumb back and forth over what was still warm and a little frothy.

Funny, what you couldn't get out of things.

What stains were permanent.

CHAPTER SEVEN

Four Lakes Estates
Caldwell, New York

As Tohr re-formed out in the middle of a fucking blizzard, he got attacked by snow, his eyes blinded, his cheeks whipped, his clothes flapping against his body. With a quick pivot, he put his back to the storm, but he couldn't say that improved things very much.

All he got was the kind of spanking even Vishous would have turned down.

However, the change in direction did give him a good look at Rhage, and a moment later, Qhuinn, who had both dematerialized out to this enclave of newly built mansions with him.

With the three of them on-site, he led the way forward even though he couldn't see much, and had to put his forearm up to cut the onslaught. Courtesy of the nor'easter, whole sections of Caldwell had suffered power outages, but over the roar of the storm, he caught the steady *whrrrrrrrr* of big-ticket generators burning through all kinds of fossil fuels.

At least the lights up ahead were a good thing to triangulate toward.

Only a couple of yards later—thank Lassiter—he stepped into the lee of a three-story house that was the size of a college dorm. Letting his arm fall to his side, he caught his breath and blinked his lashes clear.

Holy new-built, Batman. The mansion had to be ten thousand square feet, maybe fifteen, and size was the only thing the architect had gotten right. The place was a bad replica of an antique brick Lord of the Manor palace, the proportions of window levels, the Corinthian columns of the entrance, the angles of the roofline, all wrong.

Except they weren't here to pick on the owner's taste.

Up at the pretentious front entrance, a maid in uniform was shivering under the great lantern that hung from the portico's ceiling, her black dress and white apron offering no protection against the cold. To go along with her proper dress code, her salt-and-pepper hair had been pulled back from her makeup-less face, but the bun wasn't neat. Flyaways were fuzzed out around her lined forehead, as if her obvious distress had created its own static electricity field.

"Oh, my God, oh, my God, oh, my God . . ."

She was forcing out the words through her rattling teeth, and as Tohr mounted the steps, he noted she'd left the door partially ajar behind her.

"Let's get you inside," he said in a low voice.

Her eyes stopped bouncing around and focused on him properly. "I'm *not* going back in there."

The gentlemale in him made him want to take off his leather coat and put it around her shoulders. But there were weapons in it, and weapons all over him. The female was not going to want to see that—yet more to the point, he had no idea what they were walking into or whether he was going to need to fight.

Well, he knew some of what was waiting for them.

"Is there anybody else in the house?" he asked.

He needed to know her answer, but the conversation was also a distraction as he turned her around and eased her over the threshold. He did not want her leaving the premises, and he was also worried about her needing medical intervention if she stayed out in the blizzard much longer.

"N-n-n-no. No one else . . ." Wide, frightened eyes locked on him. "At least . . . I d-d-d-don't think so."

As his brothers brought up the rear and closed the door, he glanced around and noticed first all the security cameras. Then the interior sank in. Like the outside, the black, white, and gold foyer was grand in scale, almost-right in execution—and totally tacky with too much try-hard art, too many silk flowers, too much color. As if the owners just *had* to buy things.

On the left, there was a parlor, and a library was to the right. Out to the back, there were more rooms, but they were all obscured by archways, doors, and hallways. And finally, in the center of it all, a bifurcated staircase angled up to a second floor, then kept going to whatever was on the third level.

Lots of scented candles everywhere. But somewhere, not far off . . . he could smell the blood.

Rhage and Qhuinn fanned out, but didn't go far, leaning into spaces, checking out things while staying close.

"I want you to tell me where he is," Tohr said quietly. "And stay here."

The maid's stare shifted to the staircase and her

wrinkled hand went to the starched collar of her uniform. "H-he's in his suite. I-I . . . each night when I come in, I refresh the flowers throughout the first floor, and then I go up to change his sheets. H-he's supposed to be leaving for the rest of the week, so I'm the only one who came in to work." She snuffled and took a tissue from a pocket. "I f-f-found him . . . on his bed."

"Okay, I'm going to go up there." When she grabbed on to his sleeve, he patted her arm. "It's okay. Both of my brothers will stay with you here—"

"But what about you," she said desperately. "It's horrific, and what if there is . . . somebody still here?"

"Don't worry about me. And don't worry about you, either—my brothers are with you."

He gave her shoulder a reassuring squeeze and then nodded at Rhage and Qhuinn. And as he took the stairs two at a time, he was touched by her concern. But after centuries of the war with the Lessening Society? He was intimately familiar with death in all its forms. Mortal threats as well.

Not that he needed to spell that out for her.

"It's to the left," the maid called up. "His suite faces the garden. The view . . . is the best in the house."

Tohr got to the second story and leaned over the railing. "Thank you."

Except he didn't need the direction. The blood was ripe up here, even with the candles and the flowers—which he now recognized were real.

He'd just assumed no one would pay for so much of such a transitory thing.

As he continued down, the broad corridor was painted a soft gray, and it had bright white doors on both sides. There were a lot of security cameras, tucked up high against the ceiling molding, guarding loud, garish modern paintings that broke up the monotony—

It was obvious when he needed to stop. For one, the scent of copper was so thick, he could taste it in the back of his throat. For another, the gold-leafed crest on the slightly open door was a dead giveaway—

Okay, bad choice of words.

Before he entered, Tohr offered up a prayer in the Old Language to Lassiter: *"May the soul of the departed have found entrance unto the Fade, and be welcomed by those who have awaited his arrival."*

He pushed his way in with his elbow . . . and found himself greeted with a short stack hallway, like he was entering an expensive penthouse apartment. Everything was white. Walls, ceiling, carpet, molding, doors. And the layout opened up to a living-room-sized space that was furnished in all white decor.

"Color scheme by Clorox," he muttered as he continued farther in.

The first of the red stains was visible through an archway, the droplets on the plush wall-to-wall. It was only a dot or two, but to his eye, they were an ocular scream.

Stepping with care, he proceeded to the entry into the sleeping quarters, scanning everything, looking for any out-of-places—some pocket litter, a tread print in the rug's pile, a brush against the wall. Nothing registered, and with the decor being so monochromatic, he would have picked up on . . .

"Anything," he whispered as he rounded a corner and was able to get a proper look into the bedroom.

The partially dressed body was lying cockeyed on top of the unmade bed, head on the pillows, bare feet hanging off the edge of the mattress. The throat had been cut wide open, and blood had soaked through the collar of a partially buttoned business shirt. No other wounds were apparent. Boxers were blue.

Getting his phone out, he took pictures of where the body was in the room, of the bed, of the pillow. Then he focused close in on the clean stripe across the front of the neck. The fatal slice was at a slight angle, and he imagined the killer had snuck up behind with the knife in their right hand.

A surprise job, he thought as he texted the photographs out. Done while the male was getting dressed.

Tohr eased back. Sure enough, there was a trail of blood leading into what he assumed was a dressing room—

His phone started to vibrate and he answered without checking to see who it was. "You got the images?"

There was a rushing sound, as if Vishous were exhaling after starting one of his hand-rolleds. "Pretty professional job."

"Seems so." He went over and looked into a room-sized walk-in closet. "We're going to need you to come out here and go through the security system. There are contacts on every window and door. Cameras in all the corners."

"I'm on my way. Anything else you want?"

Tohr glanced around at what was hanging on the rods. Suits. Business shirts. Polos and casual slacks that were pressed and starched. No jeans.

Nothing that a female wore.

He focused on some scuff marks on the carpet,

and a pool of blood that had been absorbed by the wool fibers. This had to be where the job had been done, he thought.

Or at least he assumed that was the case.

"We also need Butch," he said. "This is above my pay grade."

"Roger that. He's right beside me and getting his car keys as we speak."

As Tohr hung up, he glanced back over his shoulder. Out on the bed, the body hadn't moved, but in a reality-twister, he imagined the male sitting up—and being offended at the fact that his Egyptian cotton bedding was all stained and his monogrammed shirt ruined.

Returning to the bedroom, he went over to the windows that, yup, looked out into a formal garden that would have been illuminated by the exterior lighting if everything hadn't been obscured by the swirling blizzard. He imagined the back acreage was like the rest of the place: A near-miss at the goal of old-school grandeur because the owner had more money than class.

This was the new *glymera*.

Bloodline used to be the only velvet rope. Now? Cold hard cash got you into the club. They'd had to

lower their standards after so many of the Founding
Families had been killed in the raids. After all, those
rules and social slights they lived and died by required
a critical mass of people who believed the bullshit.

Or bought into it, as was now the case.

He glanced at the body of Broadius Rayland
again. What hadn't changed?

"A murdered aristocrat is a big problem," he muttered aloud.

CHAPTER EIGHT

I t was like a museum for animal heads.

As Mayhem carried the wounded female into some kind of rustic great hall, he was under the watchful glass eyes of all kinds of taxidermied mammals. Deer, bears, bobcats, coyotes, moose—meese?—and other things with antlers he couldn't name. Given the scents, which were nil, he gathered the gruesome decorations had been mounted up into the arching elevation years and years ago.

Given what had just happened out in the forest, the wild animal shit was a little too close for comfort.

At least there was a roaring fire in the river stone hearth that ran all the way up to the ceiling, and he laid her out on the tartan sofa closest to the warmth. Then he eased back.

The female was looking up at him with wide, dark blue eyes, and talk about needing medical attention. His heart was doing the cha-cha-cha in his ch-ch-chest, and his head was swimming like someone had swapped his brain out for Jell-O. She was just so beautiful, though. Her face was heart-shaped, her features delicate and perfect, her cheeks flushed from the cold in a way that made her seem healthy even though she was clearly in shock.

Plus he'd always had a thing for brunettes. Her long, dark hair was tied back and damp from the snow that had fallen in it. He imagined it loose and wavy, down her back—

"Where's your first aid kit?"

"What's your name?"

They both spoke at the same time, but he was the only one who seemed to have to take a moment to recover from hearing the other. Sure, they had traded a couple of words out in the storm, but it had been hard to catch any nuances over the din.

Here in the quiet, her voice made him feel like she had stroked his naked thigh . . .

Abruptly, what she'd said sank in. And as he con-

sidered the truthful answer, he wished he were a Bob.
A Tom. Dick or Harry would also work.

Well—not a Dick. That was too close to what he
was having a problem controlling even though she was
injured, a stranger, and way too good for him—and yes,
he was certain that last one was true without knowing
anything about her.

And hey, he wouldn't have hesitated if his given
name wasn't a descriptor that kinda fit.

Really fit perfectly, in truth.

"Call me Hemmy," he heard himself reply.

The smile that tilted her lips amplified her beauty,
sure as you could turn up the volume on an opera.
"Like the engine."

"Yeah, that's it. How bad are you hurt—and
where?"

"My hand's the big problem." She held up a bloody
glove. "It's really throbbing."

"Okay, let's get off—" He gritted his teeth. "I
mean, can you take your—remove—"

"There's a bathroom back in that hall? Could you
go get a towel for me, please? I don't want to bleed all
over the sofa."

"Absolutely."

He was back in a jiffy, paying no attention to anything other than his mission. And after he returned, he held the towel under her glove as she took care of the hand job—

Wincing to himself, he edited that thought: *As she removed her glove.*

They both let out a sigh of relief. The cut between her thumb and forefinger was almost surgical, it was so clean, and though it had bled a lot, the injury was, in the manner of vampires, already starting to close.

"Thank God," he said under his breath as he put the ruined ski glove on the fireplace's footing and wrapped her hand in the towel. "But we've also got to check your ankle."

With a nod, she lifted up her leg, cocked it around on the sofa—

No, not cocked. She *moved* it around on the sofa so she could inspect the ragged rips in the snow pants.

God, this was hard—

"*Fuck.*"

The female's head came up with a snap at the curse. "No, no. I think all the Gore-Tex and layers stopped the bite. See?"

Oh, he was seeing things all right. Mostly how fucking ridiculous he was being.

Now was *not* the time to think about sex.

Pulling himself together, he said with an authority he didn't have, "Let's just get the boot off and check what's going on."

Hey, at least he hadn't "tugged" himself together, okay? He could do this.

Shifting down the sofa, he measured the teeth marks on the snow pant leg and tried not to think about what they would look like in her smooth skin. And then when he went to pull up the bottom of the pant leg, she flinched and he froze.

"No, it's okay." She redid her ponytail like the wrenched-around tie had been pulling at her hair. "I was just expecting it to be painful."

Mayhem stared into her eyes. "I'm not going to hurt you."

As she looked away, he could have sworn her flush got deeper. "Of course you won't."

Except the fucking pants were going to make that difficult. They were downhill-ski-grade, with two layers at the bottom: the outer, which was a pain in the ass because it was stiff, and the inner, which was a pain in the ass because it had an elastic band that locked in tight to the laced-up tops of her boots. Which he could also tell were going to be a pain in the ass.

Then again, she could have been barefoot, wearing

loungewear, and preloaded with Tylenol—and he still would have been wincing the whole time.

"Oh, thank God," he murmured as he got a gander at her mid-calf laces.

Okay, that also sounded dirty. But there were no syllable substitutes.

"It's all right, yes?" she said.

As she sat up, he leaned back so she could see. "Yup, the boot saved you."

Man, those teeth marks in the leather upper were a horrifying dental impression if he'd ever seen one.

"So they didn't break through," she murmured.

"Nope, they didn't."

Though he'd kind of guessed that because there wasn't a scent of blood from her leg, but he hadn't trusted himself—because he'd so wanted her to be uninjured.

"You mind if I work on these laces?" Oh, for fuck's sake, that sounded—

"That sounds dirty."

As she smiled again, Mayhem stopped breathing. If she was pretty when she was serious, she positively glowed with that expression.

"What's your name?" he said softly. "I forgot to ask."

Because, really, it didn't matter. When he looked into her eyes ... nothing actually mattered.

"Mahrci."

Now he was the one smiling. "It's nice to meet you, Mahrci. So what puts you in this remote house in the winter?"

When she didn't immediately answer, he hedged, "Is your mate around?"

Pleasesaynopleasesaynopleasesay—

"Oh, I'm here alone," she said. "I mean, there's the groundskeeper next door, of course, but otherwise, it's just me."

"So you're in charge of the house?"

She looked around the space. "Oh, it's not mine. None of this ... is mine."

The touch of embarrassment was totally uncalled for. He didn't care that she was a housekeeper or a maid. That was honest work, and besides, who wanted to be with some rich, useless female who sat around eating bonbons all night and ordering things from Saks.

"Is there anyone we should call?" Just so he was perfectly clear on things. "I mean, family or a boyfriend—"

"No." She shook her head. "It's only ... me."

Mayhem was aware of the tension in his shoulders easing. Yet the loneliness in her was sobering.

"Okay, well, how about we get both these boots off," he said roughly. Because he wanted to do something, anything, for her.

"Please," she said as she fell back into the couch and started shrugging out of her parka.

The way her body moved, so sinuous as she arched and twisted, so subtly powerful, did things to him that he had to put out of his mind.

At least focusing on all the glass eyes staring down at him and judging him helped. As did trying to improve his sloppy de-booting: His fingers, normally so sure, skipped and slipped, but eventually, he got the Merrell loosened and pulled the thing off. Her sock underneath was black, and she was wearing black long underwear.

And he refused to allow his mind to wander any further than that.

Flexing her foot, Mahrci moved things side to side. Made a circle one way. Made a circle the other.

"I really think I got away with it," she murmured.

Then she brought her leg up and took her sock off—

Oh, God. She had gorgeous feet. And he'd never been feet-sexual before.

Pulling the layers up, she nodded. "I wasn't sure if—well. I got lucky."

What was lucky was that he and Apex had come up on the attack when they had. If they hadn't, that wolf would have finished the job those coyotes had started. But there was no reason to bring any of that up—

The heavy front door swung wide, and the cold rushed in, bringing with it a swirl of flakes . . . and Apex. Who was sporting a glower like he was part of the blizzard itself.

As the male shut things behind himself, he dragged the temperature down with all his grim.

"Hiya, sunshine," Mayhem said dryly. "Rough day at the office?"

Apex's black stare narrowed. But then he focused on Mahrci. "You okay?"

She nodded. "My hand's already healing."

Mayhem looked back and forth between the male who'd brought him here . . . and the housekeeper who could keep him in this dead-head room for the rest of his natural life with just her smile if she wanted to.

"You know each other?" he asked them.

CHAPTER NINE

As Apex stepped into the big house, he wasn't completely sure where he was. Glancing around at the animal heads, he wondered for a moment if he hadn't entered some kind of new prison, one where they'd taxidermied the decapitated inmates, and everybody was wearing weird hats and needed a shave.

But then he focused through his stupid on Mahrci. The female was sprawled on the couch, a bloody towel around her hand, one of her boots on the floor.

With Mayhem sitting at her feet like a dog.

And after Apex asked her if she was okay, he became aware the female was looking at him with the kind of intensity that meant a message was trying to be communicated: It was like the pair of them were in an optical round of charades, where the first word rhymed with "putt," the last with "s'up," and there was an f-bomb in the middle somewhere.

What, he mouthed to her.

"Your friend wants to know how we know each other," she said awkwardly.

"Oh." He opened his mouth. Closed it. "Through work."

As Mahrci exhaled slowly, he abruptly wondered if this assignment up here hadn't been a ruse, after all. Except then he thought of the equipment in the back of the Suburban. No one, not even a male as wealthy as Whestmorel, would waste that kind of money just to monitor his daughter's temper tantrum—

As his cell phone vibrated in his leather jacket, he frowned and took the thing out.

Speak of the devil.

He looked at her. Glanced at Mayhem.

"'Scuse me."

Apex had never been to Camp Ghreylke before, but he'd studied the architectural plans to prepare for the job, so he knew where to go to find one of the five bathrooms on the first floor. Closing himself in, he accepted the call while he checked out the dark green, pinecone'd wallpaper and the rustic copper sink. There were two stalls with dark green doors, and lights that were set with copper shades.

Goddamn, he thought. This whole place was like if Paul Bunyan had decided to take up interior design.

"Hello?" came the demand over the connection. "Are you there or not?"

Well, wasn't that the question of the hour.

Apex turned and looked at himself in a mirror that was framed with birch branches. A stranger was staring back at him.

Rubbing his eyes with his free hand, he heard himself say, "Yeah, I'm at your camp."

"Is my daughter—"

"She's here." No reason to bring up the coyote attack. And he had to wonder if the guy knew his groundskeeper was a wolven. "Is that why I'm wiring up this place?"

"Put her on the phone," Whestmorel demanded. "She's not answering my calls."

Apex checked himself out again in the mirror. Nope. Still recognized the features and knew nothing about the male behind the black eyes.

"Sorry," he said, "I'm not a family therapist. If she doesn't want to talk to you, that's between the two of you."

"She lied about her whereabouts. She told me she was at—"

"Annnnd we're still talking about your kid problems. Why?"

"Because I pay you," Whestmorel snapped, "and I am *ordering* you to put her on the phone."

Apex watched in the mirror as his upper lip peeled off his fangs. "You know what one of my biggest pet peeves is?"

"Not in the slightest—"

"Authority. I fucking *hate* authority. So if you're trying to muscle me, how 'bout you get somebody else to wire your house. I'll leave the equipment here since you paid for it all—"

"*Wait.*" There was some rustling, like the male was switching ears because he was frustrated, but too classy to curse. "Surely you can understand the concern a father has for a daughter who—"

"Nope, can't say as I do—and I'm never having children so I have no intention of learning. Now, what are we doing here? Am I completing the work you're paying me for, or are you going to keep throwing around the word 'order.'"

The exhale that came over the connection had a begging quality to it. "The mating ceremony is in less than a month."

"Again, not my business."

In the quiet that followed, he imagined his "boss" was weeding through various avenues of coercion and manipulation. But here was the thing. The whole subordinate label required a two-sided arrangement, and Apex was a part of that handshake deal in name only. So the aristocrat was playing with himself.

"She must come back to Caldwell," Whestmorel announced.

"That and a bowl of soup is your lunch, not mine."

Another pause. Then, "All right, fine. But you are not an easy male to deal with."

"This is *such* a newsflash, you have no idea," Apex said dryly. "And I'll take care of the project here as long as whatever is going on with your daughter stays between the pair of you. Good talk, great. I'm out."

He ended the call, and then he braced himself on the lip of the pretentiously woodsy-casual sink.

Hanging his head, he breathed through his mouth. All he could see was the wolven on that floor up in his quarters above the garage, bleeding, naked . . . a blast from the past that knocked Apex on his ass, and sent him tumbling into his memories.

None of them good.

Like it was just yesterday, he remembered waiting by that bedding platform in the prison, the minutes creeping by, the prayers leaving his lips, his eyes burning because he didn't even want to blink in case he missed something.

God, I can't breathe, Apex thought as he unzipped his jacket with a yank.

How could something that was so long ago feel as recent as last night?

Pulling himself together, he left the bathroom and went out into a hallway that had honey-colored pine wainscoting, an evergreen carpet, and crimson drapes on diamond-paned windows. Painted landscapes framed by raw birch bark and old black-and-white photographs of people in Victorian garb stretched out in all directions.

Given that Whestmorel had bought this place and everything that was in it two years ago, those were men and women, not vampires.

Someone else's family, not the male's own. But the images were right for the decor.

And hey, the guy was always more worried about looks than his own bloodline.

Apex walked back out into the great room with the animal heads, and found Mahrci alone on the couch by the hearth. The female was staring off list-lessly into the flames, and he knew how that felt.

"Was it him," she asked in a dull voice.

"Your father?" He measured the height of the ceil-ing and hoped there were ladders tall enough to reach it somewhere on the estate. "Yeah."

"Is he coming up?"

"Not that he said. But if you don't want to deal with him in person, I suggest you call him."

"I can't . . ." She covered her face with her hands. Then looked through her fingers with eyes that gleamed with unshed tears. "I can't see him right now. Can't you put him off?"

How in the *hell* had he become some kind of fam-ily counselor? he wondered.

At least he liked Mahrci. Or felt sorry for her, was more apt. Although he'd never much thought about—or bought much into—the whole "poor little rich girl" routine, he did not envy her life in the slightest. Like all daughters in the aristocracy, she was a status symbol to be bartered with. Not a person who'd ever be allowed to live her own life.

And the male who had been chosen for her? Apex had never cared for Remis, son of Penbroke. So he didn't blame Mahrci for going AWOL from the upcoming ceremony.

"Again," he said, "my advice is for you to get on the phone with him. That's your deal, though. You got to decide for yourself."

As the female continue to stare up at him helplessly, he was *not* about to get involved with her love life drama.

"You've got to understand." Her voice cracked. "I cannot get mated to Remis, and neither you nor my father—"

He put his hand up. "Let me set your mind at ease, in case you're wondering. I'm not here for you."

"Good. That's . . . good." Except then she frowned. "Why are you here, then?"

———

When Mahrci had seen her father's head of security out in the woods, her first thought, even above the fact that he and his friend had come to rescue her from coyotes—and a white-and-gray wolf the size of a line-backer—was that he'd been sent to bring her back to Caldwell. She'd been convinced, after she was put in the rear of that black SUV, that she was going to be returned to her father like a package that had been mislaid in the mail system.

And even now she wasn't sure whether she be-lieved Apex. She was, however, still on this couch.

God knew he could have easily carried her out.

Yet she couldn't trust him—and not because he al-ways looked so scary, with his hard dark eyes and his ice-cold demeanor.

No, she'd learned in the most heartbreaking way not to trust anybody.

"So what are you doing here?" she repeated.

Apex shrugged, his heavy shoulders shifting under his leather jacket. "Just my job." Before she could press him, he nodded at the front door. "Listen ... about the groundskeeper."

She frowned. "Yes?"

"What's his deal? How long has he been working here?"

Confused by the change of subject, she rubbed over her eyebrow. "Did he do something wrong?"

"No, I'm just curious. His truck was parked out on the lane. It's the reason why we stopped, actually."

"Oh." She flushed. "You know, I haven't thanked you yet for saving my life—"

"It's fine." Apex waved away the comment. "I just wasn't told there was anybody else up here. What do you know about him?"

"Not a lot. I mean, he's been fine with me. When I arrived a couple of nights ago, he told me he was hired in September to watch everything over the off season. I think he said he planned to leave in the spring when the regular summer help comes."

"So until May."

"I guess?"

"What name did he give you?"

"Callum. But I don't know his bloodline at all, if that's what you're wondering. Why do you ask? Are you worried about something with him?"

"Like I said, I just need to know who's on the estate. It's not a big deal."

Bullshit, she thought. There was nothing casual about the male, not from how he was standing like he was ready to pounce, to that simmering calculation on his face. Her father had always hired well because he had enough money to pay for the best in any position—and as the head of security for all the properties, Apex, with his aggression and intelligence, was exactly what was required.

He was always watching—and seeing too much.

But two could play at that game.

Mahrci sat up with a groan. "You know him, don't you."

The ever-so-slight recoil sealed the deal on her own suspicion, but she wasn't surprised she was right. She had developed a sixth sense for those who kept secrets lately.

"Why are you pretending to ask me what his name is," she murmured.

"Don't get ahead of yourself. I didn't know what he was going by now."

"So I'm right—"

"Tell your father I said hello, why dontcha."

Well. There you go, she thought.

"Um . . . Hemmy's in the kitchen getting something to eat." She nodded toward the back of the house. "You just go straight through there if you want to join him."

"Hemmy?"

"That's not his name?"

"Guess he's claimed a nick, then."

As Apex looked away, she studied his grim profile. "Can I ask you one question about the groundskeeper? Are you worried he's dangerous?"

"Not to you," came the tense response. Then the male focused on her. "You're fine."

Am I, she wondered listlessly.

From the far corner, Hemmy emerged with a tray of—

"Did you have to bring the entire kitchen?" Apex muttered.

Although he did have a point. Hemmy had clearly rooted around and brought out anything you could put a piece of cheese on, drag through a dip, or layer with a couple of slices of hard salami. But hey, at least he'd balanced all those carbs with a bag of M&M's.

"There's no food in there," the male said as he came over and put things on the low table in front of her. "Did you just get here or something?"

For a second, she assumed he was talking to Apex. But no, those eyes were on her.

"Oh, me?" She tried to remember when the last time she'd had food was ... and couldn't recall. "I haven't been thinking—I mean, I need to go to the store."

"No one's going anywhere." Apex went to a window and stared out at the storm. "Not right now."

Besides, what would be open this late this far up-state, she mused.

"Well, I raided the pantry." Hemmy swept a hand over his display. "This is what we got."

"You know, I think I am hungry." She sat forward and forced a smile at the male. "And this looks terrific."

Old saltines and oyster crackers. Fritos that had expired in November. Boxes of Triscuits and Wheat Thins. But she was suddenly starved, so it was a feast.

Breaking open the saltines, she looked back and forth between her two new roommates. Hemmy had gone over to the hearth and was throwing some more hardwood on the fire, his brows down low like log placement and BTU production was something he was going to be graded on. Apex was still staring out that window.

That looked across the circular pebbled drive to the garages. And the expression on his face was as if he'd seen a ghost.

Maybe she was just applying her own unrest to him.

She glanced at Hemmy. And then tilted her head to the side. "You have a mullet."

The male looked over his broad shoulder. His smile was slow, and you know, suddenly the temperature in the grand hall seemed much, much warmer.

"It brings out the color in my eyes, don't you think."

Mahrci didn't mean to laugh, and it was like the food. She couldn't recall the last time she'd gotten her giggle on.

But it had been a long, long time since she'd had anything to even smile about.

It felt . . . magical to laugh. Especially with the bright-eyed, blond-mulleted male who was staring over at her as if he really, truly *saw* her.

CHAPTER TEN

*The Black Dagger Brotherhood Underground Housing
Complex
a.k.a. The Wheel
Caldwell, New York*

Tohr arrived back at the Brotherhood's cul-
de-sac about ten minutes before it was BBQ
time. And not as in Last Meal, and short ribs
were on the menu.

Dawn was coming like something from Scuderia
Ferrari.

As he re-formed by one of the five houses that
had been built aboveground to keep the suburban,
nothing-special ruse up for the humans, he could feel
every inch of his skin prickle, even the stuff that was
under his clothes. Likewise, his eyes started tearing up
even though he'd deliberately become corporeal with
his back to the east.

There were a lot of things in life that you could fudge. The great, glowing death ball in the sky was not one of them—

"Sire! You must come in!"

At the sound of the voice, he pulled a pivot-and-hustle, zeroing in on the command. And as he shot through the side door of the Colonial and into a homey kitchen, Fritz, butler extraordinaire, started fanning him with a dishtowel like he was already on fire.

"That was a little close," Tohr said, as the breeze did feel good on his flaming cheeks.

And thanks to the special reflective coating on all the window glass, the harmful rays were mostly blocked. The relief was instantaneous.

"Mistress Autumn has been—"

"You're here! Oh, thank Lassiter."

His *shellan* bolted out of the basement door, and his arms opened without him even thinking about it: Those lovely gray eyes that were usually full of calm warmth were frantic, and her blond hair, which she usually knotted high on her head, was streaming behind her like a halo of anxiety.

"I'm sorry," he said as he pulled her in close. "It's been crazy tonight."

After they reconnected for a minute, his mate

pulled back, and touched his face as if reassuring herself he was really alive.

"Too close," she whispered.

"I'm sorry." He pressed a kiss to her forehead and felt like an absolute asshole. "I won't do that again."

It was a lie, and they both knew this, but he didn't know what else to say. His job was dangerous, unpredictable, and almost always in the way. There was no getting out for him, though. He was Wrath's second-in-command, and the Elmer's glue of the Brotherhood, as Rhage always said.

"Okay," she murmured with resolve.

"Okay," he echoed with love.

And that was why he could only ever be mated to her. Of all the people he had met, his Autumn was most like water. She flowed over difficulty, and not weakly. No, never weakly. There was great strength in her calmness and the way she accepted that which could not be changed.

Like his past, and the loss of his first *shellan*. Like his present, and his job.

She inspired him every night, lifted him every day, loved him like they had an eternity in front of them and only one more second at the same time.

Another hug, he thought as he pulled her in again. She was smiling when they eased apart.

"Butch and V are waiting for you downstairs in our family room." She glanced pointedly at Fritz, who was worrying at the apron that was tied around his waist. "Where we are all going to enjoy everything that has been so thoughtfully prepared."

"I can make more?" Fritz's wrinkly face was pitched like a tent off the tip of his nose, and his clear concern for the adequacy of his efforts made everything seem looser. "Perhaps another dessert?"

There was a "please" dangling in the breeze, as if he needed to work out his anxiety on a flan or something— and Tohr hated that he'd worried the elderly butler, too. *Fuck.*

"Absolutely." He forced a smile at the *doggen,* as regret soured his stomach. "And you know what I feel like I need? A fresh apple pie."

"Oh! Sire!" Fritz clapped his hands like someone had offered him a winning scratch-off. "I have the most beautiful Braeburn apples. And I can sweeten them up with some Galas. And if I start now, I shall be able to provide it warm in ninety minutes!"

The butler was already turning away and going for

the Crisco. Handmade and flaky as ever was the only way a crust was happening in this, or any Brotherhood, household.

Tohr pressed a quick kiss on Autumn's mouth.

"Before you say it," she murmured as they went over to the cellar door, "I'll be staying for the conversation with Butch and Vishous. And yes, I know you hate it, but I live in your world alongside you. Reality is what it is, and I have a right to know."

For a split second, Tohr entertained a fantasy that there was another zip code, far, far away from Caldwell, where there was no violence, no need for the Brotherhood's official duties, no war with Lash and the *lessers*. In his utopia, he would sequester all those who he loved—

"And I just made some fresh vanilla ice cream," Fritz announced.

"Thank you," Autumn said. "That would be lovely."

The pair of them descended together, and as he held the warm, vital hand of his mate, he was grateful for the here-and-now. And he really was going to try to not burn himself to a crisp in the future.

At the bottom, they hooked up with the Wheel's outermost ring, and they didn't have far to go. The next door was their quarters, and he jumped ahead and opened the way in. As Autumn stepped through, he closed his eyes and breathed in. She smelled like a summer night, clean, fresh, tinted by rosebuds.

His blood stirred, and he found himself craving another kind of dessert—

"You could have cut that closer," came the dry greeting from the sitting area. "I mean, really, you had at least three or four minutes' wiggle room."

Tohr leveled a stare at Butch O'Neal, but as usual, the former homicide cop was impervious to a good pipe-down-sonny and merely smiled back. Next to him on the couch, the brother's roommate and best friend, V, was going back and forth between a cell phone and a laptop as if he were watching an argument and not sure who to back.

Vishous was always sharp as a dagger. "I was about to break out the ranch dressing—"

"Enough."

As Tohr made a pointed can-you-please-not-freak-her-out-more glance at his mate, the two of them winced.

And Butch stammered. "Ah . . . yeah, so anyway, I . . . hey, is it time to eat?"

"Last Meal will hold," Autumn said as she took took her place on the love seat across from the brothers.

"Fritz has it in our warming drawer. What happened tonight."

Tohr glanced around the cozy living room with its relaxed furniture and many throw blankets. Autumn liked their home to be the kind where people could kick their shoes off and curl up—and he wanted it that way, too . . . especially because so many of the conversations were so damned heavy. Like tonight's.

This morning's, rather.

And yes, he wished he could talk about this shit out of earshot from her. But he respected her enough not to play the chest-thumping *hellren* who demanded that her delicate ears be protected from subjects not suitable for the fairer sex.

"What have we got, boys," he asked in a low voice.

Butch brought his rocks glass up to his lips and took a sip of the Lagavulin in his traveler. "I went through the entire scene at Broadius's. Very professional job. The killer knew where the security system was, knew how to disarm it, knew the layout of the house. Also knew the schedule of the staffing. He—or she—picked the dead zone right before the maid arrived."

Tohr glanced at Autumn. Her eyes were locked on the cop. So he just cleared his throat and continued on. "What about the body?"

"Again, our murderer was very confident in their work. No defensive wounds, no disruption in the closet except for a couple of scuffs on the wall-to-wall, and minimal blood. They're also strong enough to carry deadweight without knocking into doorjambs or dragging the body to the bed."

"Why bother with that," Tohr said. "I mean, you could have just left him in the closet—"

Butch held up his forefinger. "I think there's a message being sent. You lie in the bed you make. I'll bet dollars to dickheads that the killer was making an example of Broadius, and took a couple of pictures to send to people. The male who did this—"

"Or female," Autumn pointed out.

The brothers nodded at her before Butch corrected, "That's right. *Whoever* did this also took a souvenir. Broadius was only wearing one cufflink. I didn't find the other one."

"Where's the body now?"

"At the morgue." Butch tilted his glass forward. "Now it's your turn. What do we know about our victim?"

Going over to his *shellan*, Tohr sat on the arm of the love seat, and rubbed her shoulder. "From what Saxton and I were able to discover, he was part of the new group welcomed into the aristocracy about thirty years ago. Not mated. Money made in bitcoin. No controversies—"

"Here we go." V sat forward and turned his laptop around. "This is our killer."

Everyone leaned in as the surveillance footage was played on the screen. The grainy images didn't show much because of the fucking falling snow, but after Tohr's eyes focused properly, he could make out a figure in white battling the blizzard's fury, curved in against the gusts as they approached the garage.

"The ski mask covers the face, of course." V hit replay. "And they weren't stupid. The first thing they did when they got inside was turn off the system so this trek to the side of the garage is all we have. The interior cameras go black right after this."

"Like I said, it's a professional," Butch murmured as they watched things for a third time. "I mean, no fingerprints anywhere—but then I'm working under the assumption it was one of our kind anyway. But no boot prints, either. I did find two puddles on the floor just inside that door. I'm guessing they jimmied the lock, got in, and slipped on some treadless pads."

"Any sense what they did with the security stuff, V?" Tohr asked.

"They knew the code." V sat back on the sofa and stroked his goatee with his gloved hand. "It's a pretty standard system. You have a minute to disarm it any time you open a door or a window. The log was easy to access and review, and it shows entry from the garage at five thirty-eight p.m. and shutoff with the code less than thirty seconds later."

"It was twenty-two minutes before the maid arrived for the night," Butch cut in. "And she confirmed the alarm was off when she arrived, which was unusual."

"After those digits were entered"—Vishous shrugged—"they they were in like Flint."

"I loved those movies," Tohr said under his breath.

"Zowie." The cop lifted his glass. "Cheers to Coburn."

"So who wants Broadius dead." Tohr looked at V. "I only scratched the surface on his identity. I need you to go further."

"No problem." Vishous tapped his lappy. "By noon, I'll know a lot. By nightfall, I'll be able to tell you even what his favorite fucking color was."

"I love you," Tohr said under his breath.

"You should." V started touching the screen. "Because while we're on the subject of surveillance footage, I know who left that envelope in the Audience House's waiting room. Lady and gentlemales, I'd like you to meet our courier."

As everybody went forward again, the Lenovo was turned back around. "Meet Candice, daughter of Meiser."

This time, there were four images in a square, each offering a different angle of the waiting area. When V hit the play button, a short female in a wool coat entered and checked in with the receptionist, her voice well modulated and quiet. Then she nodded pleasantly to the male and female who were seated on the couch, and took the single chair by the door.

"I'll speed it up," V said as he tapped something.

Abruptly, the little clock in the lower right-hand corner went into flight mode, and the three vampires twitched and jerked through their movements, their feet tapping, their hands shooting up to cover a cough, a series of tiny, split-second tilts of heads punctuating the Alvin-and-the-Chipmunks-octave, staccato convo that was exchanged.

And then the couple was called out. After which a male came in with a female and a tiny baby in a pink blanket. They took the place of those who'd departed on the sofa.

More time passed at a dead run, and more super-sonic chatter twittered along.

Then one of Saxton's paralegals came in and the female in the single chair stood up. As she did, an envelope fell out from under her coat and got wedged in the juncture between the arm and the seat.

Tohr frowned. "She didn't know it was—"

"Wait for it." V tapped the upper right quadrant feed, which showed the door. "Wait . . ."

Just before the female stepped out, she glanced back—and not at the couple with the young.

Her worried eyes went to where she had been sitting.

And the envelope she had left behind.

"She knew what she was doing," Tohr said.

V nodded. "She did."

"So why'd she deny it?"

"Well, there's the fun part. I tried to call her back? She didn't answer. Phone's a burner, address was a lie, and there's no record of that name in any of the databases."

"So who the hell is she?"

Vishous shook his head, and shut the laptop. "At this point, your guess is as good as mine, true?"

CHAPTER ELEVEN

When the sun was properly peeking over the horizon, Callum pulled on his parka and stepped out of the garage's second-story living quarters. As he went to shut the door, he caught sight of something on the newel post at the top of the staircase.

With a frown, he picked up the yellow and white tube. Turning it over, he read the label: Polysporin.

He put the ointment back where it had been left for him—and with the next step he took, he felt the pain in his ankle as if it were a fresh bite.

Funny, how you could ignore something as long as you weren't fucking reminded of it.

Yup, on the descent, he was definitely limping, and

as he exited the garage, he inherited another physical inconvenience: Snow-blindness.

Covering his eyes with his bare hands, he thought, *Well, hell, all I need is a good knee to the balls to finish things off.*

After his retinas calmed down, he lowered his arms, but still had to fight the squint as he headed to the truck. Overhead, the last of the storm clouds had moved off, and the sky was a brilliant, robin's-egg blue. With nothing to block the sun's rays, and everything covered with snow, daylight was amplified to an unbearable brilliance.

Breathing in deep, the inside of his nose hummed, and when he exhaled, he created his own cloud that hung in the still air in his wake. Odd, that there was absolutely no wind. It was like the intensity of the blizzard had used up all the energy in the elements, and there needed to be some kind of recharge before there was so much as a breeze.

Before he got behind the wheel, he looked over at the big house. The safety shields were down for the day all around the rambling structure, the reflective skins providing dozens of snapshots of the winter landscape. Even with them in place and keeping the sunlight out of the interior, he was willing to bet the vampires were all underground, in those newly built subterranean bedrooms.

Screw the creepy crypts of human lore. Modern Draculas had Wi-Fi, nice sheets, and indoor plumbing.

He refused to think about which room Apex had chosen. Or whether the male had decided to sleep on top of one of the king-sized beds . . . or if he'd decided to strip down and get under all the duvets—

"Get going," he said in a low voice.

Instead, he just stared at the Ford. The truck needed a bath, all kinds of snow streaks and salt grime dusting its flanks and hood and front windshield.

As he considered where he was headed, he recognized that there was a time when he would have shifted and traveled on paws to his destination, but he didn't trust his other side anymore. A month ago, his wolf had broken out and he'd ended up back on Deer Mountain, where the clan was. He'd woken up naked in the cave he'd once called his home, the heated spring just as it had once been, the furniture he'd put in it more than forty years ago totally unchanged.

It had been the last thing he'd wanted to revisit. And then one of his cousins, who he hadn't wanted to see, either, had shown up with questions and kindness.

Both equally unbearable.

So, yeah, when he'd merely come to next to the plow last night, he'd counted himself lucky.

Forcing himself into action, he yanked open the door—

And found the keys he hadn't realized he'd left behind in the drink cup holder.

Hefting himself up, he thought, Well, fuck, some groundskeeper he was, not protecting the estate's equipment. Although in his defense, no one would have been out in that storm.

On that note, not many were this far north at all this time of year.

After starting the engine, he hit reverse, and then realized the plow was still on—and keeping it on would be a waste of gas, and a pain in the neck on the highway. Getting back out, he went around and disengaged the thing, leaving it where it was, right in the way of the garage bays.

Once more with feeling.

It was not long before he was on the Northway heading south, and he made slow time, traveling the single lane of tire ruts that ran down the center of I-87. Efforts had been made to clear the snowfall in a rudimentary way, and no doubt there would be other passes by the big municipal plows as the day went on.

Maybe he should have left his plow on—

"Just shut up," he muttered. "And also, stop thinking while you're at it."

Unfortunately, all he had was the highway ahead to focus on.

No music to Bluetooth—because he'd left his cell phone on the bureau by the bed on purpose. No radio—because he didn't want to deal with what would be mostly static. No Sirius—because this was a work truck and the aristocrat who owned it might be willing to pay hundreds of thousands of dollars on the kitting out, upkeep, and human-world taxes of the old Adirondack estate.

But that monthly subscription was too much for a lowly worker.

Not that Callum cared.

In fact, he wasn't much aware of driving, even though his hand was on the steering wheel and his right foot angled down on the accelerator—and the snow-covered peaks and forests of white-dusted pine trees were streaking by him. He couldn't have said whether he was hot or cold, couldn't have cared less if the heat in the cab was on or not. And not even the brightness of the sun bothered him anymore.

In his mind, he was in darkness, and not the kind that came with the night.

And shit was getting darker by the mile.

When he got to the exit he'd come for, he floated down a slippery descent, and as the stop sign at the bottom approached, he pumped the brakes and was gentle with the steering. As much as he didn't care about his own health and safety, his destination was an obsession and ending up in a ditch on the way was not part of his plan.

Left or right? Of course, right.

He shouldn't have been surprised that he knew the way so well.

Willow Hills Sanatorium had never left him. Not its location. Not its five stories of patient porches or its tower-like core. Not the rotten, moldy smell of the place, or the layout, or the landscape.

Six miles farther down and he hit the brakes again. Hard.

The turnoff into the unkempt property wasn't plowed, and as high off the ground as the truck was, he didn't want to run the risk of getting stuck on his way to the chain-link fence—assuming the thing still ran a circle around the place.

Pulling forward to get closer to the road's snow-packed shoulder, he measured whether there was enough room for traffic to pass. The county plows, the big boys, had already gone through properly, so as long as none of those had to squeeze by, things were okay.

Getting out and locking the truck, he pocketed the keys and lithely jumped over the mound—

On the other side, he sank into the pack up to his knees—and for a moment, he just stayed there, in a snare of snow. As he looked up, he studied the piercing sky, then he measured the pine trees standing so docilely in the cold.

Once again, he could have shifted or dematerialized.

He didn't.

As he pulled up one of his boots, and forced his leg down again, he wanted the exhaustion that was going to come with trudging through the acreage. Maybe it would help him finally sleep a little.

Starting across the wintery landscape, he felt like there were miles to go, especially with his bad ankle—

Right on cue, his brain kicked up a memory of Apex, walking through the blizzard toward the garage, emerging from the buffered, blustery night in all that black leather.

Like a stalker.

Then again, the male had been tracking Callum ever since he'd come back to the Adirondacks, a shadow cast by the past that fucked him up at the weirdest moments, the memories the kind of thing where he would be minding his own business, chopping wood, clearing snow off one of the main house's flat roofs, making a meal . . . and an image of the vampire would slice through whatever he was doing and take over, an opaque shield that he couldn't see through, couldn't get around, couldn't burrow under.

And now that he'd actually seen the male in person? It was worse—

Apex's voice was the same. Deep, with a slight rasp, his accent characteristic of vampires.

And he was always frowning. Still.

"I didn't feel anything," Callum said into the cold, still air. "Not a thing. I did not feel . . . anything . . ."

Except he was lying.

He had felt too much. Which was why he'd had to come here.

To the prison.

CHAPTER TWELVE

Back at Camp Ghreylke, Mahrci sat at the foot of the bed she'd been sleeping on top of for the last couple of days, her bare legs dangling off the end, her socked feet turned in as they always had. In her cupped hands, her cell phone was like a grenade with the pin still in, the kind of thing that wouldn't explode as long as she didn't turn it on.

Apex was right. Her father was going to show up here if she didn't do something.

What the hell had she been thinking, coming up to his property here? Then again, he had so many estates, apartments, and buildings, it was nearly impossible to keep track of what he owned, and he didn't come to Connelly even in the good months. As usual, the acquisition and the transformation of the property had been what had interested him.

Not the enjoyment. Never . . . the enjoyment.

The arrival of her unanticipated roommates was a reminder that, however far she could go, there was no escaping her reality. Not with Whestmorel as her father.

Not with the male he wanted her to get mated to.

Not with what she had done.

Taking a deep breath, Mahrci hovered her thumb over the button on the side of the iPhone. Then she pushed the thing in harder than she had to, and set the cell aside on the flannel duvet.

Looking around, she had no emotional reaction to the space. She had picked this room only because it was the first one she had come to as she'd bottomed out on the underground level. Like all the other daytime suites her sire had insisted on building, as well as the house above, everything was done in interior-decorator-Adirondack, the colors evergreen, crimson, and gold, the woodwork left natural, the furniture made of polished logs and branches with the bark still on them. Yes, technology controlled the temperature, the Wi-Fi, and the lighting, but every effort had been made to hide the screens and even the ductwork.

No expense had been spared, even though he didn't care about the property.

And in this respect, she was just like his real estate portfolio. His art collection. His cars.

Well, she didn't have a monogram branded on her butt like a head of cattle. And considering everything, that was kind of a surprise.

Putting her hand out to the side, she palmed the phone, and turned the goddamn thing over. As the cell connected with the Wi-Fi, calls, voicemails, and texts came in, the banners running like water—

Until things were cut off by a phone call coming through.

Closing her eyes, she swiped her finger across the screen and put the unit up to her ear—

"No voicemail this time? Is this really you, Mahricelle?"

The long vowels, clipped consonants, and high altitude attitude went through her nervous system like a charge of electricity, and she straightened her spine and set her shoulders back.

I can do this, she told herself.

Clearing her throat, she said, "Hello, Father—"

"I am sending a car at nightfall. I expect you to get

in it and come back to Caldwell promptly. I will deal
with you when you—"

Her heart thundered. "No."

In the pause that followed, she imagined him at
his desk in his study in Caldwell, a dark red, monogrammed robe tucked around his trim body, his black
hair styled in a side part with nothing out of place, his
elegant hand removing the reading glasses that sat at
the end of his straight nose.

"I beg your pardon," came the icy response.

She shook her head, even though he couldn't see
her. "I'm not coming back—"

"Yes, you are. And you are going to apologize to
Remis, and beg him to forgive you. Then you are getting mated in a month."

"I'm not d-doing any of that."

There was another stretch of silence, as if her father
were translating her words into a language he could
understand.

"Then you are a trespasser." The brisk throat
clearing was something she had heard before. When
he was addressing a subordinate. "And I will have my
head of security remove you from my premises—and
let us think that through, shall we. Where will you

go? What will you live off of—and before you say the love and support of your aunt, I control the finances of this entire bloodline. If you think for one minute anyone will take you in or give you funds, you are mistaken."

"I can find my way—"

"No, you cannot. The sooner you realize this, the faster we can all put this folly of yours behind."

She got to her feet. "I'm packing my bags right now. I'll clear out at sunset."

There was a third pause. And then her sire's voice gentled some. "Mahricelle. Be reasonable. The mating has been planned for—"

"And I won't trouble you again."

"Darling, I worry over you. I want only good things for you, so please, let us resume our course. Remis is a fine male of worth who can provide quite readily for you. Your future is with him—and your *mahmen*, if she were here, would be saying the very same thing."

Lowering her head, Mahrci rubbed over her eyebrows. "I can't do this. Anymore."

That cold tone, the one she hated because it frightened her, came back. "I did not realize being provided for and having your every desire catered to was such a burden. I have invested in you. I have supported you your entire life. I would hate for you to know what it is like to be without that—"

"Support?" she snapped. "Is that what this is? Because it feels like coercion to me. What I want to know is why Remis is so important to *you*."

As another call beeped in, she could guess who it was and she was not answering it. "If you like him so much, I think you should mate him yourself."

Mahrci hung up on her father and got to her feet in a rush.

But it was daytime, so she was going nowhere fast.

She was stuck in a gilded cage.

———

"Well, look who's winning the OCD award this morning."

Directly above Mahrci, in the study, Apex looked up from the floorboards he was kneeling on. Mayhem was leaning against the room's archway, a tall figure whose godforsaken mullet was damp, suggesting he'd just had a shower. With a chocolate pudding cup in one hand, and an ornate silver spoon in the other, he was sporting a royal blue bathrobe that was marked on the pec with the same crest that was on the estate's gates. The plates. The sheets.

Like Whestmorel was afraid guests would forget who was paying for everything. Or maybe he felt like he owned people while they were under his roof.

"Why aren't you putting yourself down for some beauty rest," Apex muttered. "Maybe your hair will fix itself if you sleep on it wet."

"You love my hair."

"No, I don't."

When one of the male's bare feet started tapping, the repetitive beat took Apex back to the drive up here and the damn drum set the guy made out of everything.

"What," Apex demanded.

"Hm?" That silver spoon got licked clean. "Oh, nothing."

As Mayhem just stayed where he was, with the tapping and the fucking pudding and the stupid pretentious robe, it was a case of NOT AGAIN: For the second time in twenty-four hours, Apex wondered how the problems of other folks were suddenly all over his proverbial windshield.

"What's wrong," he grumbled.

In response, Mayhem's eyes traveled around the voluminous—natch—room, like he was taking note of the collection of old hardbacks. In reality, it was doubtful anything was registering. He was doing the same thing with the spoon, going around and around the plastic pudding cup, the little scraping noise like the cymbal to that bouncing foot thing.

"Can you stop that?"

The guy shook himself to attention. "Huh?"

Apex drew circles in the air. "The goddamn spoon, and your foot—and fuck off with that robe? You think this is a spa?"

"You need a vacation."

Apex let his head fall forward. "That is not what I—"

"And the sauna was nice." The guy pointed to the floor with the spoon. "I recommend a little relaxation down there."

"I don't need to relax!"

"Really? 'Cuz that's a cute little lineup you got there. Are you getting ready to teach those pocket-rocket security cameras math or something? Nice classroom rows you've made."

Apex motioned at the cameras—intending to fuck that one right off. Except . . . well, he had to admit things were pretty frickin' tidy. He'd even lined up the four duffles he'd emptied.

"I had to count them to make sure I have what we need," he groused.

"You didn't do that before you left Caldwell?"

Of course he had. "No, I didn't."

"So you can't sleep, either, huh." Mayhem motioned with the spoon again. "So I'm guessing our job here is to mount them everywhere so they can take pretty pictures of things."

"Look at you go, Einstein. What's next, quantum physics?"

"And here I thought you brought me for my charming personality." Mayhem came farther in, and tossed the container in a wastepaper basket by one of the leather chairs. "Why's this such a secret?"

"Discretion is part of my job."

"Even for people you're hiring to help you?" Mayhem put the licked-clean spoon in the robe's pocket. Then he went over to the last duffle that was set aside. As he started to unzip the top, he said, "Besides, I thought we were friends—"

"*Stop*." As Mayhem went statue, Apex thought fondly of a deserted island, somewhere in the middle of the ocean, where no one could reach him. Even by cell phone. "That's just my clothes. You can leave that alone."

The male put his hands up. "Okay, boss. And have I mentioned I'm touched that you picked me, out of everybody else, to be the one who holds your step-ladder while you screw these suckers in?"

"You're gonna do more than that."

"Annnnnd now we get into the meat of things." Mayhem headed over to the cold hearth and paused to scratch the chin of the bobcat that was mounted on the river stone. "Finally."

"You're in charge of making sure the motherboard pulls it all together, and channels the feeds where they need to go."

"Oh, that old bollocks again?"

"You're good at programming." Tragically so. "I'm not."

"Why, thank you." The male put his hand over his heart, right by that stupid stitched crest. "But again, you could have told me this before."

When Apex grunted, the male leaned in. "You want me to change the subject, right?"

"Yes."

"Fine, so who is she."

Apex frowned. "Who—Mahrci?"

"No, the other female who's under this roof with us." Mayhem wandered over to the rustic desk and clicked the old-fashioned green-shaded lamp on. Off. On. Off. On. "She's not just a housekeeper—"

"*Will you quit it.*"

"What?"

Apex waved his hand around like he was batting at bees. "The goddamn noise. Jesus, the tapping, the clicking, the—"

"You live alone, don't you."

"*Yes.* And you're reminding me why—turn that *fucking* lamp off and step away from the desk before I shoot you."

Although no doubt the guy'd find something else to flick around with: A wall-mounted switch. That door over there. Maybe the fucker would go poor-man's-Neil-Peart on the coffee table with that spoon.

Mayhem's pensive look was not a good sign. "Tell me who she is."

"Oh, come on—"

Click. The lamp turned off. *Click.* The lamp turned on—

"You know," Apex pointed out, "they're going to name a medical procedure after you if you keep that up. And it's going to involve removing a light fixture from someone's asshole."

"Tell me." *Click.* "I got nothing better to do—"

"You need to ask her. What the fuck does it have to do with me?"

P.S., wasn't that the theme of his frickin' life since he'd entered this zip code.

At least the male stopped with the lamp. "Look, I've always been fair with you. I just want to know why she's here."

As Mayhem went totally still, like not-even-breathing still, Apex let himself fall back on his ass. And before he could string a proper give-it-up together, the male cut in.

"I overheard her arguing on her phone." Mayhem pointed to the floor, like it wasn't obvious where he'd been. "Downstairs."

"Stalking does *not* need to be added to your résumé of skills and training."

"I was heading for the stairs to come find you."

Apex shook his head. "She's not for you."

"I didn't say I was interested in her."

"Really. So why're you asking me about—"

"I only want to know who wants her to leave here."

"FYI, she speaks the same language you do. I'm *not* the person you need to be asking these questions."

"I don't want to seem invasive."

"Going behind her back and pumping me for details is the very definition of that." Apex picked up one of the cameras and thought about how fond he was of inanimate objects that just did their job without drama. "We're here to set up this system and get the fuck out. That's it."

Well, that was true for Mayhem—and goddamn, he wished he had the guy's techie skills. If he himself knew that much about computers, he could have avoided this claptrap altogether.

Mayhem glanced out of the archway he'd come through. "She was scared. The scent of fear was so strong, I smelled it out in the fucking hallway." The male looked back. "And no, I don't believe the housekeeper bullshit. You were surprised to see her. You'd have known she was up here, if you were coming to do this job and she was the staff. Also, there's no food in the house. The beds weren't made—and they would have been if she'd been in charge. I know you know the truth, and if I'm going to protect her, I want to be prepared."

"No one's asking you to do that, Mayhem."

"Well, I'm volunteering because no one else is doing it." Those eyes narrowed with a calculation that was a surprise. "You're only in charge of taking care of her father."

In the silence that followed, Apex got to his feet with a curse. He hadn't expected things to get brass-tacks real, not with Mayhem. And that laissez-faire attitude, even more than the male's IT abilities, was the real reason he'd picked the former prisoner.

Mayhem never cared about anything.

"Do you trust me," Apex said softly.

There was a long pause, the other male's stare not wavering. And then the guy shook his head. "You know, Apex, at another time, in another place, I would have said yes. If only because you wouldn't waste time lying or screwing me over. But here, in this house? With whoever she is? I don't think I do."

Apex nodded once. "I respect that. And I'll tell you something—not because we're friends, but because it's going to make what I'm doing here easier."

"What."

"Do *not* get involved with this family." Apex put his palm out, and deepened his voice. "They are not who you think they are, and you do not want their problems."

CHAPTER THIRTEEN

What was that human saying? *Through the woods and across the streams, to Grandmother's house we drove . . .*

Or was it across the woods and through the fields? No streams? And was it a bicycle? Or on foot.

Oh, who the fuck cared.

Knee-deep in snow, Callum stopped to catch his breath, locking his hands on his hips and scenting the air. The acreage all around him was a tangled mess draped in drifts and accumulation: The undergrowth was matted up after decades of neglect, and the trees were packed in tight, alternating between pines that showed some green and oaks and maples that were gray and skeletal. Clearly, even bare minimum landscaping had been given up, and the chain-link fence had also been abandoned, the lot of it nothing but collapsed sections and posts now.

He was finally in range, though.

Through the interlocking bushes, branches, and boughs, the looming, glooming front facade of the Willow Hills Sanatorium was straight out of an eighties horror movie. And as his gut sank, he would have taken a step back if his boots hadn't been locked into the snow.

Ah, yes. This was why he hadn't dematerialized.

He'd wanted to reserve the right to turn back.

Looking away, he caught a glimpse of a deer struggling to get out of his sight. Off to the left, a hawk soared over a little clearing, obviously in search of breakfast. Otherwise, nothing moved, and he felt as though the entire layout was a snare trap, luring him in just to snap on a limb and keep him in place for the hunter who was going to claim him.

"Why the fuck did you come here," he muttered.

In lieu of a verbal answer, his body kept going on its own, his feet lifting high and sinking back down through the snowdrifts once again, his hands reaching up and pushing branches out of his way. When he hit the edge of the forest, he paused once more . . . and then he stepped out onto what once must have been a rolling lawn that ran all the way up to the brick sprawl.

This part of the property had been maintained. Of course it had, because it increased the defensive position of the structure.

Maybe the Brotherhood still owned the place after all these years.

God . . . damn. The degraded building was exactly as he remembered, its central core the anchor for two flanks that had been the real purpose of the place. Back before antibiotics, the treatment for tuberculosis patients had been fresh air, so each of the wings' five levels was a long, open porch, onto which the afflicted, in their beds, could be rolled.

He didn't know the full details of the sanatorium's history. But he was dead clear on the fact that, some thirty years ago, it had been used, for a short time, as a hidden prison for a bunch of vampires. And after the liberation? It had been a clinic for the treatment of said prisoners, who had been, for the most part, falsely caged and used as drug processors. There had been a lot of disease and malnourishment among the males and females, and the Black Dagger Brotherhood had given the survivors everything they'd needed to recover.

Now the facility was apparently back to a steady state of being empty.

At least that was what the departing seasonal staff of the Ghreylke estate had told him back in the fall, when he'd just had to ask.

But he'd never intended on coming for a visit.

Resuming his trek, he closed in on the towering center part. He wasn't sure what his plan was, and didn't decide, until he arrived at the entrance, that he had to go inside.

It was like poking an open wound to see how bad the infection was. You just had to mess with your injury.

The double doors were locked, and as he looked up at the facade, he realized strategic investments had been made. Though the surface appearance of degradation had been preserved, the place had been shored up with new windows, and security cameras were mounted all around the decorative frieze that ran between the second and third floors. The Brotherhood had to still own the place. God knew they possessed the financial resources to keep anything forever, even if there was no one inside—

When there was a buzz and a click, he frowned.

This time, when he tried the right side of the doors again, he was able to pull things open. Clearly, he'd passed muster with the security guard, even though he hadn't been in the vampire world for how long now?

Guess those Brothers had long memories—or databases full of identities.

Had they taken his mug shot when he'd been . . . recovering—

Okay, wow. Talk about your reno jobs.

Back when the hospital had been a going concern, more than a hundred years ago, the first floor of the core had clearly been a check-in and waiting space, and courtesy of some serious effort, it was once again sparkling clean, the floor polished, the walls freshly painted, and the ceiling patched.

No furniture, though. Also no people.

As he wandered around, motion-activated lights came on, but he didn't need them. There was plenty of daylight streaming through the triple-paned glass, and as he went farther in, everything continued to be well maintained.

The next thing he knew, he was down a hall and standing in front of a door that made his blood run cold.

He was exactly where he didn't want to be.

Except this was the reason he'd come, wasn't it.

The scene of . . . the crime that had been perpetrated on him.

When Apex and the others had decided to overthrow the head of the guards and free the prisoners, he'd joined in on the attack on the latest in a series of despots. Why? He was used to fighting and he liked it. As a wolven, combat was a way of life, whether it was defending the clan's territory from other wolven or killing poachers before they killed members of the clan. Besides, pain had never scared him, and he was fast on his feet—and his paws.

Not fast enough that night. Not that time.

In a trance, he put his palm flat on the door. On the other side? The private quarters of that female who had tied him down and used him until he had separated from his own flesh.

Images filtered through and registered viscerally in his body, hands touching him, rolling him over face-down, a male body mounting his own.

In a sickening rush, he remembered that female watching him as he was fucked ... before she turned him back over and threw a leg across his hips to ride him.

After a while, all he had known was whether his face was in the mattress or he was staring up at the ceiling.

Eventually, he hadn't even felt any physical sensations anymore.

It was as if a hole had been dug with each session and his soul had sunk further and further down, away from the corporeal world.

Into a prison inside of himself.

At some point, he'd lost consciousness. And he only knew that because, eventually, he'd woken up.

A scent had been what had brought him back.

"Apex . . ." he whispered.

The vampire's presence had been his beacon to return to the physical world, and he'd followed it back for reasons he hadn't understood. And at first, he'd refused to open his eyes—because he wouldn't have been able to bear seeing the male he had been so attracted to.

Lying there on that bedding platform, he'd gotten stronger with the passage of days, his body rebounding thanks to the nourishment Apex had forced down his throat. And that hadn't been the only thing provided to him. His wounds had been carefully looked after, his base bodily functions attended to with diapers, his skin ever so gently cleansed and rebandaged on a regular schedule.

As he'd noted the contrast with the way his body had been treated by that female, that was when the first claw of sorrow had dug into him.

So he'd refused to think about it again.

Instead, he'd concentrated on the sounds of the voices, the comings and goings of the medical staff, and where Apex was—which was never far. Through his eavesdropping, he'd learned that the liberation of the facility was sticking, that the guards who had been commanded by that female had all run off or been killed, that the site was secured by the Black Dagger Brotherhood, and that the prisoners who hadn't died of starvation and disease were being treated.

He'd also known Kane was around. Lucan, too. And their mates, especially Nadya, who was a nurse.

He'd memorized the schedule, knew when darkness fell because that was when Apex always brought in the first round of food—and then the male would leave for a stretch of time, returning freshly showered with something that Callum, until he'd finally opened his lids, had assumed carried a spritz of perfume.

Not perfume, though. White blooms.

The night he had decided he was strong enough to leave, he had waited until Apex left to go get the first of the meals. Then, he had finally opened his eyes.

He'd been on his back, and the sight of that ceiling? It had ripped him back to that female riding him—for a split second, he had blinked and seen her straddling him again, felt the sensations, jerked at binds that no longer existed.

He could still remember the battle it had been to stay in the present. And his wonder at the flowers had helped him focus.

All around the bedding platform, set in little glass containers, there had been roses and carnations and sprigs of baby's breath.

It had been spring in his sorrow.

And that was when he'd cried.

Not for long, though. He hadn't had a lot of time if he wanted to avoid a goodbye he didn't have the strength for . . .

A goodbye he still didn't have the strength for.

"Apex," he whispered—

"No, I am afraid that is not me."

Callum spun around. The male who had come up behind him was a striking figure, tall and lean, dressed in a black robe that fell to the floor, his black hair long and straight. At first glance, you might mistake him for some kind of ascetic, a religious figure who wafted through the physical world doing good deeds. Not it. Those gleaming dark eyes were calculating in a banked-nuclear-bomb kind of way.

Funny, how appearances could be deceiving.

The male's nose flared and there was a flash of surprise. "Oh, it's . . . you."

"Excuse me?"

"I know you." The figure drifted forward as if he were floating, bypassing Callum and pausing at the door. "Come in. Join me for a meal. It's the least I can do to pay you back."

Callum blinked. "For what?"

"Your hospitality."

Shaking his head, Callum blurted, "You must have me mistaken for someone—"

"Oh, no. I haven't."

"Who the hell are you?"

The male bowed. "Blade, blooded brother of Xhexania. And it's true, you do not know me, but I know you."

As the entrance was opened, Callum's entire body was suffused in fight-or-flight, echoes of the past whipping at him.

The male regarded him steadily. "You were hurt here, then?"

"Yes," he replied in a rough burst.

"And you've come back to see if the pain is still with you?" The smile was part sly, part soulful. "Hard to get stains out of the soul, isn't it."

"How do you know me?"

"I stayed in your cave. Up on Deer Mountain."

The male touched the side of his nose. "I recognize your scent."

Lights flared in the interior, and even though Callum didn't want to see, his eyes locked on what was revealed.

The exhale that came out of him was not relief, per se. But it was a release of some kind.

Nothing was the same. There was no bedding platform. No weapons on racks on the walls or lying about on tables. No combat clothes, no combat rations, no combat-clad guards waiting for a turn with him.

No female watching him get violated with hungry, angry eyes.

Just a lot of elegant, sleek furniture—and a white shag carpet that he had the absent, stupid thought was absolutely inappropriate in the middle of an abandoned goddamn sanatorium.

The bitch would be hard to vacuum, too.

Callum stepped forward without thinking, as his brain was too fucking busy trying to figure out what he was looking at.

"I have redecorated," the male said dryly.

"You have," Callum blurted.

There was even a white marble and brushed steel kitchen.

The male walked over and opened the Sub-Zero refrigerator. "I was going to pan-fry some scallops and steam my asparagus. I have a fresh loaf of French bread—and for dessert . . ." That calculating stare shot over his shoulder. "I'm feeling naughty. I have Ben and Jerry's mint chocolate chunk."

Callum walked around, putting his hand on a chair that was slipcovered in cream and white. And the back of a sofa that was done in the same damask pattern. He touched a cashmere throw blanket. Lingered at the foot of a king-sized bed that was draped in fine white and cream cotton covers.

"Not what you expected?" the male prompted.

Callum turned around. There was something . . . different . . . about the male. But he didn't feel threatened. "That cave you stayed in hasn't been mine for years. I've just moved back to the area."

"That makes two of us. I've been here for about a year." The smile that flared offered more of that sly warmth. "I stayed in your cave a long, long time ago."

"Me, too," Callum whispered.

"Well, aren't we two peas in a pod." Blade motioned to his stove. "And you either stay for dinner or depart, it's your choice. Either way, I need to eat."

CHAPTER FOURTEEN

One hour after nightfall, Tohr traveled in a scatter of molecules to the west, to a solidly middle-class neighborhood a good ten miles away from the Wheel. When he re-formed, it was in the shadows between a little Cape Cod and a ranch. Moments later, Qhuinn joined him.

"Across the street?" the brother asked.

"Yup, that's the house."

"Let's do this."

The snow dump from the blizzard the night before had been properly plowed and shoveled from the streets and walkways, but that didn't do much for them as they hoofed out across a lawn toward the street. Getting over the piles on either side of the road was a thing—and the first clue something was off was that the driveway and walkway they were heading for were not shoveled.

In fact, 2168 Foote Avenue was the only house on the street that hadn't gone the snow removal route. The split-level was well-tended enough, with a solid roof, trimmed bushes and shrubs, and a fit-in-with-the-humans Christmas wreath on the front door. But the little place was totally snowed in still. Of course, as a vampire lived there, you could make the argument that getting a car in and out of the garage wasn't neces-sary. Except when as Tohr measured the darkened windows? Yes, interior shutters could explain that, too, but—

"I don't think anyone's home," Qhuinn said as they stopped next to the mailbox. "Or has been for a while."

Tohr glanced around. It was a cold night, so most of the humans had their drapes pulled to keep the heat in, and this was good news. Also, no traffic com-ing and going on the street. Everyone was still hun-kered down, in recovery from the weather drama.

"You ready to do a little breaking and entering?" he said.

Qhuinn nodded. "Yup, I think it's come to that."

The two of them walked down the property line

on the right, heading for the back corner of the garage. Off in the distance, a dog barked, and the scent of spaghetti sauce wafted over on the breeze, like the people next door were running the hood over their stove as they heated up *nonna's* gravy.

When they made the turn and got to a door, Qhuinn stepped up with a lock kit and went to work. He didn't take long, and then they were in the garage.

There was a very faint smell of gas in the air, but no car. As Tohr triggered a penlight, some faded oil marks in the center of the one-car space soaked up the illumination.

"Looks like our friend Candice left . . ." Tohr murmured as he walked over to the entry into the home. " . . . waaaaaay before she went to the Audience House two nights ago. If this is even her place."

At this point, he had no idea who the hell the female was. The name she'd given when she'd registered to see Wrath? False identity—and the irony was that she'd come to get it verified and entered into the species database. Or at least that was her excuse to get in the door and drop off that package.

"If she has a security system," he said as they went over to the interior door, "it'll be interesting to see who shows up when the alarm goes off."

Maybe whoever it was could answer some questions. As this was clearly a vampire house—because there were no human scents anywhere—it wasn't going to be ADT and the Caldwell Police Department, for sure.

"Let's try to get inside," he said.

As he trained his light on the door, Qhuinn worked his lock kit at both a knob and a dead bolt. And then they were in a pitch-black kitchen that had been scrubbed clean: In his bright little beam, there was nothing out of place, the counters cleaned off, the little table shut down with its three chairs tucked in tight, the trash bin empty.

And no alarm.

When Qhuinn opened the refrigerator, the light went on—so there was electricity coming into the place and being paid for by somebody.

"Nothing," the brother said. "Not even ketchup or an old mustard container."

"Let me check the cupboards." Tohr found stacks of plates and lineups of glasses, but no food. "Nada."

"Is this a rental?" Qhuinn glanced over his shoulder, the piercings in his ears glinting in the light. "Or is that Candice's name on the deed?"

"Don't know. It's just the address she listed when

she registered with Saxton's paralegals. He's researching the property records as we speak."

The pair of them made quick work of the floor
plan: Living room, sitting room with a TV, two bedrooms, two full baths. Upstairs, there was a primary
suite, and what do you know, there were no clothes
in the dresser or the closet, no toiletries in the bath,
no photographs of the female or her family.

Back downstairs, Tohr stood at the base of the
steps and stared at the front door as he took out his
phone.

Vishous answered on the second ring. "Empty?"

"Like a ghost town. And you still haven't found
anything about her? At all?"

"Nothing. Whoever that female is, she's a ghost."
When Tohr went quiet, there was a chuckle on the
other end. "So you're thinking the same thing I am?"

Qhuinn came up from the basement. "Nothing in
the cellar except a pair of washing machines."

"She doesn't live here," Tohr concluded. "This was
a lie, too."

None of it made sense. Female comes in, to register a name that was fake and an address that was a lie,
into the species database. She leaves those papers behind and disappears.

"What're we doing now?" V said over the connection.

"I want you to send me a really good still of her from the footage," Tohr said grimly. "And the address of Broadius's maid, the one who found him."

CHAPTER FIFTEEN

L et me help you with that."

As Mayhem tossed the offer out into the breeze, he wanted to sound casual—when in reality, his fangs were tingling with aggression and he was surreptitiously checking that the gun he'd tucked at the small of his back was where he'd put it.

He'd slipped the weapon into his waistband and covered it with his fleece as soon as Mahrci had started putting on those red-and-gray ski pants and the matching parka.

"Really," he prompted when he got no response. "I want to help."

She looked up from the bag of livestock feed she

was humping off the mudroom's floor. "Oh, no, it's okay. I've got it."

And sure enough, she did. Even though it involved some grunting and straining, she managed to get the fifty-pound deadweight on her shoulder, buttressing it with a solid palm.

That landed like the slap on a bare ass.

Okay, that's hot, he thought as he eyed her braced stance.

"I'll let you open the door for me, though?" she said.

He was so distracted running his eyes down her body—and trying to pretend he wasn't checking her out—that he didn't realize she'd spoken. Then her expectant expression registered and he snapped to attention.

"Oh, yeah. Sure." Pulling on his own parka, he hustled for the back door of the mudroom. "And sorry, I'm just . . . I've got PTSD from the bite marks on those ski pants, k?"

Mahrci glanced down at herself. "It's just a couple of little pinpricks? They're still good enough to use. Now, how about that door?"

"Right, yup." He futzed around before the locks released. "Ladies first."

As she passed by him, he shut his lids and breathed in. Her scent was a combination of fresh air and female spice, and for a split second, it was all he knew.

Then the cold hit him and he whipped back into action.

There was not going to be a repeat of last night. Nope, not on his watch—

Thump!

Mahrci dumped the bag in the snow, and reached for one of the sets of snowshoes that were hanging on pegs on the side porch. When she bent down to strap them on, he had to look elsewhere, otherwise he felt like a fucking letch—so he focused on the moon overhead. It was just a sliver, but it was super bright because of the clear night.

As he grabbed a set of the shoes, too, she glanced over from her crouch. "So you're really coming with me?"

He let the tennis rackets fall to the snowy porch boards. "You mind? I've been cooped up all day. Need some fresh air."

She straightened. "And you joining in has nothing to do with—"

"Your little furry forest friends? The ones with the matched sets of dental daggers?" He made a pshaw with his bare hand. "Naaaaah."

Mahrci tilted her head as she stared up at him, in that way she did . . . and her dark blue eyes were so lovely in the moonlight, he briefly forgot his own name.

But stayed clear on his priorities.

"Please don't argue with me." He didn't bother to hide the hard tone behind his words. "I'm not rolling any dice with your life, especially ones that come on four paws. That wolf? It's still out there."

And so was whoever had scared her so badly on the phone.

"All right," she said roughly. "Thank you."

As they just kept staring at each other, it was the oddest thing. He felt as though there were ties binding them together, physical ones, wrapping around and around their bodies.

"No problem," he said.

Straightening, she cleared her throat and held up her forefinger. "I carry the bag, though."

He saluted her as she hefted the weight up on her shoulder again. "Yes, ma'am."

They set off as soon as he finished buckling in— and holy fuck. The snowshoes required coordination. As he pitched and Pisa'd, beat the air with his arms, and nearly ate the ground a couple of times, she waited for him and tried not to laugh.

"You're doing great—oh!"

Catching himself a bush, he shoved himself back to level. "FYI, if this is your definition of 'great,' that word means something entirely different to me."

"It takes some getting used to." She blew a strand of hair out of her face. "But you'll get the hang of it."

"Yup. Absolute—fuck." He clapped a hand over his mouth. "Sorry, fudge."

Now she didn't hide the giggle as she started off. "Please don't edit yourself for my benefit."

Well, that's a relief, he thought as he followed after her. *I've always sucked at that.*

"I feel like one of those dogs with booties on their feet."

Mahrci glanced back at him and smiled. "You kind of look like it, too."

The mental sound of an old-fashioned camera shutter preceded what he knew to be a permanent memory: Her hair was tied at her nape again, and the ponytail was tangled in the high collar of the parka. Her cheeks were bright red from the cold and her eyes were such a resonant blue, they appeared to glow in the darkness.

She was so beautiful in the winter landscape, his chest ached.

"Why are you looking at me like that?" she whispered.

Taking two bad clomps forward on the snow, he reached out and brushed that strand of hair out of her face. As he tucked it behind her ear, the end of it caught the breeze and curled around her lips.

He couldn't help but stare at her mouth.

"I was just thinking," he murmured, "that that grain bag really brings out the color of your eyes."

Her laughter was loud and a little honky, and he found it so frickin' endearing, he was the one who started walking again. Snowshoeing again? Whatever—he knew he had to get moving or he was going to do something too soon.

"So how long have you been working for the guy who owns this place?" he asked casually.

"All my life," she muttered. "How about you and Apex?"

He wasn't a fan of liars, but reminded himself that he was a stranger to her. She didn't owe him shit about herself.

A stranger for now, at least.

"I'm an independent contractor. I work with Mr. Personality sometimes."

"I noticed you guys screwed a lot over day." As

Mayhem fumbled his feet, she barked a laugh. "I mean, the cameras. You screwed in the—oh, forget it."

"We got them all up, but the job's only halfway done. I've got a lot of programming to do before we leave."

And he was going to take his sweet goddamn time at it. Maybe even have to work through a couple of software "crashes."

"No more secrets in the big house, huh," she said as they entered the tree line.

"Nope."

"Little much for a summer place that's hardly used, don't you think."

"Those kinds of questions are way above my pay grade."

With a hop and a grunt, she repositioned the grain bag. "And what do you do when you're not screwing"—she glanced over with a smile—"*in* cameras."

"Oh, I'm a pretty simple male. I like long walks on the beach, rom-coms from the nineties, and pink cocktails."

Her laughter was like a goal line he wanted to get to over and over. And then she looked at him and he found another motivation.

"How about you?" he asked as he stared at her lips.

"I've never been to the beach before, I'm not a big fan of pink or alcohol—but I did see a Sandra Bullock movie once and liked it. Does that count?"

"Depends on which movie. I mean they're ancient now, but there were eras, if you know what I mean."

"I can't remember exactly. I think there was a guy in a coma and she falls for the brother—"

"*While You Were Sleeping.*"

"—who's a furniture maker?" She smiled again. "Is that the title? And there was the guy who liked her shoes?"

"Joe Junior."

"That's the one."

"And that's a classic, so yes, it counts."

They both started laughing, and Mayhem thought back to the last time he'd been with a female who made him feel lighter in his spirit.

Never. Try never.

"What's your favorite food?" he asked as they kept going, with him holding pine boughs out of her way.

And that was how it went. Back and forth, easy, but exciting. And when the platform came into view, Mayhem wished the damn thing was across the state.

"I just feel bad," she said as she let the grain bag fall to the ground.

"Because you like mass-produced American choc-olate? There's no shame in M&M's, you know."

"No, the deer." She looked around. "I'm leaving, and I worry that they won't get enough to eat."

"Where are you going?" he said softly.

There was a long silence. "I know, I know, they've been foraging for years through the wintertime, but I want to do something to help . . . someone."

Out came a Swiss Army knife, and she made quick work of the top of the bag's knitted fabric. With another grunt, she barrel hugged the weight up onto the platform and let the grain pour out. When things were empty, she shoved at the pile, flattening it.

"I think the birds get some. The squirrels." Mahrci picked up the empty bag and rolled it into a ball. "I want them all to have a full belly—"

Off in the distance, a set of headlights flared through the trees and came down the lane. As Mahrci glanced at the strobing, her expression tightened with fear.

"Who do you worry's in that car?" he asked grimly.

CHAPTER SIXTEEN

God knows how many hours after Callum turned down Blade's invitation to eat, the sound of the front entrance of the sanatorium opening woke him up. As he lifted his chin off his collarbone and opened his eyes, he was momentarily confused as to what time it was. But he knew where he was, even though the hallway outside of the private quarters was cast in shadows.

And his sore ass and stiff shoulders suggested that, yes, he had fallen asleep sitting up against the wall.

Maybe it was Blade coming back.

Sometime after the scent of scallops and asparagus had wafted through the door's jambs, the other male had stepped out and said he was leaving for a while, but that any wolven on the property, especially ones who were—in his words—tense, wall-eyed, and twitchy, were welcome to stay as long as they liked.

Evidently, the male had bought the place from the Brotherhood after years of roaming—and was willing to be hospitable.

"I'm not wall-eyed," Callum muttered into the dark.

Out in the waiting area, the motion-activated lights came on and the glow rounded the corner. Bending his legs up, one of his knee joints popped and he winced as his butt repositioned itself on the hard floor.

It was time for him to go, anyway.

As he went to get to this feet, he had to lock his molars. Funny, how you could turn into a board just by sitting on them—

Apex stepped into the hallway. "How's your ankle."

Callum froze.

Blink. Blink. Blink—"You came all this way to check on my leg?" he muttered.

"It's not that far. As the crow flies."

"How did you"—Callum grunted as he got all the way to vertical with the help of the wall—"know I was here?"

The vampire took that tube of Polysporin out of his leather jacket. "It wasn't that hard."

"You figured it out from an antibacterial lotion?"

Apex eyed the stuff. "It's an ointment, not a lotion. And the tube was not in the same place I'd left it on the newel post, so I knew you'd seen it. And I figured if you took the plow off the front of the truck you were going on the highway."

"But how did you know I was coming . . . here."

"Where else would you go? I show up unannounced on your doorstep—"

"That is not my doorstep—"

"—and I bring baggage." Apex shrugged. "There have been a lot of things in my own life that are with me whether I want them to be or not. Sometimes you need to go back, if only to know whether it was all real."

"Of course I know it happened," Callum snapped.

The vampire looked away. Looked back. "But memories become dreams after a while. We live with them in our minds, and the edges get blurred until you're not as sure as you once were exactly what happened versus what your brain made up just to torture yourself more." Apex cursed and crossed his arms over his chest. "And like . . . the shit really cripples you, traps you, sinks you, and you think, am I doing this to myself? Or . . . was it done to me. For real."

Callum was dimly aware of his heart stopping.

"That's why you came back here," Apex concluded. "And that's how I knew where you were."

As a heavy silence stretched out, Callum went for a little walkabout, pacing back and forth.

"I don't know what to say to that."

Apex shrugged again. "You don't need to say anything. The truth is what it is, whether we comment on it or not—"

Before Callum knew what he was doing, he was right in front of the other male. And as he looked into those glittering black eyes, they flared so big, it was a wonder they didn't pop out and hit the floor.

Don't do it, he told himself. *Don't—*

His hand reached up and hovered beside the vampire's face. And when his palm closed the distance of its own volition, and he felt the warmth and the subtle friction of beard growth, he thought about the division between memories and dreams.

"Have you ever come back here?" he whispered. "To see if things were real."

Apex shook his head, and in doing so, caused a brushing touch to flare between the pair of them. "No, I haven't."

Callum dropped his hand. "Oh. Well, good for you. Glad you moved along—"

As he went to turn away, Apex grabbed his arm. "I think about you. Always."

The words were spoken with such urgency, there was no pretending to have misheard them or misunderstood.

And then there was the pain on that hard face. A special kind of agony radiated out of those eyes and flattened that mouth, and as Callum regarded the emotion, he felt the strangest unlocking in the center of his chest.

He was not alone.

He hadn't . . . been alone. In the suffering.

Callum swallowed through a tight throat. "You remember."

The vampire nodded and answered hoarsely, "Everything."

———

It had been the touch Apex had craved for so long, and the sensations did not disappoint. Though that palm had rested on his cheek for just a moment, he had felt it all through his body.

And now he knew a different kind of heat, as Callum lowered his head in shame and retreated internally. Even though the distance between them did not change, the male seemed to shrink where he stood—and that made Apex want to kill that fucking female all over again.

"It happened to me, too," he heard himself rasp. "Every time I pushed that food between your lips . . . with every towel I passed over your skin . . . for every hour I sat beside you and worried you were dying, what was done to you happened to me . . . too."

Apex's vision got blurry and he wiped his tears harder than he had to. And then with him being able to see, he had to look away from the wolven, from those icy blue eyes.

"I'm sorry I left like I did." Callum shook his head. "That night, thirty years ago. I couldn't—I just didn't have it in me to . . . say goodbye to you."

"I understand."

Even though he didn't, even though he hadn't. But now that he thought more about it, he supposed that was just because it had hurt so badly.

"You had to take care of yourself."

Their eyes held—and the sexual undercurrent surged. As it once had, all those years ago.

And it was too fucking weird. After all this time, he'd played this scene out in his head in so many different ways: There had been reunions of chance, like on the streets of downtown Caldwell some night, or in a restaurant, or in a supermarket. There had been the unexpected phone call, the out-of-the-blue contact that opened a random door. And then there had been his favorite, where Callum came and found him at his little bullshit house on the outskirts of town.

Maybe with a white rose in his hand because all those stupid fucking flowers he'd brought the guy had been remembered as the heartfelt gifts they had been.

There had been other fantasies, too. Like Lucan bringing the male over. Or maybe Kane doing the connecting. Both of those former prisoners knew where he lived, after all.

The last scenario he'd fantasized about had been the most impossible . . . and the one that had, on occasion, led him to have to do something to relieve himself: He had pictured himself going up to the summit of Deer Mountain, and walking into that cave, the one where the wolven had lived, the one with the hot spring. He always arrived just as Callum was emerging from the water, naked and dripping, as beautiful and haunting as he had been when he'd been naked in that road.

In that moment the two of them had first met.

"Never here," he said softly.

"What?"

"When I imagined seeing you again, alone . . . it was never here, in this hellhole." He glanced around. "I hate this fucking place. I'd burn it to the ground if I could."

"It's not a hellhole anymore." Callum smiled in a flat way. "They've got Thermopane windows and lights now."

"I don't give a shit if every inch of paint is new and the roof is retiled with gold bars." Apex shook his head. "It's always going to be a fucking mausoleum to me."

As Callum just stared at him, he shifted his weight back and forth on his boots. "What."

"I didn't know that . . . it lingered for you."

"Not it." Apex's voice cracked, and he reached out for the male's hand. Placing that broad palm in the center of his own chest, he said, "You. *You* were with me."

CHAPTER SEVENTEEN

O ut in the front acreage of Camp Ghreylke,
as a vehicle went by them on the lane,
Mahrci's instinct was to run. But maybe it
was just the groundskeeper coming back? The truck
had been gone, the plow left behind. It wasn't neces-
sarily her father. Or, as the humans called them, her
fiancé.

Ex-fiancé.

"Who are you afraid of," Hemmy said into the
darkness. "And how can I help you."

Not a question. A statement of intent.

"Let it go." She shifted her eyes to him. "Let me . . .
go. I'm nothing to you."

"Who decides that—"

"You don't even know me."

The male shook his head slowly. "And you're out here, humping fifty-pound bags of grain in the snow for animals *you* don't know."

Exhaling a curse, she breathed, "You don't know what he's capable of."

"I'm not worried."

"You should be," she whispered. "You just don't understand."

"Try me."

Mahrci looked away. Looked back. "I'm sorry . . . I can't talk about it. And that is the truth. It's also all I can give anybody right now."

There was a long silence. Then he nodded. "Okay. Fair enough. So are you dematerializing out of here right now? Or are we going back together."

"You could leave now—"

"No, I don't run. From anything." His eyes searched her face. "You can go to my place in Caldwell, you know. Take some time to figure out whatever this is. No one needs to know you're there, and I'll leave you alone, too. If that's what you want."

"Why are you doing this."

He reached out and took the grain bag from her. Then just held it up.

Taking a deep breath, she closed her eyes. "I'm going back to the big house to pack."

She wanted to beg Hemmy to race off to wherever he lived in Caldwell and forget all about her. She wanted to protect him—even though, as she measured the heft of his shoulders, like he needed defense from the likes of her?

"And I'm going back with you."

As his words were carried away on the wind, it was hard to calm herself, and when she wasn't readily able to dematerialize, she wondered if she was going to have to walk back. Except then she was flying through the cold air in a scatter of molecules, returning to the vacation house her father never went to. But was now outfitting with security cameras?

What the hell was he up to?

When she re-formed, it was at the front entrance, at the base of the steps—

It wasn't her father. Or Remis.

Or the groundskeeper.

"Jesus! Sneak up on a man!"

Over at the side porch, the human farmer jumped back from his truck bed and grabbed the front of his chest like he was having a heart attack. Mr. Yates was in his sixties, and wearing the same blue-and-black-check wool jacket, knee-high barn boots, and black cap he always did. With his white beard and white hair that curled around the edges of that little hat, he was like Santa's thinner brother—except for the fact that he was cranky as a mule.

And crap, in her distraction, she'd almost sprung an out-of-thin-air on him. Thank heavens she'd picked the front and not over there.

"Sorry," she called out roughly.

Glancing around and not seeing Hemmy anywhere, she headed across the snow in her snowshoes.

"Thanks for bringing all that grain," she said as she came up to the man and his truck.

She got a grunt in reply as he hauled another bag off the bed and onto the pile he was building under the porch's cover.

Glancing around for Hemmy, she knew better than to ask Mr. Yates if she could help. Back in the fall, she'd come up for what was supposed to have been a romantic weekend with Remis—and she'd first met the farmer then, promptly offending him by stepping in to grab a bag. His expression had been a combination of you-said-*what*-about-my-mother and clearly-you-are-from-downstate. She'd have gotten a better reception if she'd stomped on his bare foot.

Still, she'd come to like him.

"Lane's cleared good," he said as he threw another sack onto the stack. "That man knows what he's doing with a plow."

Wow. She was going to have to tell Callum that he'd won the upstate New York equivalent of a Nobel Peace Prize.

"He's very handy," she said as she looked over her shoulder again. "We're lucky to—"

Up on the roof of the maintenance garage, by the chimney, a figure materialized—and even with the distance, she could tell Hemmy was glowering.

She motioned across the distance that This Wasn't A Problem.

Fortunately, Mr. Yates wasn't paying attention to anything overhead—and when Hemmy nodded and squatted into a sit on the roof ridge, it looked like, of all the crap she had to worry about tonight, explaining that vampires did in fact exist to an old-school farmer was not on her list of things to grit her teeth and get through.

"Woulda had this to ya earlier, but been plowin' for the county myself."

"Thank you for bringing it all." Although the four

bags were going to wait until spring. And someone else. "I can get you the money now—"

"I'll bill ya," Mr. Yates said gruffly. "You stay warm in there. Going to be below zero for the next couple of days. You got my number if you need anything."

"Thank you again. So much."

She got another grunt, and then the man was back in his truck, cranking the diesel engine over and driving off. He did offer her a wave through his window, though, even as he didn't glance at her.

When the red brake lights rounded a corner and disappeared into the trees, she looked up to the garage's roofline. Hemmy seemed to be focused on the lane from his perch. Was he watching the truck? Or . . . wondering how much she wasn't telling him?

God, she felt awful.

"Would you like to eat something?" she called up to him. "I could make you . . . a plate full of Triscuits?"

Hemmy glanced at her. Then he got to his feet and strolled down the roof pitch until gravity got ahold of him. As he lurched forward, she shouted and put out her hands—like that was going to do anything—

Just before he fell, he dematerialized.

And then he was standing calmly in front of her. "Aren't you leaving?"

She pictured her father showing up here—and what the male would do to Hemmy if she were gone and the two clashed. Nothing good could come of all this misplaced chivalry. She had to get Hemmy to leave everything well enough alone.

"Not yet."

———

Back at Willow Hills, Callum was staring into Apex's eyes, and feeling like he was airborne. But not in a soaring way, in a falling-down way. He couldn't break that stare, though, and as the words that had been spoken to him registered, he tried not to believe them.

Not it. You. You were with me.

If what the vampire said was true, if it was real . . . the idea that Apex had been eaten alive, too, was unsustainable—

Without thinking, he grabbed the male's shoulder. "Listen to me. It was not your fault. Don't take this shit on, okay? What happened to me thirty years ago isn't worth ruining your own life over."

Apex shook his head. "Doesn't work like that."

"It should."

"Do you say those things to yourself? And believe them?"

Fuck. No, he didn't. But he couldn't live with the idea that both of them had been ruined. That just couldn't . . . be where they ended up.

"I'm not worth the pain," Callum said as his voice cracked. "Let yourself be free."

The vampire looked down the hallway. And then focused on the door of the private quarters like he was seeing through it to the other side.

"Looks like we're both still in prison, doesn't it. Life sentences, side-by-side cells. No chance of parole—"

Before Callum knew what he was doing, he grabbed the lapels of that leather jacket and dragged their faces together.

"I don't want you on my conscience."

"I can't help you with that." Those eyes dropped to Callum's mouth. "Just like you can't order me to forget about . . . you."

Desperation was a such strange thing, Callum would think later, when he was feeling more rational. It could pivot from one angle to another in the blink of an eye, pulling sexual need out of a hat that only had choking sorrow in it a split second before: The sensation of heat that ran through his body was an echo from an earlier era, and the need that went along with it was the same. He was like a rusty engine, though, clunky and slow to respond, his lips trembling before they parted.

"Are you sure you want this," Apex whispered.

"I don't know."

And yet he was the one who closed the distance between their mouths, pressing his own to the male who was holding back. The contact was firm, the lips were soft, and his breath got tight fast.

Although the tightness in his lungs could have been caused by a lot of things.

It was all just so confusing. He was instantly hard, his cock straining in a way it hadn't for decades. But his brain was scrambled, the past and present contorting so that he wasn't sure where he was in the timeline, whose body was against his, where he was. And then Apex tilted his head, and there was a lick. And another. And—

Callum stepped back sharply. Banged into the wall. Shied like a spooked horse from that contact. Careened around until he knew he either stopped moving or got vertigo so badly he fell over.

As he panted into the silence, Apex put his hands up and looked down at the floor.

"I'm sorry," Callum choked out. "I'm . . . sorry."

"I know." The vampire cleared his throat. "And I'll . . . leave you alone. No questions asked. I get it."

Apex backed up a couple of steps. Then he turned away.

Then he . . . jogged away, his heavy footfalls rounding the corner and dimming as he traveled through the waiting area. After a moment, the sanatorium's front entry opened and closed.

In the aftermath of the departure, Callum's shoulders slumped, his head dropped, his erection deflated—

The door behind him opened. "You're still here."

Was he, he thought as Blade's voice registered through the roar in his head.

"I'm going back," he mumbled.

"Are you?" There was a stretch of silence. "Then why aren't you leaving?"

Well, Callum thought, at least he knew the answer to that: It was because he was worried if he returned to the estate right now, he was liable to hunt down that vampire and apologize.

By getting down on his knees in front of the male.

"Will you please come in and have something to eat," Blade drawled. The because-you-look-like-shit was left unspoken. "I have leftovers from that meal I made at dawn, you know. It was quite good. Or you can have some eggs with me."

Callum pivoted around. When all he could do was blink and breathe, the other male shook his head.

"I know, I know, you're not hungry. You don't care about anything. You're leaving right this second." Blade shrugged. "And yet twelve hours later, you're still here. So perhaps we start with a little food and then maybe you can dematerialize back out to that truck you left on the edge of my property."

In the rear of Callum's mind, a connection was suddenly made. "You're a *symphath*, aren't you."

Those eyes narrowed. "Changing the subject so fast? Afraid I'm going to mention the fact that Apex just left and this hallway smells like sex?"

Callum recoiled. "How the fuck do you know him—"

"Don't be jealous. It's not like that." The smile was smooth and even. And yet the offense had been taken. "And I know him because his and my paths have crossed professionally, you might say. Caldwell can be a very small town, especially if you're talking about the—shall we say—otherworldly community."

There was another period of tense silence.

"I'm not eating your food," Callum grumbled.

"So that's the reason you've starved yourself for the whole day outside my door? You think I'll tamper with your entrée because of what I am? My dear boy, I can assure you, if I wanted to fuck with you, I don't need you to be chewing to ruin your life."

Callum laughed in a hard rush. "That's already happened." Then he pushed past the male and entered the *symphath*'s quarters. "You got it right the first time. My appetites are shot—appetite, I mean."

All he knew was that he couldn't go back to Camp Ghreylke.

And who knew this fucking place would ever be a better alternative.

CHAPTER EIGHTEEN

O h, good evening, s-sire. You have more
questions for me?"

As the anxious inquiry was posed by
Broadius's maid, Petrie, Tohr stepped closer to the door
of her third-floor apartment. Gone was the uniform,
the flush from the cold, and a lot of the panic. She was
wearing jeans and a comfortable sweater, and her salt-
and-pepper hair was loose down her back.

But of course, she was tense. Anybody would be
when a couple of brothers showed up on their stoop.

"Just one." He smiled to try to reassure her. "May
we come in?"

"Yes, of course." The female moved back with

deference and indicated the way forward. "Anything I can do to help."

The building she was in was on the outskirts of the downtown, and it was filled with vampires, the fifty-unit development a nonprofit that was owned and managed by the Brotherhood for the benefit of the species. All kinds of domestics lived in the converted hotel, the maids, chauffeurs, butlers, and bartenders servicing the new *glymera* and all their new-built mansions, glitzy parties, and vacation homes.

And whereas most of their employers adhered to the old-school tradition of aristocrats taking advantage of the help, here, the civilians and *doggen* were watched over and protected.

"May I get you some coffee?" She glanced at Qhuinn and did a double take at all the piercings in his ear and his black-and-purple hair. "Tea?"

Tohr shook his head and noted that something smelled delicious. Stew? He'd comment on it, but no doubt she'd feel obliged to offer them some, even if she didn't have much.

"I think we're good, but thank you," he said.

"Okay."

The living area was tidy, the pale blue sofas and creamy rug making him think they were on a cloud.

Winsome pastel drawings of fields of flowers and cute cottages marked the walls, and the fact that there wasn't a TV suggested maybe the female was a big reader, and if she did do a movie or a TV show, it was on an iPad.

Everything about her made him think she was an old-fashioned Merchant Ivory kind of girl.

"I'm afraid I'm not dressed properly," she said as she swept her graying hair back and tucked it in at her nape. Like she was hoping her sweater's collar would hold the makeshift bun.

"There's no need to worry. We weren't expected, and even if we were, this is your home."

"I was going to call you, actually."

As he sat down on one of the couches, he set his butt on the very edge of the cushion. In his black leather-and-dagger duds, he felt like an ink spot ruining a nice tablecloth. Meanwhile, Qhuinn stayed by the door, as if he recognized his presence was overwhelming to her.

The maid did not sit down. At least not until Tohr indicated the armchair across from him—and as she finally took a seat in her own place, he gave her a gentle smile. Yup, she was one of the traditional types who were in the New World, but still living the way things had been done in the Old Country, and he wondered if Broadius had ever appreciated the graciousness.

Thinking about all the gaudy in that house, he doubted it.

While she twisted her hands in her lap, he said, "How are you doing after last night?"

"My daughter is coming up from Philadelphia to stay for a week." Petrie pointed toward her little kitchen. "That's her favorite Last Meal on the stove. It's just beef and potatoes and carrots, but young have their comfort foods—I'm sorry, I'm babbling. I've never had members of the Black Dagger Brotherhood in my home before."

As she looked down at her hands, Tohr took out his phone. "You said you were going to call us?"

"Well, I thought of something." She stared off into the middle distance between them. "But maybe it's nothing."

"Tell us. You never know?"

When she just sat there, worrying her lip, Qhuinn crossed over and sat at the other end of the sofa. Another ink spot. "That's my son's favorite meal, too."

"I'm sorry?" she said, as she returned from wherever she'd been in her head.

"Beef stew." Qhuinn flared his nostrils on an inhale. "It smells fantastic—and it makes me think of him."

"Really?"

The brother nodded. "When he was little, he was a picky eater—and it lasted right up to his transition, actually. Sometimes stew was the only thing we could get him to eat."

Her body relaxed a little and she crossed her ankles, tucking them into the kick pleat of the chair. "Well, I can give you what I've made. It would be an honor."

"Oh, you keep that for your daughter." Qhuinn smiled. "But I think I'll have my mate's *mahmen* whip some up. No one beats *granmahmen*'s cooking, even though my son's a grown male."

"How old is he?"

"Rhamp is ten years out of his transition—and I can't believe I'm saying that. I had him and his sister young myself. And yes, they're twins."

"You have twins?" Petrie put her hand on her collarbone with a rush of surprise. "My sister and I are twins."

"No kidding! Identical?"

"No, but we do look so much alike and we're so close. She lives next door."

"That's really cool." Qhuinn laughed. "I bet your sis has been over here a lot in the last twenty-four hours. My two kids are inseparable—especially when times are . . . stressful."

The maid took a deep breath, but not like she was bracing herself. "Anna stayed with me all day long. And she's coming back after she gets off her shift. I . . . don't have work right now."

As the female's face tightened, Qhuinn leaned forward onto his knees. "You know, we'd be happy to talk to some people. We have a lot of contact with folks, and if you're concerned about . . . things like that . . . we'll put a word in. Won't we."

Tohr nodded immediately. "Absolutely."

"I have some savings." She retwisted her hair. "But I am worried about the future. I'm just feeling a little ragged. I'm not sure I trust my composure, if you know what I mean."

"I do," Qhuinn said. "And it'll get easier, I promise. You'll never forget what you saw, I'm not going to lie. It'll get draped over by other, more normal things, though."

"Really?"

"Is your daughter mated?"

The maid blinked as if she were surprised at the subject change. "Ah, no. She isn't. But she's dating a very nice male. I think things are headed in that direction—and he lives in Caldwell, so she'd come back here. I'd love that. My *hellren* passed seven years ago."

"I'm really sorry." Qhuinn nodded gravely. Then he

shook his head in a wry way. "I don't know if either of my kids will ever get mated."

"No?"

"My son works hard, but he's always at the clubs with his friends. My daughter . . . well, she's a free spirit. I don't know who's ever going to tie her down. He'd have to be a helluva male."

"Fate has a way of working miracles. I wish them the very best."

"And I do the same for your daughter."

Well, what do you know. Qhuinn still looked fierce as hell, especially with all the metal in that ear—oh, and his eyebrow was pierced, too. But it was amazing how bringing up young could level all kinds of playing fields.

And now there was nothing awkward in the pause: As the maid looked over at Tohr, it was clear she was ready to talk.

"I'd like to show you a picture of someone." He put his hand up. "There's no pressure. I just want to know if you've ever seen them before?"

"Of course."

He already had the still snapshot from the waiting room at the Audience House up on his phone, and he turned the screen around.

As Petrie's eyebrows pulled together over the bridge of her nose, he motioned forward with the Samsung. "Here, take my cell."

She nodded absently and they met in the center of her area rug for the exchange. The female eased back slowly, concentrating on the image.

"Am I supposed to know her?" she asked as her eyes lifted.

"So you don't recognize the female."

The maid slowly shook her head. "I'm sorry. I've never seen her before?"

"You're sure?"

"Yes. I am."

"Have you ever heard of anybody by the name of Candice, daughter of Meiser?"

"No?" She glanced back and forth between him and Qhuinn. "Should I have?"

"Not at all. I'm just following up on possible leads."

Tohr was aware of an acute disappointment as he took his phone back, but come on. Just because it wasn't every night that a member of the aristocracy was murdered in an apparent hit after someone left a bunch of mysterious paperwork in the damn waiting room . . . did not mean that the two things were connected.

Sometimes the mind made ties out of thin air.

"I'm sorry," she said as she settled back in her chair. "Who is she? Do you think she's connected to . . . what happened to Master Broadius?"

Tohr shrugged and got to his feet. "We're investigating all kinds of leads and this was a long shot. So no, I don't. We thank you for your time."

The maid got up, too. "I'm here. For anything, for any way I can help—"

"Wait," Qhuinn cut in. "You said you were going to call us?"

"Oh, yes." Her worried eyes seemed to cling to the brother's mismatched stare. "But I don't know . . ."

"It's okay," the brother said softly. "Whatever it is. And if you're worried about discretion, be assured that anything you tell us will not be shared widely."

"Thank you." She nodded. "I only worked for Master Broadius for about a year. I think I was among his first domestic help? There's a cook and a chauffeur, too—you must talk to them as well?"

Tohr nodded. "They were contacted last night just before dawn and they're being interviewed right now."

"They had been given the week off."

"Because Broadius was leaving," Tohr murmured. "On a trip, wasn't he."

"Yes, that was on his schedule."

There was a long silence. Then she glanced at Qhuinn again. When he inclined his head, she squared her shoulders and leaped.

"I never understood where the money came from." She put her hands up. "I didn't judge him. I needed a job and it paid well so I was grateful. But I never understood—I mean, he didn't seem to work, and yet he made a big deal about how he was a self-made male. How he didn't come from a Founding Family. He didn't have a desk or a computer, though, and he never talked about an office or a profession, had no associates over for dinners or social events. I'm not a sophisticated female, but . . . I mean, all he did was buy things for the house. Paintings, art, furnishings. It was a churn of deliveries all the time, so he had to have income of some kind . . ." The maid seemed to retreat into herself. "And then one night, about a month ago? I found the guns."

"Guns?" Tohr tilted his head. "Like for his personal security?"

The maid shook her head and focused very, very clear eyes on his own. "Crates of them. An entire U-Haul truck full."

CHAPTER NINETEEN

How did you know where this supermarket was?"

As Mahrci spoke up from the SUV's passenger seat, Mayhem put things in park and killed the engine. Even though locating the store hadn't been rocket science—all he'd done was Google "24 hr grocery stores in Plattsburgh, NY"—he took a certain satisfaction in the female next to him thinking he was a fucking genius.

A lot of people thought a lot of things about him. "Genius" was usually not it.

"Just like magic," he said. "And honestly, I think we need some real food, and I like to cook."

Bullshit. All he really cared about was getting her to hang around a little longer and he was willing to leverage anything he had. Even if it was her own digestive tract.

"Okay, Chef," she said.

Then Mahrci laughed a little, but not in the easy way he liked so much. There was a determination behind the sound, just like there had been a forced pleasantry pushing the conversation she'd shared with him during the forty-five-minute drive here.

"But I should be the one offering to make you a good dinner." She opened her door. "Not the other way around."

While she hopped out and closed things, he followed her example, landing in the salty slush of a parking lot that was big enough to play football on. No problem getting a parking space right up close. There were only five other cars on account of the time of night and the frigid weather.

Meeting up with her on the opposite side of the SUV, he had a stupid impulse to take her hand—and he cured the problem by shoving his fists in the front of his jeans. He told himself that it was better to keep them physically separate as much as he could. He was not *hellren* material, and going down some kind of rose-colored rabbit hole with a female he didn't know, who was keeping secrets like an FBI agent, and possibly on the run from somebody dangerous, was not going to be a good outcome for him or her.

Well. Wasn't that a nice little pep talk.

Too bad his libido totally middle-fingered the shit—

"What do you fancy," he asked, to get himself to stop thinking.

"How do you feel about meat sauce on a big ol' plate of pasta?" she countered.

He glanced over. Her stare was fixated on the glowing Hannaford sign over the entrance like it was the promised land, her rapt concentration the kind of thing someone sported when they were desperately trying to convince themselves that Everything Was Just GREAT.

"Great, that would be great," he said.

Fuck.

"You're so easygoing," she murmured.

"I'm not sure Mr. Personality would agree with that."

"You mean Apex? Yes, he is intense. I mean, he's always seemed disapproving to me, too."

Mayhem looked over sharply. She was still staring at the entrance—and no doubt hadn't heard her own words.

"You got a freezer?" he asked. Before he followed up

on things that shouldn't have been any of his business.

"Oh yes. A walk-in."

That was right, he thought. He'd—well, *walked into* it last night when he'd foraged for food.

"We can get some Tater Tots, too. I love those little—"

A scent filtered through the wind from behind him and shut him up. Frowning, he glanced over his shoulder. A human man was getting out of a truck, and pulling a broad-billed trucker's hat down on his head. His field camo flak jacket seemed like it was two sizes too big for him, the folds billowing out as the guy leaned back into the cab.

Flaring his nostrils, Mayhem tested the air again.

"Whoa!"

Mahrci threw out a hand as she slipped on some black ice. With a quick grab, he caught her and pulled her against him—and for a split second, all he could feel, all he knew, was the sensation of her coming up to his body, his arm around her waist, a wisp of her hair tickling his chin, her thigh brushing against his own.

With a laugh, she locked a hold on the front of his jacket—and then they were looking into each other's eyes.

Clearing his throat, Mayhem kicked his own ass as he set her on her feet properly. "Close call."

"Ah ... yes. It was."

As they awkwardly entered through a preliminary set of electric glass doors, they were greeted with a rush of warmth and distant Muzak, and he glanced at a lineup of little two-level pushcarts. "We're going to need something more heavy-duty than that."

"We are?"

Heading for the big-boy version, he yanked one free and pinned a let's-do-this on his face.

"I say we take this one row at a time."

"Oh, you are serious."

"I don't mess around with meals." He clapped himself in the six-pack. "Energy is required to keep my God-given talents upright and moving, and though there is no shame in frozen dinners, I say we home-make everything but the pasta."

On that note, he indicated the way through the next set of doors, where a surface-of-the-sun-bright interior filled with seventeen thousand different brands of twenty million different comestibles awaited them.

Hopefully, it would clear the air some.

"Let us forage together—"

From out of nowhere, the guy with the trucker hat and the camo jacket plowed through the space between them, catching Mahrci with his elbow.

The effect was instant. One minute, Mayhem was pretty much coloring inside the lines. The next, his fangs were descending, and he actually took a step out and around the cart, his head lowering, his shoulders coming forward over his hips—

The touch of Mahrci's hand on his arm was enough to stop what certainly would have been murder—and a bloody one at that.

"I'm fine." She put her face in his, like she wanted to make sure she was the only thing he could see. "Really. I am. So how about we hit the bread aisle."

Mayhem nodded absently—and tried to pretend he wasn't searching for that rude asshole in the fruits and vegetables department immediately to the right.

"Sounds great," he said in what passed for a fairly non-growlish voice. "I love bread."

What he didn't love? What he could absolutely have done without?

Was him acting like he'd bonded or some shit. But have fun arguing with your internal wiring.

And that human better stay out of range, if he knew what was good for him. Some people just had the wrong vibe, all the way around.

CHAPTER TWENTY

As Tohr re-formed at Broadius's McMansion, Qhuinn was right behind him. Big changes onsite from the night before: No lashing snow. No open door with the maid about to get frostbite. No dead body inside.

But this was still a crime scene.

As he took out a copper key, Qhuinn was assessing the neighbors on either side and across the lane, those other estates set way, way off and isolated by stone walls and plantings. Good thing, given how much activity had been going on over here. After the remains had been taken to the morgue in Manny's mobile surgical unit, V had changed all the locks and installed his own cameras with an entire team of people.

Stepping into the tacky interior, Tohr hit the panel of light switches on the wall. All kinds of oversized, over-crystaled fixtures came on, making him think of the BDB mansion up on the mountain. He missed that imperial palace, he really did. And man, he'd never appreciated its elegance before, but next to all this miss-the-mark? That place really had been divine.

"Garage bound?" Qhuinn asked as he shut them in together.

"Yup."

The pair of them headed for the rear of the house. The stillness of the rooms was ominous, in a way that an emptiness that was temporary just didn't come close to: The owner was never coming back. The clothes in the closet were never going to be worn by him again. The mail was going to remain unopened, the phone calls unanswered—

Tohr stopped.

"What?" Qhuinn asked as he took out one of his guns.

"Where's the cell phone." Tohr motioned for the brother to put his weapon away. "Everyone has a phone. Where's Broadius's phone?"

The fact that they'd all spaced the detail was kind of like what had happened with the maid: Someone coming across a U-Haul full of rifles and autoloaders should have been top of mind if their employer was murdered. But the brain only had so much processing capability at any one time, and it also had its own priority list. As things were framed and released, cognitive space was created, and shit popped up.

"Let's see if we can find the armory first," Qhuinn remarked. "Then we look for a phone."

With a nod, Tohr started walking again.

The kitchen was all business, no cozy family stuff anywhere, not even a table and chair set for the staff to eat at. The fact that the appliances were all restaurant grade wasn't a surprise, but they were never-been-used brand new. Likewise, the red tiled floor was gleaming, and the stainless steel saucepans hanging from a rack over the island were just-out-of-the-box sparkling clean.

"I don't think this guy has even had a bowl of cereal in this place," Qhuinn said.

Tohr nodded. "No food in the pantry, the cupboards, the fridges and freezers. What did the cook do?"

"We'll find out after Butch is through talking to him." Qhuinn paused and opened a random drawer—which, of course, was empty. "It's like a stage set."

There was an industrial laundry room off the far side of everything and—no surprise—it had no detergent on the shelf above the massive machines, nothing on the ironing board, and no pile of dry cleaning on the way out the door.

When they finally came to the garage door, they opened things and motion-activated lights came on—

"Okay," Qhuinn said. "I'll give him the cars."

A dozen Porsche 911s of various vintages and styles were lined up in rows, their paint jobs glowing, their sloping back ends and round headlights making them seem like dogs sitting on command.

Tohr walked down the far wall, passing by all kinds of Porsche posters and Porsche models set on clear shelves. "Man, he got into some buying ruts, didn't he."

"Helluva rut."

While Qhuinn lingered over something that had a rear tail so big you could have pulled chairs up to it and called it a four-top, Tohr headed for a door about three-quarters of the way down.

Locked solid.

"We need your little kit."

"Coming." The brother jogged over. "Sorry, I got distracted. I wonder what happens to all of these now? Maybe Shuli'll buy 'em from the estate."

He went to work on the upper dead bolt.

"So Rhamp's not focused on the getting mated thing, huh?" Tohr leaned back and idly looked at the cars. "Not yet, at least?"

Qhuinn rolled his blue and green eyes. "Not in the slightest. And honestly, Lyric's the same. I don't have a problem with it. Not everyone feels that way, though."

"Blay's *mahmen* ready for great grandyoung?"

The brother switched tools and went back to work, the soft sounds of metal scraping metal rising up. "Oh, she's not the problem. Not by half."

"Layla?"

"She wants them, sure, but not over and above our kids' happiness."

Tohr frowned. "Blay's dad?" When there was a shake of the head, Tohr did a double take. "Blay?"

"Nope." Qhuinn straightened. "Your half brother, Xcor. He's baby daft."

"I'm . . . okay, that's a surprise." Tohr smiled as he pictured the big male with his distorted upper lip. "I mean, a good surprise. But yeah, wow."

The head of the Band of Bastards wanted to be a grandpappy already?

"He's a softie, for certain." Qhuinn nodded at the lock. "But you know what isn't? This frickin' door."

"My turn." Tohr pushed a hand into his jacket.

"Now that I think about it, Xcor was awesome with Rhamp and Lyric. I heard through the grapevine that he did it all, the diapers, the baths—step back for me, wouldya?"

"He was really great." Qhuinn got out of range and crossed his arms over his chest. "He truly was. Do you need a charge?"

"Got one, but thanks." Tohr set the C-4 plastic explosive between the dead bolt head and the steel jamb. "That's what I always love about your family. All four of you—you and Blay, Xcor and Layla—really pulling together for those kids. Nobody was ever raised with so much love."

"Thanks. We're a good team—hey, did you get that C-4 from the new stock?"

"Yup." He inserted the detonating fuse. "Z really prefers the new supplier. It comes down from Canada."

The fact that they were alternating between talking about young and him setting up a breach involving enough explosive to blow both of them up was par for the course.

Just another night on the job.

"On three."

Both of them backed all the way to the door they'd exited from. When they were sufficiently out of the blast zone, Tohr initiated the detonation program on his phone.

"One . . . two . . ." He nodded at the brother and they both plugged their ears. "Three—"

A sharp, cracking sound echoed all around the cars, and then came the *slam!* of the steel panel slapping onto the polished concrete floor.

They jogged forward in unison, and Tohr entered the stairwell that was revealed first. It was nothing special, only a short stack of steps that were super deep, and when he bottomed out at their base, he hit the light on his phone because he didn't know where the switch was.

Talk about your letdowns. Just a ten-by-ten space that was lead-lined concrete, low-ceilinged, and empty.

"I can smell the gunpowder, though," he said as Qhuinn joined him.

There had definitely been an arsenal stored here recently.

"Look at this wall." Tohr ran his hand over some scratches in the paint that were chest level. "This was crates on crates."

Qhuinn nodded. "I definitely think we found his day job."

"Arms dealer."

"No wonder the hit was professional. Buyers and sellers of that shit have connections in all kinds of bang-bang places."

Tohr did the math out loud. "No office. No work associates. No one in the house except for a maid, a cook who never used the kitchen, and a chauffeur who's polishing bumpers in here instead of taking his boss anywhere." He looked at the set of concrete steps. "But why did he let the maid see that U-Haul backed up outside on the lawn?"

Qhuinn's mismatched stare narrowed. "She was lucky Broadius didn't know what she caught him doing."

Thinking back to the sweet older female, Tohr nodded. "Yup. And as for the murderer's motive? Broadius must have tried to muscle the wrong person."

As they went back for the steps, Tohr imagined the space filled with the kinds of wooden crates V kept in their own armory at the Wheel, the long ones stamped with black paint, their origins from all different countries depending on what kind of weapon had been purchased in bulk. And it was the same with the bullets, although those tended to come in heavy cardboard lots.

"I've got a bad feeling about this," he said in a low tone.

Qhuinn, who took the lead on the ascent, glanced over his shoulder. "Why the fuck wouldn't you."

"I mean . . ." He met the brother's stare. "I got a reaaaally bad feeling about this."

CHAPTER TWENTY-ONE

Well, weren't they a great twosome, Mahrci thought a mere fifteen minutes later.

As Hemmy pulled their cart of groceries up to the self-checkout lane, she was impressed. They'd managed to fill the thing with an almost military approach to the store, splitting up to cover lanes, with quick agreement on choices—

She glanced at her watch again. "Surely this has to be some kind of record?"

He started swiping barcodes over the scanner like he was being timed. "Efficiency is everything. And we make a great team."

"I was just thinking that."

His eyes shifted to her quick, and then he grabbed

a bag of Tater Tots. "If there's ever a supermarket shop race, we are entering."

The words were casual, but falsely so. Underneath them, the same tension that had made her blabber too much about absolutely nothing on the way here was simmering. And God, she wanted to tell him everything, she really did. But the more time she spent with him, the more she wanted only good things for him. Safe things . . .

Not the kind of stuff she was bringing with her.

"I wish I'd met you a year ago," she whispered.

As he froze in mid-scan of the hamburger they were going to use to make the sauce, she hadn't intended for him to hear what she'd said.

Hemmy straightened. "Why's that."

Taking a deep breath, she glanced over the other checkout lanes, all of which were empty. The slots were separated by candy displays, stacks of magazines no one read anymore, and soda refrigerators that were Coke branded. So normal. So regular.

The kind of life she wished she lived.

"Things were a lot simpler a year ago."

There was a pause, like he was waiting for her to explain. And then he started scanning again, going even faster.

"Well, I'm sorry about whatever," he said.

As she focused on him, she could feel his frustration, and she contrasted his mood with the way he'd been as he'd carefully carried her inside the night before. She was responsible for the change. Sure, she didn't owe him anything, but at the same time, you could only leave so many hints until the other person just felt strung along.

At least he wasn't going to be in Connelly long. On the way north, he'd told her it was just a night or two, at most. She should be able to put off her father for forty-eight hours.

"I'd like to be friends." She offered him a smile. "You and I."

With a frown, he reached into the cart and took out an armful of things. If it was possible to make quadra-time, he somehow managed it, the little *beep!* that was released every time going a supersonic *beep! beep!beep!beep!*—

And then it stopped.

For the first time since they'd left the big house, he seemed to really look at her. "Sorry. That would be great." He smiled a little. "Let's . . . be friends."

When he stuck his hand out, he said, "Hi, I'm Mayhem."

She stared down at his palm. As she clasped it, she smiled again. Or tried to. "Not Hemmy, then?"

"It's a nickname—that I figured might make a better impression than something that, if you looked it up in the dictionary, means damaging disorder and chaos."

"I like Hemmy."

He bowed. "Then Hemmy I shall be."

After they shook, he let go first. And the next thing she knew, she was stepping up to the screen with her credit card.

"It's on me." She put the thing in the slot. "It's the least I can do for . . . everything—"

"Mahrci."

"Hmm?" She looked over at him. And instantly stilled. "What's wrong?"

Mayhem was half-turned on his hips and staring at the entrance, which was about thirty feet away. His stare seemed to be on a man who had just walked in, and there was nothing casual in the way he was tracking the human.

"What's going on?" she asked.

The customer, who was dressed for the cold in a knit cap and parka, didn't seem to be anything other than a regular Joe out late at night, just like the rest of the people in—

The keys to the SUV were pressed into her hand. "I want you to go out and wait for me. Lock the doors—"

"Why?"

Hemmy's face was suddenly in hers, and everything about him got through to her, especially the way his eyes were so intense on her own and the tone of his deep voice, all the I'm-not-fucking-around spearing into her brain.

"Okay," she said with a nod. "All right."

"And stay there. If I'm not out in five minutes, drive away."

As he started to walk off, she grabbed his arm with alarm. "Wait, where are you going? What's going on—"

"Go out, and get in the car. *Right now*."

———

The plan had been to go back to work.

When Apex returned to the great camp from Willow Hills, he'd intended to snag Mayhem and make the guy work his magic on the back end of the security setup—so they could get the fuck out of Dodge. Naturally, the SUV had been gone, and when he'd hollered down to the cellar, no one responded. No calls were returned, either.

So he'd pinged Mayhem's location. A Hannaford in Plattsburgh.

Food. Of course.

Or at least the guy's phone was trying to get dinner.

Apex had then gone into the basement, knocked on Mahrci's door—and discovered that the female's clothes were still in that closet.

Fates in the fucking Fade, he thought, *please let her not be out there feeding the deer and getting herself eaten again.*

Or having been kidnapped by her father. Her fiancé.

Santa-fucking-Claus.

Returning upstairs, he got to the first level just as a flare of headlights pierced through the windows. Couldn't be Callum. Not unless that wolven could somehow dematerialize a Ford truck back here. Not Hemmy, who was still playing hunt-and-peck at Hannaford.

And as far as he knew, Mahrci hadn't brought her car up.

It was with an utter lack of enthusiasm that he went over and opened the front door—

Out in front, a matte gray BMW sedan looked like a great white shark that had been rolled in powdered sugar. The male who got out from behind the wheel was slick as the car, his dark hair pulled back in a man bun, his face sporting designer beard stubble that he no doubt mowed like a golf fairway every nightfall. In his dark suit, he looked like a model who'd gotten lost in the sticks.

"Aren't you finished yet," Remis, son of Penbroke, said as he came around the car's ass.

The fact that his Gucci loafers had hot soles from the heater meant he went for some Three Stooges, on-ice action, and wasn't that deeply satisfying. Too bad he caught his balance on the posterier of his pretentious-mobile.

"Almost fell on your butt there," Apex drawled as the guy hit the walkway.

"Well?" Remis was considerably more careful as he came up the path of packed snow. "Are you finished with the job yet?"

Apex turned and went back in the house, leaving the door open. He was halfway to the hearth when the thing was shut loudly.

"You got a helluva n'attitude, Apex."

"Your boss doesn't hire me for my personality." From the cord of wood set into a nook in the river stone, Apex gathered a couple of logs. "And relax, I'm still on schedule. Most of the cameras have already been installed."

"What about the feed?" The male looked around with his hands on his hips, a tattletale all grown up and ready to be petty. "When is that going to be online."

Ignoring the supercilious bastard, Apex took an armful of logs to the hearth. The banked ashes were hungry for food, and the instant he restocked the glow, flames licked up as if they were taste-testing things and finding the hardwood very palatable.

He turned around. "The programming's coming along."

"When."

Not a question, a demand. But he didn't work for the guy. "It'll be ready. I was told I have plenty of time."

"You've got forty-eight hours."

Apex frowned. "That's not my understanding."

"It is now." The male waved around. "So . . . get going."

Apex looked down at the wool rug for a moment. Nice rug. Red, green, and gold. Like everything else in the house.

All things considered, he was surprised it didn't have a border of birch bark.

When he was ready, he took three steps forward

so that he and Remis were nose to nose. "I don't work for you. And if I did? I can guarantee you that tone of voice wouldn't be used again in my presence."

Remis went full-bore hauteur, his stubbled chin raising. "I'll address you any way I want to. And you do work for me. I'm Whestmorel's right-hand male, so when I tell you the schedule has changed, you're going to make it happen or you're out."

"Oh, I'm so sorry. You're right."

On that note, Apex went into the study and picked up the duffle that hadn't been opened. As he carried it out, the male had an expression of satisfaction on his superior face—

Which changed as the luggage was dropped by the front door and Apex went for his leather jacket on the coatrack.

Fucking hell, where was Mayhem with that SUV?

"What are you doing?"

Apex glanced over. "You gave me two choices. Stay and—how did you put it . . . 'make it happen.' Or leave. So I'm leaving."

As soon as Mayhem got back. On that note, he got out his phone—

"You can't go." Remis started pointing at the cameras. "These need to work—we can't have the meeting up here unless they—"

Apex's phone made a series of little tippity-tappy noises.

"You don't have to text him." Now the tone was more reasonable. "You just have to do your job—"

"Oh, I'm not talking to our boss." Apex smiled—truly smiled. "I'm going to let you handle what's going to happen when Whestmorel tries to have the Council meet here and isn't able to record every move of those traitors—so he has leverage to hold their feet to the fire if they rethink what they're doing because it's illegal."

"Now, hold on—"

"Have fun with that, by the way. If the schedule has changed, and you only have two nights before they think they're arriving? You're going to have a totally easy time finding an IT guy who specializes in security systems. Dime a dozen. Especially one who you can trust not to fucking blab all over the place." He leaned in and went *sotto voce*. "If the great Blind King finds out this group is convening, you all are going to have serious problems."

Remis's eyes narrowed. "Is that a threat?"

"Nope. Hey, I work for Whest, too. It's a statement of fact."

"Whestmorel," the male said absently.

"Tomato, tomata. Or whatever the human saying goes."

Remis put his hand up to his head, like he had a pounder behind one of his eyebrows. "I'm sorry. If I came across wrong. There's just been a lot going on, and this needs to go well. Lot of stress."

Flaring his nostrils, Apex caught the scent of something that, given what he knew of the male, was a surprise: Fear.

Rank fear.

Then again, if you were part of a treasonous plot to reestablish the Council and try to overthrow Wrath, son of Wrath, you had a right to be shitting yourself.

"There was a murder," Remis said. "Back in Caldwell. One of ours."

With a frown, Apex said, "Who?"

"Broadius."

"No ... shit." Apex whistled under his breath as he pictured the male who had been mission critical to the plot. "How'd he die?"

"Someone came into his house and slit his"— Remis glanced around as if checking to make sure there was no one else with them—"they slit his fucking throat."

"When?"

"Last night. His maid found the body." Remis cursed again. "Broadius was an integral part of all this. So things just got harder."

"Do they have any idea who did it?"

"One of my maids is the sister of the one who found him. So I'm getting all my information secondhand through my butler. Right now? No. Thank God we got the product off his property last week."

That last bit was spoken absently, like the guy was talking to himself.

Apex crossed his arms over his chest. "Well, that explains it."

"Explains what."

"Now I know why your first question when you came through the door wasn't about the female you were set to mate in a month."

Remis didn't seem to hear anything further. Then again, that made sense. The guy was playing dangerous games.

And the prizes were death, dismemberment, and debridement.

Not in that order.

CHAPTER TWENTY–TWO

Mayhem waited until Mahrci was out of the store before he went over to the woman who was in charge of the self-scan lanes. Dropping his voice, he said, "Call the police."

Her eyes bulged. "Excuse me?"

"There's about to be a robbery." When she started to tremble and put her hands up, he shook his head. "No, not me. I'm not robbing anything. C'mere."

Drawing her through the lane, he nodded toward the pharmacy, which was in the far front corner of the store, all the way down on the other side.

"You see those two men—hey, it's going to be okay." He moved her back out of sight. "I want you to go behind the customer service counter, and get down while you call their description in. One in a trucker's hat, the other in a knit beanie. Both in camo flak jackets. They're about to hold up the pharmacy."

"How do you—"

"Trust me."

"Y-y-yes, sir."

"Go."

The woman hightailed it over to the customer service department, let herself in, and disappeared.

With that settled, Mayhem moved quickly, jogging on the balls of his feet. As he passed by the canned vegetable aisle, a man with a handbasket was headed toward the checkout.

If only there was time to warn him.

The guy Mayhem had seen first out in the parking lot, the one with the John Deere trucker hat, was standing at the pharmacy's staff-only door at the far end of the lockup room, his right hand inside his coat, the bill of that cap moving from side to side, as he twitched back and forth on his boots. The other guy, who'd just come in and sealed the deal that something was about to go down, was hovering in front of the drop-off counter, searching his pockets as he stared at the pharmacist.

The woman in the white coat seemed confused.

She was frowning and leaning over her counter, as if trying to understand all kinds of mumbling.

Mayhem almost got there in time.

He was still a good twenty feet away as both of the men got guns out at the same moment. The pharmacist immediately put her hands over her head and started stammering.

"Open the door!" the man in the knit hat hissed at her. "I'll fucking kill you—you open the fucking door—"

Mayhem held off for a count of three—which was the amount of time it took the frightened woman to unlock the glass-fronted room where the drugs were kept. When she did, her body was briefly shielded by the doorjamb.

That was when he went airborne.

Using his momentum and body weight, he leapt at the assailant at the counter, zeroing in on that gun. Double-handing the weapon, he tackled the guy—

At which point, Trucker Hat at the other end started waving his nine millimeter around. "Fuck you! Let him the fuck up! I'll fucking kill you right now!"

"You shoot me, you shoot him," Mayhem yelled as he got control of the robber under him. "You want to kill your buddy?"

With a quick shift, Mayhem looked over his shoulder and locked eyes with the guy who was still on his feet. Burrowing into that scattered mind, he had a sudden concern that the brain running things was going to be too compromised by drugs to get into and control.

"I'll kill you!" the man shouted.

"No, you won't. You're not going to do anything—"

"You're going to die—"

"—but lower your gun to the floor—"

"—I'll fucking—"

"—and kick it to me. Right—"

"Fuck . . . you . . ."

"—now."

The man started to breathe heavily. Then he winced like someone had poked him in both eye sockets. His next move was to look at his hands and the gun in them with a kind of shocked horror. Sure enough, that muzzle started to go down. Meanwhile his whole body was shaking, like he was fighting some invisible force—because he was.

He was in conflict with his own neuropathways.

And he lost.

When the nine millimeter made contact with the floor, he gave it a push in Mayhem's direction. Then he straightened up and stayed where he was, shaking in his Timberlands.

Mayhem took a deep breath. Keeping the other aggressor down didn't require a lot of effort, but he wasn't moving. He had the bastard pinned, and he wasn't taking any chances—

"Who are you?"

He glanced up again. Over at the drop-off counter, the pharmacist had poked her head around the jamb, and she didn't seem to know what to look at.

"The police are coming," he said to the woman. "But I want you to lock yourself in there, okay? In case there are others in the store right now."

She nodded with such vigor, her dangly earrings danced. "I've never seen anybody do that—"

"Lock yourself in. You'll be safer there. When the cops arrive, that's when you can come out. Go on, now."

She nodded and disappeared. Then there was a click and the shift of a dead bolt.

"Can you get off me, man," the assailant under him groused.

"Nope, I'm quite comfortable right where I am. Thanks for asking, though."

———

Mahrci left the supermarket, but she didn't make it out to the SUV. She stopped in the slush as soon as she got to the handicapped spaces. Turning back around, she stared at the front of the Hannaford, all the lights glowing like the moon had crashed to earth. As she closed her eyes, she saw Hemmy telling her to leave.

She headed back for the entrance before she was aware of deciding to change direction.

As the glass door slid to the side for her, all the carts were still lined up in their chutes, and the mats were where they'd been on the floor, and through the next set of doors, everything was just as it had appeared.

Including all the bags of food she'd been about to pay for.

The Muzak was still playing softly overhead, and there was a man approaching one of the scanners with a basket full of canned vegetables—

The shouting came from deeper in the store, to the left.

She ran before she could think better of it—

And skidded around a candy display just in time to see Mayhem throw his body at a human man who had a gun pointed at a woman behind the pharmacy counter.

"Hemmy!" Mahrci raced forward.

Except she stopped as her male focused on another man with a weapon. With the roar in her ears, she couldn't hear what was being said between the two— but she knew what he was doing as soon as the perpetrator put down his gun, pushed it across the floor, and then just stood there, as if he'd been shackled to the spot.

The woman who'd been in charge of the self-scan checkout rushed by. "I've called the police! They're coming!"

And then from the back of the store, a male voice: "Off-duty PPD!"

From out of the frozen foods section, a man in blue jeans and a navy blue parka shot forward. Along the way, he ditched his cart so that the thing rolled into a display of toiletries and L'Oréal cosmetics—but on the fly, he managed to grab two extension cords off a pop-up bin marked "Household Essentials."

He ripped the packaging off and jumped in behind the man who was still on his feet.

"You're under arrest." The cop grabbed one arm and pulled it to the small of the robber's back. Then he took the other. "You have the right to remain silent. Anything you say can and will be used against . . ."

As the cord got wrapped around those wrists fast, Hemmy shifted his position and brought the man underneath him up to a standing position.

"Cord me," he said as he held out a hand.

The cop tossed the other extension pack over, and within moments, Hemmy had wound things up and tied the ends together.

"He saved us," the pharmacist said as she pointed at Hemmy. "He made sure we were safe!"

"It's true," the checkout lady said. "He told me to call nine-one-one."

The off-duty cop nodded. "Fast thinking. Good job—"

Off in the distance, the sounds of sirens grew louder and louder. And then a pair of women in uniform jogged in.

As the humans all started talking at once— the two who were detained each protesting that it was the other guy's fault, the cops telling everybody to take a deep breath, the supermarket workers explaining everything—Hemmy looked over, and Mahrci's first thought was to run to him. Instead, she held herself in place and lifted her hand in a stupid "hi."

"Happy to hand this guy over," he said to the cop who stepped in to take his place. "And we'll go wait over there to get our statements taken, if that's okay?"

"Thank you," the female cop replied. "That'd be great."

Mahrci couldn't help but run her eyes up and down as Hemmy approached her. Except there had been no shots fired, he wasn't bleeding, and he probably didn't have anything more than a bruise on an elbow or a knee from the takedown.

"Are you okay?" she whispered.

"Yup. Come on, let's get out of here."

Everyone else in the store, from the deli manager and a pair of stock boys to a couple more shoppers, headed over to the drama. Meanwhile, the only two vampires in the place bucked that trend.

And one of them was on a stroll. Like there hadn't just been a couple of AWOL humans with guns prepared to hold up the place, and he hadn't just saved a bunch of people from an active shooter situation.

"I-I don't know how you did that," she stuttered.

Another couple of cops steamed by them, hands

on the guns at their hips, eyes trained on the pharmacy department.

"I wish you'd stayed outside." He shook his head. "You could have gotten hurt."

"The same's true for you."

Hemmy made a dismissive sound. "I'm fine. I'm always fine."

As they came up to their cart of groceries, he held his finger up. "One sec."

Before she could respond, he got his own credit card out and quickly finished the transaction. Then he locked a pair of grips on the cart.

With a shrug, he started pushing. "We still need the food, right?"

Mahrci opened her mouth. Shut it. "Ah, yes. Yes, I suppose we do."

Outside, there were all kinds of blue flashes from the Plattsburgh Police Department cars that had been parked nose-in at the entrance. Hemmy's strides were long and quick as he shoved the cart through the slush, and over at the Suburban, she helped him with the bags. Within a minute or two, they were driving off, just as another pair of patrol vehicles shot into the parking lot.

In the SUV, everything suddenly seemed very silent to her. Which was what happened when there were things you wanted to say, but you weren't sure how to phrase them.

"That was an incredible kindness you did," she murmured. "But how did you know? That those men were trouble?"

He shrugged and kept his eyes on the road ahead as he followed signs to the Northway. "Let's just say I'm good at picking out felons."

"I didn't even notice them."

"Well, it all worked out. That's all that matters, right?" Hemmy glanced over. "And besides, we got groceries. Mission accomplished."

When he refocused on what was ahead of them, she glanced in the back at the bags. All she could think about was . . . what if things hadn't gone well. What if he'd been shot. Killed.

The violence terrified her. But the idea he might be gone? Well, that did something to her soul. And yet . . . he was just a stranger, right?

Once they were on the highway, she stared out the window at the drifts of snow, the pine trees, the hills in the distance that loomed in the clear night sky . . .

If he had died, there in front of the human pharmacy, in a wrong place, wrong time kind of thing, what would she have missed?

The pain in the center of her chest was a shock, and she did her best to rub it away.

Now was not the time to meet the love of her life.

It really wasn't.

CHAPTER TWENTY-THREE

It's funny what you'll do when you're avoiding something else.

As Callum wiped his mouth with the napkin he'd been provided, he sat back from the table. "This was good."

The *symphath* across from him laughed in the low way he did. "You sound so surprised."

There was a lot of this that was surprising, Callum thought.

"And now you're ready to go." His host also sat back in his chair. "I'm proud of you. For staying in this room as long as you have."

The conversation had been easy, even too easy.

And he knew why. *Symphaths* had a way of putting people at ease, usually before they manipulated the fuck out of them for their own purposes. Yet none of that was going on. At least not that he was aware of.

Callum glanced around at all the nice furnishings. "Me, too."

He thought of Apex. And that kiss.

Maybe it was the wine . . . maybe it was the feeling that he'd broken this place's hold on him . . . but he felt himself warming under his skin as he remembered their mouths meeting. How could he go further, though? It was impossible to separate Apex from everything . . . that had happened.

The rescuer was part of the disaster.

"I feel like I should pay you for this," he said briskly as he nodded at the empty plates. "And yes, the asparagus was really good, even left over."

"I suspect it's been a while since you've eaten properly, so your standards are low." Blade lifted his wineglass with a nod. "But I will take the compliment because I'm a narcissist, and compliments are better than food to me."

Getting to his feet, Callum carried his plate over to the sink. A quick rinse and he put it in the dishwasher.

After he slipped the silverware into the machine's little basket, he pivoted around and leaned back against the counter. Time to go—

"Answer me this," Blade murmured. "Did you come back for your male?"

"Apex?" Callum frowned. "He's not mine. I didn't know he was here in Connelly."

"Oh, it is fate, then." Blade tilted forward. "How magical that you've reconnected."

"We haven't—"

"You will." The *symphath* toasted in Callum's direction again. "And may I give you a little advice? You are going to be leaving at a dead run in about two minutes, so consider it dessert—and I promise it will be more useful than ice cream, even if it doesn't taste as good."

Crossing his arms over his chest, Callum shook his head. "I still don't understand how I even ended up having dinner with you."

"Life is a mysterious trial, isn't it." Those eyes grew serious. "And here is my advice. Redecorate that male."

"I'm sorry?"

"This room . . ." The *symphath* glanced around pointedly. "Is little different than your male."

Callum tilted his head. "So you're suggesting I turn him into an armchair? Wrap him in wallpaper?"

The shake of that head was grave. "No, I'm giving you permission to make new memories of him. With him. Think of him as a room you're redesigning. You do not have to keep him draped in the past."

Callum scrubbed his face.

"It's all right," the *symphath* said. "You are allowed to move forward. You don't have to stay where you're stuck, with the pain."

It was a while before Callum could find his voice. "Can I ask you something?"

Blade motioned around his face. "Why I am so captivating?"

"Why are you trying to help me."

There was another long silence, and as the calming, elegant space sank into Callum, all the new decor suggested the male had a point.

"It's a bit of a Catch-Twenty-two, isn't it," Blade said with a little laugh. "Good advice from a *symphath*. Do you trust it or not."

"That isn't an answer to my question."

"Hmm. True. But I'll tell you something else. You won't believe whatever answer I give you, so I'm just going to keep my secrets. We are given only so many breaths, and I'm not going to waste any of mine on an inquiry that will never, ever be satisfied."

Callum straightened. Walked over to one of the couches. Picked up the jacket he'd laid on its arm.

"Tell me your lie, *symphath*. Why are you trying to help me?"

That wineglass was set down with the kind of precision usually reserved for bombs that had pressure charges.

"I once did a terrible, terrible thing to someone who did not deserve it." Blade touched his sternum. Then started rubbing things as if he had a pain there. "I was forgiven—and oddly enough, over the ensuing decades . . . that grace has proven to be as unbearable as the guilt. Perhaps more so."

The male stared off into the distance. "I am helping you as part of my atonement. I see you and your suffering, and I must do what I can to ease it. You might say . . . it is a calling for me now. The way I stay in my own skin." Those eyes shifted over. And suddenly the pensive tone was gone, the sharpness returning. "Quite at odds with what we *symphaths* are known for, isn't it. And now you, dear male, shall have to decide whether to believe what I have told you. Or not. Whichever will you choose, I wonder."

Callum drew on his jacket. Then he walked over to the table.

Looking down at the male, he waited. And sure enough, those eyes couldn't stay on his own.

After they shifted away, he said, "Thanks for dinner."

"It proves nothing, you know," Blade cut in. As if he'd guessed the conclusion that had been arrived at.

"Worry not, *symphath*. Your secret pain is safe with me."

Callum went over to the door. As he opened the way out, he heard in the background: "Don't be a stranger. Come back anytime. With that male of yours, too."

He pivoted around. "He's not mine."

"He will be, if you're smart enough to keep him." Blade finished his wine and put the empty glass back down. "And you can, if you want to. You're the one he's been waiting for as well."

As Callum left the private quarters, the words trailed after him, streamers that seemed tangible.

He told himself that he'd been wrong, that lack of eye contact meant nothing, that it was just a *sym-*

phath, seducing him into some kind of fucked-up situation that was going to crash and burn on him. But somehow . . . that paranoia didn't stick.

There was a healing being offered to him. If he just had the courage to take the plunge into the present.

And leave the past to die where it lay.

CHAPTER TWENTY-FOUR

After Mayhem piloted the Suburban through the gates of the estate, he glanced up into the rear view to catch the two halves closing, resealing ... becoming once again a barrier to entry.

He kept their speed low, because of the snow.

His light foot had absolutely nothing to do with the fact that as awkward as this silence was, he didn't want to get out of the damn vehicle. His stupid mind had decided that the second he pulled up to that big old Victorian house, Mahrci was going to fly away.

And he was never going to see her again—

"Can you slow down a little?"

He snapped to attention and looked across the

console. The female was staring out the front windshield, her profile a study in tension.

"Oh, yeah. Sure."

The lane was plowed, and there was no wind or snow making things hazardous. But sometimes speed was not just m.p.h., but perception. Maybe she didn't want to be back, either.

He wasn't asking, though—

"Can you . . . go slower."

This time, it wasn't really a request, and he lifted his foot off the accelerator completely. The SUV rolled for some number of yards, and then it just stopped, the idle unable to move the heavy treaded tires through the snow pack.

Glancing over at her again, he tried not to memorize what she looked like, that profile so achingly beautiful that his chest hurt, the dark tendrils of her hair curling up around her face, her lips parted as if she were on the verge of speech.

Or a kiss—

"I'm Whestmorel's daughter." She took a deep breath. "And the reason I'm here—well, one of them, is that I am refusing my arranged mating and I have no other place to go."

The sound of an exhale was loud in the interior.

And then he coughed because he realized that he was the one who'd released his breath like that.

"I just need a place to think." She smoothed her hair back, and hung her hands on her shoulders. "My father is livid because I'm embarrassing him in front of all the families that matter so much to him. But see, it's not about me, really. He wants me to get mated to the male because it's important for him. For . . . the things he's doing. I tried to fall in love, I really did. And I thought I had some feelings for my intended at one point. Some things you can't live with, though. Some things are just . . . wrong."

Mahrci glanced over, and there was a strange light in her eyes: Tension . . . but there was more to it than that.

"I'm sorry," he said. Even though a part of him was glad she'd had the backbone to get out of the situation.

"Hemmy, I'm telling you, this is . . . a bad mess that I'm in. And I don't want anybody else sucked into it. That's why I didn't want to talk to you about myself." She shrugged. "Also, it's nice to just forget about things for a little bit, you know?"

He nodded. "I do. I get that."

Her eyes swung back out to the lane ahead, a glowing white path cut between two mini-mountains of banks. On the far sides, the trees seemed to crowd up to the natural fencing, the snowfall from the night before lingering both in the boughs and on the bare branches.

"What about your *mahmen?*" he asked.

"She died in childbirth." She put her hand on her heart. "Not mine. My infant brother's, and he went unto the Fade, too. Since then, it's just been my father and me. Well, I was raised by the *doggen*, and my father has always been . . . busy. But it's been only the two of us."

"I'm sorry for your loss."

"I was ten at the time." Mahrci continued to focus on the winter landscape. "The truth is, it did not affect me as much as you might think. I was raised by *doggen* nannies before she died. I mean, I was shown to her and my father from time to time, but that was pretty much the extent of it. She was a ghost before she passed, and I say that with no malice, honestly. My nanny was my *mahmen*, and she is still in my life even though she doesn't live in my father's house anymore."

With obvious resolve, she glanced over at him. "My father is very angry at me. And that's why . . . I'm begging you to leave as soon as your work here is done." There was a slight pause. And then she blurted, "What-aboutwhenyouwereayoung?"

He knew there was more to things by the way she rushed her question. But at least if they were talking, she wasn't disappearing on him.

"I was an orphan, but everything worked out." Mayhem shrugged. "My parents left me at a Spring Festival as a nine-year-old—"

"They *left* you?"

"Mm-hmm." He wanted to hold her hand, but not because he felt like he needed the support. He just . . . really wanted to touch her. "I ended up being taken in by a baker. He let me sleep at the shop."

"Oh, that was kind of him."

"I'm not sure kind was the reason behind it all. He was looking for an extra set of hands, not another son. By taking me in, his real son didn't have to work and was allowed to go to school."

"I'm so sorry," she whispered. "That must have been hard."

"Are you kidding me?" He pointed to his chest. "I didn't want to go to school. I had a roof over my head, and all the bread and pastries I could eat. It was awesome."

Mahrci frowned as she seemed to study his features for clues as to whether he was hiding pain from her. From himself.

"Really, it was all right," he said. "What."

"Ah, you're telling me you were essentially dumped at the side of the road by your parents—"

"Honestly, I had no more a fucked-up childhood than anybody else does. Like young in so-called normal households have it easy? Just because you're checking off all the 'normal' boxes doesn't mean that everything is hunky-frickin'-dory."

And the same was true if you grew up with all kinds of bread at home—and not the loaf stuff, but the green, stacked variety.

"Well, I'm glad you told me—" She cleared her throat as her voice cracked. And then she rubbed her eyes, clearly so no tears fell. "I'm so sorry . . . my emotions are all over the place."

"Sure they are. That was an intense situation back there in the supermarket, and this conversation— we're not exactly talking about the weather, are we?"

She nodded in what looked like an absent way. Then she turned to him again.

Unlike the silence on the highway, now the quiet seemed to wrap around them, moving them closer together, even as neither of them changed positions.

"I'm really . . ." Her words trailed off. "Lost right now."

He reached up and brushed a piece of her hair back. "You're going to be fine."

"I don't think I am." That gaze drifted down to his mouth. "I'm not . . . okay, and I don't know what to do about it."

"Yes, you do." His voice deepened, his blood starting to thicken with arousal. "You know exactly what you're doing. You also know . . . what you want."

"Do I," she whispered.

He traced her face with his eyes, lingering on her lips. "And my answer is yes."

"I didn't ask a question—"

"You can use me, if you want."

Mahrci looked away sharply. "That's wrong."

"No, it isn't. I totally consent to being your rebound. Your revenge, your rebellion. Whatever it is. Use me."

"Why in the world would you let yourself . . . be treated like that?"

"Easy." He waited until she looked at him again. "I want you, too. And that's enough for me."

The female's eyes flared. And then she turned to him.

"I'm not right," she repeated. Like she was confessing to something. "In the head."

"You're right enough for me."

That simple truth was so powerful that a part of him threatened to reveal even more. Because how had this happened so fast between them? Then again, that didn't really matter anymore. For him, the journey was over. He was at his destination: From the moment he had first seen her, Mahrci had been different. And he wasn't going to miss his chance.

He'd rather have a little time with her.

Than none at all.

On some level, Mahrci had known this moment was coming. She hadn't been sure where or when, and certainly couldn't have predicted it would be here, in an SUV full of groceries, in the middle of the drive up to the big house. But she had known they would find themselves alone, in a privacy that was electrically charged.

"You shouldn't trust me," she said softly.

"Trust isn't relevant in this case."

Okaaaay, so maybe he only wanted a one-night stand, she thought. The question was, what did she want?

Well, he was right about one thing. At least part of that could be answered really damn easily.

"And no, you're not going to hurt me," he murmured as he brushed her cheek. "So you don't need to worry about that."

She shook her head. "I'm not using you or trying to hurt you. That's not the kind of person I am."

"And I live in the present. That's the kind of person *I* am." He stroked the side of her throat inside the collar of her fleece ... then lingered on her collarbone. "So I don't worry about what was, I don't care about what's coming. I have the here-and-now. This moment. Here ..."

He leaned in a little. "And ... now."

His eyes were hooded and hungry, his big body throwing off all kinds of sexual signals. But he stayed right where he was, in that tilt, on the cusp.

Mahrci parted her lips. "I'm sorry."

With a nod, he backed off. "Well, you know where to find me. And everything is good with me. All, nothing. A little."

He reached forward to put the engine in drive—

Mahrci launched herself over the center console, grabbed the front of his jacket, and pulled him in. As their mouths met, she wasn't gentle. Neither was he. It was an explosion of contact, and as she buried her hands in his hair, it was just such a relief to let go and feel.

No thinking. No planning. No worrying.

Just the sensation of his lips and her own meeting, and the scent of his arousal, and the urge to be naked and under his surging body.

As he penetrated her. As he filled her up.

Hemmy had a point about living in the present. And she hadn't ever felt this free.

As his tongue licked into her mouth, she moaned and thought about that big bed she'd been lying in alone—

For a split second, she had a spike of reversion, a return to her life of *What would people think?* But considering what she had done right before coming up here, this kiss wasn't a betrayal.

And it felt soooo good.

Hemmy slowly eased back. "How we doing?"

"You are . . . an amazing kisser."

The beaming smile that came back at her was a charmer. "Tell me more."

Mahrci ran her hands through his blond hair. Stroked his strong jawline. Put her hand on his thick shoulder. "Fishing for compliments, are you?"

"Fine, let's just do that some more."

Now he took control, cupping the nape of her neck and bringing her to him—and she was happy to close in on him, reaching down and releasing her seatbelt so she could all but drape herself over the drink cup holders that separated them.

The kissing got explosive again quick, and as she arched into him, she understood what he meant: Here and now . . . was everything: The scent of his arousal in her nose, his lips against hers, his body so close, yet so tantalizingly far away . . .

With the promise of everything she wanted just a bedroom away. Or a back seat. Or maybe his front seat.

When they finally broke apart for air, they were both panting and the windows were steamed up.

"You are . . . a really, *really* good kisser," she said roughly. "Not that I've kissed a lot of males."

Hemmy smiled in a lazy, sexy way. "Well, I feel the same way about you. And I haven't kissed any males."

She laughed as he ran his thumb over her lower lip. "I'm glad you approve."

"I more than approve," he growled. "And I have to say, this is not the way I expected this to go. Well, the groceries in the back, yes—"

"I'm not going to take advantage of you."

"Oh, sweetheart, you are welcome to take *all* of my virtue. Not that I have much left—" Abruptly, he shook his head. "Uh-oh. Nope. No, don't do that."

"Do what?"

"Overthink anything. I can see it on your face. Just be here with me now. I promise you, fate will take care of the rest—"

A flare of headlights pierced through the SUV, lighting the side of his face.

"Looks like we have company," he grumbled.

Mahrci stiffened and looked out the back, but all she got was blinded.

"I think your groundskeeper had made his return," Hemmy said as he put them in drive and continued along.

"Are you sure?"

Wouldn't that be a thank-God. As opposed to the list of people she didn't want to see.

"Those lights are too high to be anything else but that heavy-duty Ford."

"Oh. Good. And he's not my groundskeeper. He's my father's."

As they made their way down the lane, some of the mood was lost for her, and she tried to get it back, touching her mouth with her fingertips. Still, she couldn't ignore the fact that she had a lot of music to face. Sooner or later, she was going to have to—

"And it looks like we have company."

She shook herself back into focus and looked out the front windshield. Sure enough, parked right in front of the big house, was a low-slung, gray BMW—

A very unladylike curse left her on a frustrated exhale.

"Not who you expected?" Hemmy said as he pulled in front of the sedan.

No, she had expected this. Or should have.

"Unfortunately, no," she whispered.

"Are you okay?" He put the SUV in park and turned off the engine. "Mahrci?"

"That's my ex-fiancé." She glanced across at him. "I didn't know he was coming, I swear. He hates me now."

Hemmy glanced into the rear view mirror at the BMW. "Can I ask you a question. Before we go in."

"Yes, of course. But there isn't much to ask. I broke it off, and shamed him and my father—"

"No, that's not what I want to know." Those pale eyes that had glowed with such a sexual charge narrowed into slits. "Did he hurt you. In any way. Ever?"

"No." She shook her head emphatically. "It was never like that—nothing violent. Actually, there wasn't much between us at all, which was one of the problems we had. At least on my side."

There were others, too. Plenty of them.

"Good," he said in a pleasant voice. "That'll mean we don't have to call a crime scene cleanup team."

As he opened his door, she did her best to decode his words. "I'm sorry? I don't under—"

Hemmy got out and then planted his palms on the driver's seat and leaned back into the interior. "I'd have to fucking kill him if he hurt you."

Mahrci's breath caught. And if it had been anybody else, she would have chalked the words up to hyperbole.

With the way the male in front of her was looking?

They were a vow.

She covered one of his hands with her own. "Thank you. It's been . . . a very long time since anyone, well . . . I'm grateful. Even though there's no reason to go after him."

Hemmy squeezed her palm. "I gotchu, female. Anytime, anywhere. I'll be there for you."

He straightened and closed the door. Then he seemed to freeze.

Twisting around, she watched him call to the groundskeeper, who had pulled the truck into the space where the plow had been left.

The other male got out and looked over at him. Neither moved.

It was clear they knew each other, and Hemmy started walking forward first. But then the grounds-keeper joined him.

As they met and embraced, tears sprung to her eyes. She didn't know whether they were for him . . . or for her.

But there was nothing like finding an ally . . . when you least expected it.

CHAPTER TWENTY-FIVE

W here is Mahricelle."

As the douchebag with the BMW and the shark suit threw the demand out there, Apex kind of wanted to break the guy's nose. Just on principle. There was something about tense, entitled assholes that put his hackles up, and God knew he'd already had enough of dealing with Remis back in Caldwell.

Cue the headlights.

Two sets—so unless they were getting more visitors of the unwanted variety, that wolven was returning as well.

"Something tells me she's back now," Apex said as he started for the front door.

His arm was taken in a hard grip, and Remis's eyes were direct to the point of being threatening. "You get her the fuck out of here."

Apex pointedly looked down at the male's hand. When it was removed quickly, he was almost disappointed.

"I'm here to do cameras and linkups. That's it."

"Fine," the guy hissed as he took out his wallet. "I'll pay you."

Up came a fan of hundreds, and Apex rolled his eyes. "That's your solution for everything, isn't it."

"A thousand dollars. C'mon. Take it—"

"You put that money away right now, or it's going somewhere other than back in your billfold." Apex leaned in. "You want her to go, you can talk to her yourself. I'm not doing your dirty work just because you're waving Benjamin Franklins in my face."

Remis jabbed his forefinger. "You're not the only tough guy I know. Be careful. I may call for the kind of reinforcements that can put even someone like you in a choke hold."

Baring his fangs, Apex growled, "Don't threaten me with a good time."

At that moment, the door opened and the cold came in. Along with Mayhem and Mahrci—

The third figure was identified first by scent, second by sight, and lastly by a sudden thickening behind his button fly that he really could have done without. But, yup, Callum was also entering through that heavy old door, both hands laden with Hannaford bags, limp very noticeable.

Fun fact: Did his wolven side limp, too?

Guess that was more a question.

Mahrci stopped short, even though she had to already know her ex was here, given the car outside—and Callum had to sharply swerve around the female. As the wolven stumbled, he looked up.

Right into Apex's eyes.

And didn't that suck all of the oxygen out of the entire house . . . maybe out of a radius of fifteen miles. Meanwhile, as they stared at each other, Apex was vaguely aware of some truly awkward moments unfolding around him, but the Remis drama could wait.

His wolven was the only thing on his radar.

Walking over to Callum, he said, "Let me help you."

"I'm okay." The wolven nodded out the front door. "But there's more in the back of your car."

"You're limping worse than you were and need a doctor—"

"No, I'm not and no, I don't—"

"—and where the fuck are your clothes?"

They stopped talking and looked over at Remis. The aristocrat was ugly-flushed, and not bothering to hide it as his stare raked up and down the female.

"She looks dressed to me," Mayhem drawled.

"Who the hell are you?" Remis snapped. Then he poked that stupid finger in Mahrci's face. "You and I are going to have a talk downstairs. *Right now.*"

Annnnnnd cue the intervention.

Before Apex knew what he was doing, he stepped in front of Mayhem, clapped grips on those rock-hard biceps, and pinned the other male against the beadboard.

"Easy there," he muttered under his breath.

"Oh, I'm not gonna hurt him."

This was said as Mayhem fixated on Remis like he was already ripping the front of the guy's throat out with his bare hands.

"Riiiiiiight—"

"Yes, Remis," Mahrci cut in roughly as she put the bags she was carrying on the floor. "We do need to talk."

Leaving all the males behind, she turned away and headed for the stairs into the basement. In her wake, everybody she'd ditched on the first floor had a moment of put-in-their-place. Naturally, the biggest dickhead in the group recovered first.

Remis sniffed a couple of times, like someone had blown pepper in his face. Then he straightened his jacket, popped his cuffs, and headed down after her.

"No," Apex said as he didn't move. "Forget it."

"Step off," Mayhem demanded. "I'm just going to go get the rest of the groceries."

"Okay, but let's make that a team effort."

On that note, he let go of the guy, and then followed Mr. Helpful out to the Suburban. The second they got back in the door with the last of the bags, Mayhem dropped his load next to the ones Mahrci had left behind—and went for the stairs down into the basement.

"Don't try to stop me," he announced. "And no, I'm not doing shit. Unless he does."

Apex stood there, surrounded by crap he hadn't bought and had no intention of eating, being filmed by cameras, the feeds of which were going nowhere, and getting stared at by all the glass eyes in those fucking heads . . . and all he could think of was—

"Callum?" he called out.

Picking up some of the bags, he followed the scent of the wolven into the kitchen, and found the male at the counter, unpacking things.

"Mayhem's gone downstairs," Apex said as he hefted the groceries up on the counter.

"You couldn't stop him?"

"Didn't even try." He idly started taking things out, paying no attention to what he was throwing around the stainless steel counter. "I don't want her down there alone with the asshole, anyway. Remis does something stupid, he's going to get what he deserves."

Callum stopped. Turned around. "So it's just you and me."

Apex found himself halting, too. All of a sudden, everything became crystal clear, almost painfully so, from the boxes of Barilla pasta, the carton of eggs, and the half gallon of milk . . . to the restaurant range with all its burners, the deep stainless steel sink, and the double ovens . . . to the wooden rafters, the aged oak table, and the pans that were stacked in an orderly pile on the shelf above the center island.

Still, only one thing truly registered on him.

Callum was staring across the space, his husky-like eyes gleaming with something that Apex didn't really trust himself to interpret properly.

"How are you doing?" he heard himself say. "You want some food?"

"I already ate with a friend."

The stab of jealousy was so ridiculous, he had to laugh.

"Why's that funny?"

Apex shook his head. "Nothing—no reason."

Nah, it was just that the universe seemed determined to keep kneeing him in the balls. Like it was any of his business, who the wolven had been—

"Do you know Blade?"

The laughter dried up fast at the name. "Yeah. I know him. Is that who you were with?"

An image of the *symphath* came to mind, and it was not a welcome one. Apex had run into the striking, highly intelligent—and very dangerous—male down in Caldwell a couple of times in the past decade.

Fucking wonderful.

"His leftovers aren't bad." Callum shrugged. "And he gives good advice."

Apex frowned. "Wait a minute, was he at the prison?"

"He owns it now, I guess. I just met him, so I don't know the details."

Linking his arms over his chest, Apex said in a low voice, "And what kind of advice did he give you."

There was a pause. After which Callum crossed the distance that separated them. "He said I should be with the male I want. He told me . . . the past needs to stay where it happened."

All the breath in Apex's lungs left in a slow rush. "Well ... I agree with him. On both fronts."

"And you don't have to ask."

"Ask what."

"Who ... it is I want." Callum hesitated with his hands just hovering over Apex's shoulders. "I think it's you. But I'm just not sure that I can get there ..."

There was a slice of pain at hearing the confession. Yet it was more than he could ever have hoped for, this opening, this tender, vulnerable chance.

A bloom in winter.

Biting his lower lip with his fangs, Apex swayed. Then he whispered hoarsely, "Touch me, please. Oh, fuck ... just touch me if you can. Anywhere, I don't give a fuck."

The fingertips that trembled over his cheeks, his jaws ... his mouth and throat ... were calloused and gentle. And the eyes that watched the exploration were softly focused, as if Callum were witnessing a third party's movements, rather than directing his own hands.

"What happened to your gold fangs?" the wolven asked.

"I had a vampire dentist take the caps off. I don't live that life anymore."

"Oh . . ."

For a moment, Apex wished he'd left things as they were. Assuming the male liked those little mouth daggers.

"I'm sorry," Callum murmured.

"For what?"

"I don't know. I guess I don't know what else to say."

"You don't have to talk, then."

When the wolven tilted his head to the side, Apex's heart rate doubled, but there was no kissing, no meeting of hungry mouths. Instead, the other male's fingertips continued down onto his neck, and as they hesitated over the jugular, he knew Callum was feeling that pump-pump-pump.

And then the touch went even farther, to his chest. His stomach.

There was no way Apex could hide what was going on at his hips—and just as the thought occurred, a palm cupped his erection.

The pressure on his cock made him hiss and close his eyes—and fuck *yes*, he finally felt a pair of lips brush the pulse that flickered at the side of his throat.

"You're so hard," the wolven groaned.

Apex babbled some kind of response—because holy fucking hell, the male was stroking him through his leathers, feeling his erection, exploring as that mouth nuzzled and sucked at his neck. He couldn't help it. His hips started thrusting up and back, up and back, so that that palm was turned into a very poor substitute for the kind of friction he really wanted from the male—

At that point, Apex totally lost the plot, and before he could think better of it, he pulled the wolven closer, to feel more, to do more, even though this wasn't a good place—although hey, there was a pantry with a solid door over there—

Callum let out a strangled sound. Then there were two jerks against Apex's body, like . . . pumps. And then a scent that there was no forgetting. Ever.

As the wolven went still, Apex released his hold and just stood there, in case there was any panicking.

"I . . ." Callum stepped back and looked down at himself. "I came."

Apex searched that stark, surprised face. "Yeah, you did—"

The phone going off was just perfect fucking timing really, the vibration in Apex's ass pocket, the demand from God only knew who, absolutely not welcome as it shattered the moment.

"It'll go to voicemail." Apex shoved his hand at the thing and silenced the interruption. "It's nothing."

Callum glanced around the kitchen as if he didn't know where he was. Then his eyes passed over the groceries like he didn't know what they were.

And of course the fucking phone started ringing again.

"You better get that," Callum mumbled. "It's important—"

"You're important."

"Will you excuse me? I have . . . to . . ."

The wolven tore off like he was the one having to take a call for work.

Left to his own devices, Apex swung round, braced a hold on the counter, and leaned into his arms. In the silence, the cell phone's sarcastic purring was like a scream in his ears.

CHAPTER TWENTY–SIX

As Mahrci closed herself and Remis in the bedroom, she made sure to stay next to the door. She hadn't lied to Hemmy about there having been no violence between them during their relationship, but there was a lot going on. A lot that she knew now that she hadn't before.

And as Remis's nostrils flared and he looked at the messy bed she hadn't yet made up, she realized she had made one mistake.

His expression went dark. "You . . . fucking *bitch*."

She forced herself to hold his glare. "Do you honestly care I was with someone else—"

"You're fucking the *help?*" He slashed a hand through the still air. "*That's* why you ended it with me?"

The sad thing, she thought, was that as topics went, this was better than so many others.

"Just stop," she said with exhaustion. "I know you didn't come up here to fight for me."

"Is that what you want?" He gestured around. "For me to beg you to come back? Is this whole drama some kind of attention-getting bullshit? Because you're right, that's *not* why I'm here."

"So why did you make the drive," she said in a low voice. "What are you doing this far upstate in the snow."

"Your father sent me."

"Ah, yes. I should have known—"

"You've made him *so* proud. I mean, who wouldn't want a daughter like you, who doesn't give a shit about who she disgraces."

Fuck you, she thought as a wholly uncharacteristic rage hit her.

"Oh, I care about that," she shot back. "Trust me. I'm pretty happy I disgraced you. It's the best thing I got out of our relationship."

That actually shut him up for a moment. And as he stood there, blinking like an idiot in that slick, dark gray suit, she just—

"I wanted to make it work," she blurted. "Even though I knew you didn't love me. I wanted to be the good female, do the right thing, but then I realized . . . I don't know who you really are. Underneath your fine clothes, and the manners that hide your true nature, you're not what you pretend to be. So I'm not sacrificing myself anymore to the lies—"

"Oh, spare me the vestal virgin shit," he spat. "You're not innocent, and I know that firsthand, don't I. You're lucky I was willing to stick around after that little news flash."

Mahrci shook her head and told herself to shut up.

She didn't. "And you only love my father, that's who you care about. I was just a way for you to cement your connection to him—"

"In case you haven't noticed"—Remis leaned in—"he and I are doing just fine without you. The only thing that's changed is you're out of his will, and I'm right by his side."

Mahrci smiled as she lowered her lids. "That so."

"Yes, that's so." He smoothed his tie. "You can get off your sacrificial mount. You're the only one who's impressed by it. And while you're at it, you need to leave this property immediately. You're trespassing."

In the silence that followed, the chuckle that came out of her was no sound she had ever made before. "You know something, I feel really sorry for you."

As he cocked an eyebrow, Remis clearly thought she was delusional.

"The *glymera* are not so kind to those who are less than." Mahrci took a step closer to him. "How was your drive up here. Pity you can't dematerialize like the rest of us—"

With a growl of rage, Remis launched himself at her, grabbing her by the front of the throat with both hands and slamming her against the wall. His expression was so furious, there was a blankness to it, as if he weren't even seeing her, and his whole body was shaking as he squeezed her windpipe closed.

Mahrci gasped for air and clawed at his—

The bedroom door burst open, and Hemmy took control of the situation, picking up Remis by the armpits and pulling him off of her. As the male started to flail and holler, it didn't make any difference.

Hemmy just walked out with his unstable load.

Mahrci sagged and caught her breath. Then she stumbled out into the hall. She was still grabbing at oxygen and tripping as she followed the pair to the staircase. Halfway up to the first floor, her vision cleared, and that was when Remis threw his head back and glared at her.

"You fucking cunt!"

Hemmy stopped short. "What did you say."

Remis twisted around, shoving and pushing, and still getting nowhere. "She's a cunt, and she fucked you to get back at me—"

One moment, the male was being held far enough off the steps so that he was kicking the handrail and the wainscoting. The next, he was being banged back and forth between the walls in the stairwell like a rag doll.

Banga, banga, banga—

And then Hemmy threw the male up the staircase, like he was heaving a bag of potatoes. The force of Remis's impact on the closed door busted the latch open and the male spilled out into the hall beyond.

All those Idaho bakers rolling across the floor.

After which, Hemmy strolled up the remaining stairs. As if he hadn't just tossed a fully grown male into a door—and broken the latter with him.

Meanwhile, Apex stepped into view and looked down at Remis, who was pinwheeling on his back like he had no idea what had happened to him.

"You know," the male remarked dryly, "this actually went better than I thought it was going to."

"Because I didn't bust the door off the hinges?" Hemmy offered.

"Well, there's that." Apex shrugged. "And he's still breathing."

———

Yeah, the fucker who had laid his hands on Mahrci was still breathing, Mayhem thought. But he was seriously considering shutting that down. Seemed only fair considering the male had gone for her throat.

He was never going to get over what he'd seen as he busted into that bedroom.

On that note, he glanced down the stairs. The female who had been unforgettable even before he'd kissed her was staring up at him, echoes of shock and fear paling her face, her eyes wide. After he noted all of that, the only thing he could see was the bruised, red band around her neck. It was like a second collar at the loose opening of the fleece she'd worn for their trip to the supermarket.

Are you okay? he mouthed.

He wasn't sure she'd understand him. But when she nodded and smoothed her hair back? Guess so.

Meanwhile, the ex was getting his shit together, rolling over and planting a pair of squeaky palms on the varnished floor so he could push his chest up.

Without thinking about what he was doing, Mayhem drew his boot back and aimed for that ass—

Apex yanked him out of range. "Nope, you're done. The message has been received and we don't need this."

"He called her a cunt. After he started to strangle her."

The change in the other male was instantaneous. Those black eyes narrowed, and those lips went straight-line. "I'm sorry—what?"

"He tried to strangle her."

There was a pause. And then Apex lowered himself on his haunches and tilted his head so he could look the ex in the face. "Did you do that? You put your hands on her?"

Remis met the male right in the eye. "None . . . of your . . . fucking business—"

"You called her a cunt?"

By this time, Mahrci had reached the top of the staircase, and Mayhem wanted to step into her, pull her against his body, and feel the warmth and solidity of her. But he stayed where he was—because he wasn't too sure that Apex wasn't about to jump on Remis.

And if anybody was going to go beat-down properly on the guy, it was going to be—

"You're a dead male."

As the vow hit the airways, Mayhem thought it was Apex talking. But then he realized he was the one being addressed.

The ex's nasty, unhinged eyes were staring up at him with a hatred that was surprising. Most aristocrats didn't have that much passion in them. Then again, this was the new order of the *glymera*, where money counted more than breeding.

Apparently, the male still had some starch in his bloodline.

"I have people," Remis said grimly. "And you're fucking dead—"

"You know what," Apex announced as he straightened and clapped Mayhem on the shoulder. "You just keep going with your workout. Cardiovascular health is *so* important, and really, when was the last time you went to the gym?"

"God, it's been weeks." Mayhem bent down and palmed the ex's face, lifting Remis up to his feet by the guy's features. "And I had a New Year's resolution. So I've been letting myself down."

As he started walking for the front door, Apex followed along casually. Like there wasn't all kinds of tap dancing going on next to them.

"Oh, yeah?" the guy commented.

"Yeah, totally—" He steered the ex around a table with a bunch of boating pictures on it. "Watch yourself there, Remis, I wouldn't want you to get hurt. That would be such a shame. Anyway, what was I saying— oh. Right. Yeah, so I was going to start going twice a week, but I couldn't keep that up—hey, would you get the door for me?"

"Pleasure." Apex jumped ahead, cranked the latch, and pulled things open with a flourish. "And I do mean that."

The cold rushed in, and so did the glare of the bright white landscape: Thanks to the exterior security lights, it was easy to see the shoveled walkway, easy to pilot the stamping, hollering douchebag to that BMW.

When they were about ten feet away from the car, Mayhem gave the ex a good push and the male skated forth, landing on the hood of the sedan like a deer that had been hit.

The recovery was pretty quick, all things considered, the male getting back on his feet—even if those Gucci loafers gave him some traction issues.

Hard to look like a badass when you were skating while holding still.

What a pity.

"You shouldn't have gotten involved," Remis said.

Mayhem inclined his head. "Thanks for your opinion. I'll file it where it belongs—"

"She's only fucking you to get back at me."

Time slowed to a stop. And Mayhem glanced down at the snow. "Now, see, why'd you have to go there—"

Apex stepped in between them. "Okay, I let you have some fun. Now he has to go—"

"Does that bother you?" Mayhem talked over his friend's shoulder. "That she's fucking me? 'Cuz if it does, good. I'm glad. I hope it keeps you up all day long—"

"I'm coming for you. Watch your back—"

Apex wheeled around on the guy. "Shut up, Remis. Get in your fucking car and go back to Caldwell—"

That finger he clearly liked to jab in people's faces swung in Apex's direction. "Stay out of this. If you know what's good for you—"

"Right now, I'm all that's keeping him from killing

you. So how about you do us both a favor and leave? I don't really like you, so I'm not sure how long I'm going to keep the peace going. FYI."

With a last look toward the house, the ex marched around, got behind the wheel—and made the mistake of trying to peel out in the snowpack. Even with those snow tires, and all that fancy, computer-aided traction, he didn't get far with that.

So he was forced to creep out, his luxury sedan making like a child's remote control toy—

A heavy arm became a bar across Mayhem's chest. "Let him go."

"I'm not going after him."

"Then why did you just take two steps forward."

Did I? he wondered.

Well, Apex was probably a better judge of his actions than he was at the moment.

Nodding, he turned back to the house. Walked back.

As he came up to the entrance, he stopped in front of Mahrci. And it was then when he realized what he'd said.

Fuck.

He glanced over his shoulder at Apex. "We're not sleeping together. Just so we're clear. I only said that to get a rise out of him." Then he turned back and rubbed his face. "I'm sorry. I probably should have handled . . . all of this better—"

Mahrci threw her arms around him and squeezed him so hard, she nearly popped his head off his spine. Not that he cared. The sound of her weeping just about tore him up—

"That was frickin' awesome!" She pulled back, and was laughing so hard she had to wipe her eyes. "Did you see the expression on his face? And what was the move around the car?"

Oh, okay. Not crying, but laughing hysterically.

All at once, the three of them were imitating Remis's slippery strides, their hands waving around over their heads, the laughter echoing all around—because clearly, they all needed it. And when the tension had been burned off, they stood out in the cold and caught their breaths.

"Okay, that was a little mean," Mahrci said.

Mayhem glanced at her throat and thought, *Not even close to mean.*

And then Mahrci was taking his hand and holding his eyes intently. "You're not the help, not like he meant it. I want you to know that."

Even though Apex was right beside them, Mayhem reached up and brushed that one strand of hair out of her face again. "I wasn't offended because I know I'm not. But thank you, for caring how I *might* have taken it."

She nodded. "And thank you . . . for coming in when you did."

"Wellllllllllll, I mighta been eavesdropping. A little bit. It goes without saying that I think you did the right thing getting out of that mating."

"I had to." Her face grew grave. "I didn't have a choice. I had . . . to do the right thing."

When she shivered, he knew that it wasn't the cold.

Slipping his arm across her shoulders, he led her back into the house, the warm, well-lit house, where he would keep her safe.

For however long she would let him.

"I'm going to cook," he murmured. "For the both of us."

CHAPTER TWENTY–SEVEN

As Mayhem took the female inside, Apex stayed out on the porch. He told himself that it was because he had to make sure that bastard Remis had really left. He told himself it was because he needed some fresh air. He told himself . . .

That it was not to look at the groundskeeping garage, and search that lineup of darkened windows or that slumbering truck for any sign of the wolven.

"So fucking stupid," he muttered, his breath wafting over his shoulder.

Because what he was really searching for was answers: For what he could have done differently not just tonight in the kitchen, but all those nights back at that bedside, so long ago.

If Callum could only talk to him . . . maybe they'd work through some things together. After all, words could be bandages for injuries of the soul, and that was a two-way street. Spoken by, spoken to. And yes, he was jealous of fucking Blade.

It would have almost been easier if the two of them had just had meaningless sex. But noooo, that *symphath* had said some combination of syllables that had unlocked Callum a little.

Apex wanted to be the help. *He* wanted to be the savior.

"That fucking *symphath* hadn't been at the bedside back in that prison—"

From out of the corner of his eye, he caught a flicker of movement at the forest edge. And he knew what it was before he turned.

Who it was.

The great white-and-gray wolf was standing just inside the tree line, its fur camouflaging the position perfectly in all the snow.

So the predator had wanted to give its presence away.

As it four-pawed the way out from the pines, Apex was acutely aware that it could run faster than he could, and he glanced back at the big house's entry. He could make it if the thing rushed at him.

Well . . .

As the cold wind blew around him and tightened the muscles of his legs, he was pretty sure he could make it.

While the wolf approached him, he became transfixed by the way its weight shifted, the power in that body hypnotic. The ice-blue eyes that had made a target out of him were right in front of the head, perched atop the long muzzle. They were a reminder that predators always had their visual center facing forward. Things like horses and cows and deer had eyes on the sides, so they could see what was coming.

Wolves and vampires were what was coming.

"Do you know who I am?" he asked. Like the wolf could speak English?

But maybe it knew voices . . . and maybe Callum was still in there.

He'd never gotten the chance to ask the male if he had any control over anything when the wolf was front and center. Were they two sides of the same coin . . . or two totally different entities who arm wrestled over the same set of cells?

Had Callum sent the wolf in against those coyotes? To protect Mahrci? Or had that been primal instinct to go after an easy meal?

Did Callum know the wolf was getting even closer . . . to Apex now?

Apex sank down onto his haunches and just stayed where he was. And that seemed like some kind of signal. The wolf came all the way forward, one paw after the other, not in the deep snow now, but on the drive that had been cleared.

By the other half of him, in that truck—

And then they were face to face, nose to nose.

Reaching out, he suspended a hand over the right flank—just as Callum had done to his face earlier. And he gave the animal plenty of time to move away, growl—snap at him. Bite his hand off.

When none of that happened, he stroked the springy, silky fur, passing his palm down the shoulder.

"Can you do me a favor?" he whispered.

The wolf snorted into the cold, but not in a way that seemed like a negative response.

"I'll take that as a yes." He continued to pet the rangy, powerful body. "If he's in there, tell Callum . . ."

He shifted over and put his other hand on the far side of the wolf's chest. "Callum, if you're in there, I want you to know that I've spent the last thirty years thinking of you every day. It's like you had died and I've been mourning you—and to deal with the pain, I made up stories about us. I made . . . a whole life for you and me. In my mind."

Staring into the nearly white eyes of the wolf, his voice cracked, but he was able to keep going. "See, I didn't know you long enough to have the little things. The cereal box in the store, the one I knew you liked. The jacket that still smelled like you. The side of the bed that was yours, the key ring you took every time you left . . . the sound you made when you said my name as you came. We didn't get any of that. So I created our life, and I mourned it all as if it had existed."

He glanced away and cleared his throat, embarrassed and yet somehow glad he was revealing all this to the wolf. "You liked Wheaties, in my made-up world. So I used to . . . buy a box, and eat it for First Meal. And when I poured the milk, I'd cry. It was the breakfast of champions, which is why I chose it for you." He took a deep breath. So he could keep going. "In my fantasy world, we fell in love in the summer immediately after the liberation. You came home with me to Caldwell and recovered through that spring, and then as the color of the leaves deepened into that darkest green of late July . . . we fell in love. We took walks down by the river at night, under the moon. So I would go there each August, and stroll by the lazy, hot Hudson . . . and mourn."

He moved his hands up and ran them over the wolf's head and down its neck. "In our pretend life, we watched *The Office* reruns when we were together . . . so I used to play them on my iPad, and pretend I could hear you laugh. And I would mourn."

A cold wind blew around the pair of them, him and the wolf, and his eyes teared up. "In our created life, you died in winter. So the winters have always been the hardest on me. The mourning . . . has always been the loudest when it is cold outside. In the time of snow and ice, I have always missed you most."

He threaded his fingers into the softness of the fur, and went so deep, the warmth of the flesh registered. Then he released his hands and thought of the way Callum had backed away, twice.

"If you're in there, Callum, I want you to know we had a wonderful life." He touched his temple. "In my mind, I did us . . . proud. And I've been loyal to your memory for thirty years."

I think it's you. But I just don't know that I can get there.

As he heard the male's voice in his head, for the first time in not just thirty years, but a hundred years, Apex looked into the future. And what he saw broke him.

He saw the male he loved trying so hard to force something that just didn't exist and wasn't meant to be.

On his side, Apex had been living and mourning an epic, breathtaking, star-crossed love story. On Callum's, the male had been frozen in a nightmare, anchored to a past so horrific, he could think of nothing less.

"That you're even trying . . ." He had to wipe his eyes. "Is enough love for me. It's the love I have always wanted to feel."

As he choked up, he shuffled back. Rose to his full height. Rubbed his face on the inside of his jacket sleeve.

"And here's the thing. I love you enough . . . to ask you to stop trying."

He looked out to the garage, to that lineup of windows. And thought of them going dark, one by one, the night before.

"All I want is for the pain to stop for you. I don't care if it goes on for me. Because some things cannot be separated, and . . ." Apex took a deep breath. "I'm sorry I came here and upset you, but maybe this was all meant to be. If it's opened up a door for you, go through it, Callum. Welcome to the present, and go on into your future with my blessing. Leave me with the past . . . and go forward. You deserve it, after all these years."

This was the trial run, he thought. *Say this shit to the wolf, then speak it to the male.*

"I'll be here for tonight and through the day to-morrow. Our time ends after this. I won't . . ." Now he lost the ability to speak, his throat closing to the point where he couldn't draw breath. "I won't come back. I won't try to find you. I'll leave us where we've always been—in the past. And pray that you will go on with-out me . . . and find some happiness with . . . someone else."

Bending down, he touched the wolf's face, and saw the male's at the same time, the two together, even though that wasn't possible.

And yet it was.

Apex smiled sadly, deciding he'd been stupid to think his heart couldn't possibly be broken any further.

Turned out being left behind was another shade of suffering.

"All you and I have ever had was a what-if," he said roughly. "But it's been the what-if of my lifetime."

He laughed a little. "And come on, that's more than some people get, you know? It's certainly more than I expected—and even if it's mostly pain, the suffering's been the way I've loved you."

Abruptly, the wolf moved closer, and then that majestic head rested on Apex's upper leg.

The weeping hit him hard, his tears flowing onto

the white fur, as the cold wind swirled around and he didn't feel the subzero temperature at all.

There was a relief, in finally saying his piece.

And at least the wolf seemed sympathetic.

———

Back in the kitchen at the rear of the big house, Mahrci was sitting on a stool at the stainless steel counter. In front of her was a beer, an open bag of potato chips . . . and a male who was making mince out of a yellow onion.

She hadn't had more than a sip of the Sam Adams, but the chips hit the spot.

The male was—

"You're not very good at that," she said as she eyed the uneven chunks with a smile.

Hemmy laughed and glanced across the cutting board. "I know, right? I suck. But here's the thing, the stuff isn't going to look any better once our stomachs are done with it, and it's going to taste the same."

"Excellent point."

He indicated her bottle with his knife. "You don't like the ale? We can get another kind. There's a ton in that walk-in."

"No, I'm good. Just going slowly." She needed to

keep a clear head. But she didn't want him to know why. "What comes next?"

"We brown the meat." He turned to the pan he'd put on the stove. "Which is a complicated process by which heat is added to meat and it turns brown."

Mahrci laughed. "You are a chef, after all."

"High level. Totally professional. Don't let this onion mess fool you."

As he poured a splash of olive oil into the pan, she blurted, "Remis is a half-breed."

Mayhem stared over his shoulder. "That's why he drove up then. I wondered."

"He hates that his mother was human, and he never intended for me to find out. When we were together, he'd have excuses about wanting to drive that car, how it centered him, how it was his form of self-care." She laughed without any humor. "One night, he cut himself while shaving, just before he came to see my father. When I greeted him, I kissed his cheek . . . and I smelled the fresh blood. I knew then."

"So you never took his vein?"

"No. My father has always arranged for my feedings, and they were always witnessed. We were waiting until after the mating, Remis and I."

"So your ex was going to make sure there was a ring on it before the secret came out."

She nodded. "That's what I suspect. By then, it would be too late. My father would never allow us to separate, and Remis would make sure that no one else knew to save himself the shame." Mahrci picked at the label on her beer. Then she looked up, across the mangled onions. "The irony is that I don't care. Most of us have some human blood in our families, even if some people make sure that those details are lost to time and pretend they never happened."

"Does your sire know? About Remis?"

Mahrci shrugged. "I'm not sure. My father has a lot going on. And as long as it stayed between Remis and me, it wouldn't bother him. Appearances are much more important—and you know, a lot of people prefer to drive their luxury vehicles."

Hemmy took the cutting board to the stove and sluiced off the onion chunks into the pan. Instantly, a fragrance bloomed that made her mouth water.

"That smells amazing."

The mulleted chef smiled over at her. "I told you. It's going to be fine."

As he stirred the mix, the soft sizzle and the hiss of the gas was white noise that relaxed her.

"I'm not proud of what I said to him." She took a sip from the open neck. "That I threw his lineage in his face. But I wanted to hurt him—and I know that's what cuts the deepest. It was wrong of me."

"Well . . ." More with the stirring. "That just proves you're a better person than I am. I'm very satisfied with my choices, particularly with the way I opened that basement door."

She had to laugh again. Then she grew serious. "You know what I like about you?" she mused. "Everything is up front. And integrity is the most important thing in this world to me."

With a gasp, he put his hand over his heart. "My middle name. How'd you guess?"

Shaking her head, she reached into the Lay's bag. "So how'd you and Apex meet?"

"Oh, we've known each other for a lifetime."

"Childhood friends?"

"Might as well be." Hemmy motioned with the wooden spoon. "See, he doesn't like me, but that's like saying grizzly bears are antisocial. Duh. He doesn't like anybody. On my side—in case you haven't noticed—I kind of go with the flow. Which he finds absolutely annoying, but is one of the reasons he can stand to be in the same room with me."

"Apex is a lone wolf, huh."

"That's one way of putting it." Hemmy peered into the pan. "I think this is ready for the *beeeeef*."

He made a show out of getting the hamburger into the pan, and then when he stirred, he swung his butt, and hummed a ridiculous stripper tune.

Mahrci had to look away as her face turned red. "Really?"

"Put your back into it. Only way to cook—"

Out in the front of the house, the door opened and closed. As footfalls approached, she had a momentary shot of fear that Remis had come back with the reinforcements he'd threatened to hire.

"Hemmy," she said softly.

"Mmm?" When she didn't immediately reply, he glanced over at her again. "You okay?"

"I want you to be careful. About Remis."

"I'm really not worried—"

She dropped her eyes. "You need to be. Please . . . after you leave here—be careful. I fear I've brought danger to your door."

"You know something"—he tossed the hamburger and onion around—"there is great freedom in not accepting responsibility for things you're not responsible for. Hey, that needs to go on a bumper sticker. T-shirt. Billboard—"

Apex came into the kitchen and seemed to stall out. As his eyes scanned the room . . . she thought back to him being in her father's house. The male had always been a silent, looming presence, watching them all. In this, he was like the security cameras he was installing in this place, she decided, recording everything.

"You okay there, big guy?" Hemmy asked him.

"Yeah."

No, she thought. And as she glanced back at Hemmy, he seemed worried, too.

"Beer's in the fridge," he said to Apex. "Gon then. Help yourself."

"I don't drink. You know that."

After which Apex went over to the cooler, took out a Sam Adams, and popped the top. As he put the bottle to his lips, he took a deep breath. Then he drank. And drank. And drank . . .

Hemmy seemed shocked, the spoon-stirring and the butt-whirling stopping.

"Slow down, son," he murmured, "and come up for a little air."

When the bottle was empty, the male went over to

the lower level of cupboards and started opening things.

"The trash is two over from there," Mahrci said as she pointed to a section closer to the sink.

"Thank you."

As he deep-six'd the bottle, Apex straightened and put his hands on his hips. "After dinner, we have to get cranking with the work. We're leaving at nightfall tomorrow."

Hemmy shrugged. "What's the hurry—"

"Fifteen minutes after sundown and we're out of here." He nodded to the stove. "So be quick about that, and eat fast."

As he left, there was a waft of something burning in the pan. But Hemmy stayed where he was, staring at the archway the other male had disappeared through.

"He is *such* a cheerful presence." Hemmy turned back to the stove. "I mean, a real ray of sunshine wherever he goes—*damn it.*"

He took the pan off to the side and agitated the beef with his spoon.

"He's right," Mahrci said with resignation. "We all have to leave. As soon as possible."

CHAPTER TWENTY–EIGHT

There's an aristocrat in the waiting room. He's demanding to see the King."

Tohr was sitting in the steel core of the Audience House when Saxton ducked into the corridor to make the announcement. And go figure, after the previous two nights, it was the last thing he wanted to hear.

"He doesn't have an appointment, does he?" Tohr shook his head as he hopped off his stool. "I mean, of course he doesn't."

"We do have time to accommodate him." Saxton glanced at Qhuinn and Vishous. "If the King wants to see him? We've been efficient tonight."

"I'll go check." Tohr tucked the back of his black shirt into his leathers. "What's the name?"

"Whestmorel."

Great. The squeaky wheel of the *glymera*. Just what they needed.

"Did he give a reason?" Although Tohr could guess. "Or a pretext."

"He's refusing to say." Saxton glanced at the clipboard in his hand. "We have over a half hour."

As V muttered something ugly, Tohr nodded at the solicitor. "I'll go ask Wrath—and tell Deena we'll handle this—one way or the other, I'll take care of him. She doesn't need to worry about the guy."

That receptionist was totally not going to be put on the front lines of dealing with an aristocrat like Whestmorel, especially if it was a "no" from the King. That male was a member of the new guard, which was not a compliment. He'd taken to sending memos on behalf of a "number of interested parties," as he called them, about issues they felt were pressing. So far it was all about festivals, social standards, and bullshit like that, but the frequency had been increasing.

And Tohr knew—he could just feel it in his bones—that something was cooking.

"Deena will be well pleased she's released of that

duty." Saxton inclined his head. "Thank you very much."

With that settled, Tohr walked down to the door that had a black dagger with the handle down and the tip pointed up on it. He knocked with a single knuckle and waited.

"Come in," came the muffled response.

As Tohr triggered the door release, the panel slid into the wall. The entry into the Audience Room from the steel corridor could be opened four different ways: To the left, to the right, and into the wall either way, depending on what was going on inside. Usually, it was just disappeared into the slot. But if something bad was happening—and everything was designed in the facility to ensure that was never what was going on— you could detach it and use it as cover. Or not—

"What we got."

Across a room that was draped in royal silks of red and black, Wrath was sitting in one of the two armchairs, and George, his golden retriever, was in his lap. The great Blind King was wearing his usual black muscle shirt, and the black wraparounds on his aristocratic face made him seem even harsher than his impatient greeting. Off to the side of him, a folding tray table was sporting a foot-long sub that had been cut into bite-sized pieces. There was also a Coke and a bag of Doritos with the turkey, lettuce, tomatoes, and mayo, hold the onions.

Well, at least he's having something to eat, Tohr thought. The King was not going to be happy about the newsflash, and hopefully having a little food on board was going to dull the—

"Tohr," came the impatient prod. "What's going on."

Tohr cleared his throat, and gave the dog a little wave. As he got a wag in return, the Marco/Polo he and George always did refocused him.

"We have someone in the waiting room who's not on the schedule."

A section of the sub was given to George, and the golden took it with his soft mouth, neatly munching the nubbins down.

Wrath's nostrils flared. "Who."

"It's a member of the *glymera.*"

"They don't exist anymore."

"Well, yes, that's right. But I was using the term more as a descriptor—"

"So what you're saying"—Wrath took a draw from the glass bottle—"is that we have an entitled toddler with a self-importance problem bullying my receptionist and demanding to see me."

"That's pretty much where we're at—and FYI, that's what *glymera* means to me." Tohr walked across and straightened the Kleenex box on the corner of Saxton's desk. "It's Whestmorel. And we have the time, just so you know. Not advocating an audience, though."

The King's black brows lowered behind his wrap-arounds, but he continued with his lunch, taking a bite for himself. Sharing another with the dog.

Finally, he announced, "Whestmorel can wait until I finish this—and the only reason I'm seeing him is because I don't want my receptionist to be in his presence when he throws a hissy fit. Has he deigned to give us a topic?"

"Nope. But I'm more than happy to go get one out of him."

Wrath nodded. Then said, "Deena doesn't need to see that, though. Tell her to go take a break first."

"Of course."

Like a lot of people who worked as part of Saxton's staff, the female had come up out of Safe Place, the domestic violence treatment center run by Rhage's *shellan*, Mary. Wrath was protective over everybody under this roof, but he was especially sensitive to Deena after learning her story.

He was like that. You came at him, he'd strike

your jugular. You were a decent, hardworking person who needed help? There was nothing he wouldn't do for you.

"Give me five minutes," Wrath said, "and then you bring him in to me. And have Qhuinn with you. Saxton, too. I want witnesses in addition to our cameras."

"You don't want me to get the subject to you first?"

"No. You and I both know what this is really about—so I don't need to hear it."

"Yes, my Lord."

Tohr bowed, even though the King couldn't see him, and then he left by the door the civilians were brought in through.

The front of the house, so to speak, was totally different than the security-focused core: The hallways that formed the loop the males and females were processed through were well lit and cheerful, with a cottage theme. Oil paintings of landscapes and still lifes of fruits and flowers and dogs from the nineteenth century, alternated with needlepoint samplers from the same period. Underfoot, woven rugs in red and black covered honey-colored pine floors, and the scents of fresh-cooked baked goods as always suffused the air.

Unlike the other Audience House, back decades ago, which had been like a museum—no offense to

Darius's incredible sense of style—they'd deliberately designed this one to be welcoming, homey, and relaxed. Like visitors were just going to their *grandmahmen's* from the Old Country.

And it works to bring down the tension, he thought as he walked into the receptionist's room.

Most of the time.

The male who was standing in the center of the waiting area had an expression on his face like he was liable to catch a disease if he sat down in any of the comfy-cozies. Talk about central casting. In his three-piece dark suit, his ascot, and those shiny wingtips, Whestmorel was a cross between an English dandy and a Wall Street money manager. Which was the new aristocracy, wasn't it. They were always trying to thread that needle, desperate to be what their predecessors had actually been: Exclusive by virtue of their bloodlines.

When all they could flex were bank accounts and stock portfolios.

And really, that wasn't saying much.

"Well," Whestmorel said. Then he made a show of kicking up his wrist and checking his gold watch.

Tohr turned his back on the guy. Behind her desk, Deena was sitting up straight in her chair, her worried eyes clinging to Tohr.

He smiled gently at her. "Would you be willing to refresh the tray? I'd be very grateful."

She bolted to her feet. "Yes, of course."

Even though it wasn't her job—not that she wouldn't do anything that was asked of her—she high-tailed it around the aristocrat, picked up the perfectly fresh supply of tea sandwiches, and disappeared out into the hall.

"So is Wrath coming in?"

Tohr frowned. And then stepped into the male. "No, you're going to go see him. In about five minutes."

Whestmorel's eyes narrowed. "This is important."

"You seem to think so. You want to tell me what this is about?"

"I didn't come to see you."

"Well, this is going to be a problem." Tohr glanced over and made sure the door Deena had left out of was fully closed. "No one gets in to Wrath without telling me what they're looking for."

"You're awfully protective of him."

"He's the King."

"Yes," Whestmorel said with calculation. "But you'd think, if he were a proper leader, there would not be so many barriers to access. It does not make one feel very aligned with the throne."

Tohr moved in very close. "Why don't you tell me why you're here. And while you're at it, step off that line you're walking. Your night's going to go a lot better as soon as you do."

CHAPTER TWENTY-NINE

I brought you a plate."

As the words registered, Apex looked up from the desk he'd been sitting at in the study for—how long had it been? He swiped the laptop's mouse square and checked the time stamp at the lower right-hand of the screen—

An hour. He'd been staring into space for an hour.

No, not space. He'd been looking out that window over there, focused on all the snow, the security lights turning the front expanse of the big house into a kind of moonscape—

"Hello?" Mayhem waved a hand around. "You still on the planet?"

Coming to attention, Apex shook his head. "Sorry. Thanks."

Mayhem set a load of pasta and sauce down. "The fork's in there."

Sure enough, said fork had been stabbed into the mound, the twists of linguini holding it in place like the tangle was a chorus of arms.

Apex rubbed his eyes, thinking, *Well, if that isn't a Hieronymus Bosch moment.*

And just in time for him to try to eat.

"I'll trade you this dinner for the laptop," he said as he held out the unit. "Get cranking on the sync, genius. This is your part of the job—"

"We don't have to be in such a hurry."

He jogged the laptop in the air. "Yeah, we do."

"I'm not worried about Remis. If that asshole comes back with a bunch of bare-knuckle reinforcements, it's not going to be a problem."

Apex narrowed his eyes. "This is not about you and your love life, okay? This is about the job. The timeline's been moved up, and we need the system double tested and fully functioning by dawn. We'll further vet it over day, so I'm sure the product works. And then we're leaving. All three of us."

Mayhem took the computer, but didn't look at it. "I'm not going to rush out of here—"

"Do you want to get her killed?"

The change in the male was immediate: Mayhem was always moving, even when he was standing still. Now he was like a statue.

"I can take care of her."

"Not against what's coming here in forty-eight hours." Apex focused on the steam that wafted up off the pasta, and told himself he needed to stop talking. "I can't tell you much more than that. Just, if you care for her, you'll get her the fuck out of here. This isn't about the ex."

Mayhem slowly lowered the laptop. "What the fuck is going on here."

Pulling the fork out of the pasta, Apex turned a twist in the center of the mound of meat sauce. "The less you know, the safer you are."

The other male dropped himself into the chair on the opposite side of the desk. When he reached toward a lineup of small carved figurines, Apex gave him a *nuh-uh*.

"You fiddle with those fucking bears"—he put the tight knot in his mouth—"and I'm going to feed them to you."

Mayhem sat back in the chair, bracing his elbow on the arm, propping his chin in his hand. "She thinks we need to leave, too."

"So follow Mahrci around down in Caldwell." He kept eating, the stuff surprisingly good. "This was never a Tinder date. That's not why we're up here. Do the job, Mayhem, and then go on about your life. But I *really* need you to do this work."

There was a long silence. Then the male stood up in a surge and tucked the laptop under his arm.

"I'll get started."

"Good, there's a document of instructions right there for you." As the guy turned away, Apex said, "You know, this ain't half bad."

He got a dismissive grunt over that shoulder.

Left on his own, Apex continued eating, watching through the archway as Mayhem opened the computer and typed one-handed. As the password that he'd been given got him into the instructions, files, and program platforms, the guy looked toward a camera mounted in the far corner, above the front door.

As he walked off out of sight, Apex glanced back to the window—

"Fuck!" he blurted as he dropped his fork onto the plate.

———

Callum hadn't intended to go back over to the big house yet.

But here he was, standing on the front porch in his two-footed form, staring into the study . . . like exactly what he was: A dog locked out in the cold.

And then Apex pivoted and looked at him.

The windows of the big house were all triple-paned, the replacements engineered to look like the old ones that had no doubt not only leaked like a sieve, but been incompatible with the light protection that had been added. So with the cold wind whistling in his ears, he wasn't able to hear the shout of surprise.

But those lips had certainly seemed to mouth *fuck*.

In the back of Callum's mind, right down deep at the brain stem part, a voice that was no voice, just meaning, spoke up:

Go to your mate.

He complied with the demand because that was why he was here, wasn't it. That was why he had come to this estate in the fall in the first place. Fate had seen fit to put him back on a track that intersected with the male who was now, at this very moment, rising up from the chair he was in. Next Apex was going to rush from the room, and run to the door and jump out into this cold, this bitter cold.

It was time Callum also did some running. And not in the opposite direction.

In three jumping strides, he was at the front door. But even with the effort, Apex was still the one who opened it.

Swallowing hard, Callum said, "You have a minute?"

Apex glanced over his shoulder. Then stepped out. "Yeah. Sure."

As the vampire closed the door, Callum nodded at the garage. "My place?"

For a second, the other male just glanced in that direction with surprise, like it was the first time he'd noticed the building. "Yeah . . . sure."

They walked together, the snow squeaking under their boots. When they got to the side door, Callum opened things and stepped out of the way. As Apex went through, the scent of the male took over the whole world.

And then they were going up the stairs.

Apex waited at the top, as if he had no intention of entering before he was invited. Like the old-school human myths about vampires.

"You're always welcome," Callum said. "In here."

The fact that he got an arched brow in response told him more than he wanted to remember about how harsh he'd been the night before.

"Can I get you a beer?" he offered. "I already made you leave your dinner."

"It's okay. I ate most of it. And I'll take the beer."

Callum nodded and went over to his refrigerator. Taking out two Heinekens, he twisted off the tops and then approached the vampire. As soon as Apex took the bottle, the guy put the open neck to his mouth and started drinking.

"Why were you crying out there—"

Apex sputtered and choked.

"Sorry," Callum murmured.

As the coughing subsided, Apex wiped his lips with the back of his hand. Then he lowered the bottle. "I didn't know . . . whether you were in there or not."

"I am. Just like the wolf is inside me now. We are one and the same."

"So you heard what I said?"

"The sounds . . . didn't really translate. But I know you were upset."

"How does it work," Apex dodged. "Somebody takes the wheel? And the other takes a back seat?"

"Something like that." Callum stepped in closer. "Look, I want you to know . . ."

His eyes traced the features he could not, would never, forget.

"I need your help," he said roughly.

"Anything."

Callum turned away to the bed. Getting down on his hands and knees, he put the beer aside and pulled his suitcase out from under. The scraping sound over the bare floorboards seemed very loud, and he almost lost his steam as he confronted the top of the valise. But then he looked up at the vampire. Apex was standing there calmly, with no judgment or pity on that harsh, beautiful face. He was just waiting for whatever was needed.

As he always had been.

"I kept this . . . thing," Callum said as he flopped the stiff fabric top open. "This . . ."

The empty suitcase had a couple of different pockets, one of which lined the back wall of the base, and the bulge in that fold of nylon made it feel as if the piece of luggage was crammed with clothes. Dirty, moldy, decaying clothes.

Baggage, indeed.

Reaching in, he took out a bundle housed in a plastic supermarket bag. And as he turned the tightly tucked twist over in his hands, he glanced across and tried to figure out what he wanted to say.

"It's okay," Apex murmured. "Whatever it is."

Callum unwrapped the thing. The black fabric inside, on its most basic level, was just a black nylon long-sleeved shirt—and not a big one. One that would fit a female. And it could be used for a lot of things, like running, for instance, the thin fabric moisture-wicking, whatever the fuck that meant. It could also have been appropriate for hiking, water sports, rowing.

To him, it was radioactive. Because it had been worn while he'd been defiled.

"When I left that night," he said roughly, "I put on some clothes that were in that room. There was a stack of them, I don't know whose they were. I took guns and ammo. I . . . didn't know whose they were, either. But this . . . was hers. I found it wadded up behind some boots. It smelled like her and I took it because . . ."

He turned the shirt over and over in his hands. "I wanted a piece of her to remind me that I got out and she didn't. I thought maybe I could own something of hers like she owned me when she'd had me. But it didn't . . . it didn't work like that. This has just been a reminder that, like so much else, I haven't been able to let go of."

"And now?"

"It's time." He nodded. Nodded again. "It's . . . time to get rid of it. But I don't know in what way?"

By way of answering, Apex walked over to the hearth. And when he pointed to the cold ashes, Callum thought, of course. Why hadn't he—

"Yes," he breathed.

With a nod, Apex knelt down on the hard stone. There was some kindling next to the stack of fresh logs, and he took the former and then layered it down with the latter. Up on the shelf, there was a box of long-stemmed matches and also a long-armed lighter. He chose the matches.

The sound of the strike was a *shhhcht* that seemed loud as a sneeze.

Apex's hand was steady as he penetrated the pile with the tiny flame—which caught and did its job. Smoke curled up first, then orange tongues licked around, tasting their meal. A moment later, the fire burst to life, throwing out proper heat and light.

Apex poked it a couple of times, making sure the base kept the top stable. Then he just stared over his shoulder.

Callum rose and walked forward, the pain in his ankle nothing but an echo. Standing in front of the hearth, standing . . . next to the male who had been with him all these years, just as that female had as well . . . he became sad to the point of tears.

The two had become what he and his wolf were. Separate, yet trapped together. Inseparable, even though unalike.

Apex was nothing like that malevolent bitch.

Abruptly, Callum thought of his other side—and how much he had worried for its suffering, too. He had tried, back in the beginning, to just let the wolf part of him take over. Surely, if all he was was the background consciousness of that predator, it would be easier because the abuse had been done to another body.

The trauma had been a poison, however, infecting them both.

Just like it had gone toxic for Apex, too.

"You're allowed to let the past go," the vampire said on a rasp. "It's all right."

Callum stared into the flames, and fell into the struggle that was starting to feel familiar: He wanted to move on, but couldn't fight the emotions, the fear, the memories, that kept him prisoner.

At least *wanting* to move on was a new thing. A good thing.

And he had Apex to thank for it.

"But like burning a shirt will really make a difference?" he heard himself say.

"So then just toast it because it takes up space in your suitcase." Apex shrugged. "If there's a larger meaning, let it come to you later. Or not at all. But you may as well start here—"

Callum's hand flicked forward, and justlikethat, the shirt went into the hearth. There was a split second of a pause, and then came a bright flare. As the flames licked even higher, he could have sworn he saw the female's face in them, the precise composition of her features dulled by time, the impact of his brain's conjuring them immediate as his heart rate tripled.

And then . . .

It was gone.

The shirt and the vision.

Wiping his face with his palm, his eyesight got wavy. And wavier. And—

He started crying. Not in a discreet way, not in a manly fashion where most of the shit was kept in. He wept. Openly. Until his eyes and his lungs burned, and his throat was raw, and his brain finally went quiet.

And as the emotion was let out, he felt himself cradled in strong arms, pulled up against a solid chest. Like a young, he was gently rocked, as a broad hand stroked his back.

In the midst of his storm, he was sheltered by the male who had always been with him, even if they hadn't been side by side.

CHAPTER THIRTY

Right before the aristocrat was brought into the Audience Room, Tohr positioned himself behind Wrath. Not too close, because that would be inappropriate. But he wanted to make things perfectly clear to Whestmorel as soon as the male came in. Wrath was the King, and there was muscle all around the throne.

And after Qhuinn and V were in position in the other corners, he texted Saxton to bring the male in.

"Time to go back to work," Wrath said as he put George down at his feet.

While the golden got settled, tucking his tail in, laying his blond muzzle on his master's shitkicker, Saxton knocked once—and after Wrath barked an "enter," the door was opened and the solicitor stepped aside so that the interloper could pass through first.

Staring over Wrath's shoulder, Tohr gritted his molars. He had a short temper with people who demanded special treatment, as if the fact that the guy was living and breathing was enough to velvet-rope the whole world.

But then there was his reason for coming.

"My Lord," Whestmorel said as he inclined his head.

Tohr glanced at a low growl that percolated up. Qhuinn's upper lip was peeled off his fangs, the brother's blue and green peepers narrowed into slits.

Sure, a proper bow wasn't required. But everyone did it as a measure of respect—and that nod was a mockery of the tradition.

Meanwhile, Wrath lowered his chin and stared forward as if he could see the male. As if he knew there was little regard being paid.

"So what brings you to my house," the King said in a smooth voice. That was somehow more threatening than if he'd yelled. "At this particular hour."

There was a pause as Whestmorel seemed to have to gather himself. Then again, the last purebred vampire on the planet was nailing him to the wall through those wraparounds, even though Wrath was blind. His ability to focus was an unexpected phenomenon, something that Tohr had seen civilians shocked by when they came in here: Somehow, the King always knew exactly where everyone was, some combination of scent and noise allowing him to triangulate bodies.

Or maybe it was as simple as the impact of Wrath's size and strength. Sitting there, in his black leathers and muscle shirt, his black hair falling straight from a widow's peak, the tattoos of his lineage running up the insides of his forearms?

He looked like exactly what he was. A war leader. A fighter. A killer.

"Get on with it," Wrath said in that tone that made even the brothers stand up a little taller.

Whestmorel fiddled with a gold cufflink, like he was nervous, but he did not back down. "I am here on behalf of a number of us. We want to know what you are doing to find the killer of Broadius Rayland."

"So he's a relation of yours?" Wrath drawled. In a way that meant the timer on his detonator had started ticking.

"No, he's not. Too many of my relations were killed during the raids. Which you failed to protect us from."

Tohr put a hand up to his forehead and rubbed over his eyebrows. This was going worse than he'd thought it would.

Whestmorel continued, "You sent out all kinds of communications years ago, about how crimes were going to be handled. We're demanding to know what you're doing about the reality that a male was murdered. Or does the fact that it was someone of wealth and position mean you expect us to solve the crime ourselves."

"There's no blood between you and Broadius, then. At all."

Whestmorel looked at the brothers who surrounded him. Then he focused on Tohr for a brief second. "No, there isn't. But that should not matter. We have a right to know—"

"Who exactly is 'we.'"

"All of us. Who are like me."

"So you're not going to say the word?" Wrath did not move in his chair, not a foot, not a hand. And Tohr almost wanted to warn the male who stood so defiantly before the King. "You can't say it? You'll claim all the rights and more than the privileges, but you won't call the *glymera* what it is?"

"That would be illegal, wouldn't it," came the laconic reply. "But no matter the term, I am not going to apologize for my status and I refuse to buy into some kind of shame because I have it." Whestmorel's eyes narrowed, making him appear positively evil. "We're thinking maybe you're staying quiet about Broadius on purpose."

There was a long pause, and Whestmorel did not look away. Did not mediate his attitude. Did not—

Wrath slowly rose out of his chair, and Tohr stepped forward. You know, just in case.

The one thing nobody needed in this situation . . . was another dead aristocrat.

"Message received," the King said. "You can go now."

Whestmorel's smile was chilling. "On the contrary. I did not come here to deliver a—"

"The hell you didn't. If you'd actually read the crime procedures, you'd know I'm not going to comment on an active investigation to a non-family member. So this is a flex that you are the representative of a faction of powerful, wealthy individuals who are meeting in secret behind my back—and you all think I had a member of the aristocracy killed."

"I did not say that, and I shall not let you put words in my mouth—"

Wrath's head jerked to the left, and V, who was

clearly having trouble holding his temper, threw up his hands—as he was obviously being warned to continue keeping his yap shut.

The King then refocused his attention on the aristocrat. "I'll meet with any of you, anytime, anywhere. I'm not worried about what you are doing in the background. The throne is mine. Try to take it. G'head."

"You think because you've got an heir, you're invincible," Whestmorel said in a low tone. "But kings only rule upon the consent of their subjects. I wouldn't take that for granted if I were you."

With a quick shift, Tohr got in between the two of them before he was aware of moving.

"You're leaving," he growled at the male. "Right now—"

The aristocrat just kept staring at Wrath. "You need your guard to speak for you? Is he going to tell me that you didn't have Broadius killed?"

"No," Wrath said calmly. "He's getting in between us because he's worried I'm going to hurt you. But I'm not going to do that. A male like you doesn't get to pull my levers, no matter what words he throws around. The reality is this, if you were a threat to me, a real threat, you wouldn't come here to tip your hand like this."

The King lifted his dagger hand and made a gun out of his thumb and forefinger. Pointing it at Whestmorel's head, he bared his fangs.

"You'd just . . ." Wrath nicked his thumb down. "*Bang*. Drop me where I stand."

Tohr was very aware of his heart skipping and then going full-tilt boogie in his chest. Especially when Whestmorel continued to hold his ground.

"I'm not hearing you deny anything," the male said. "And that's fine. Keep targeting people like us. It makes conversion very, very easy. It's a favor to us, really."

"News flash, you're not that important. I know this comes as a shock, but none of you matter. The only list you're on is your own."

"We survived the Lessening Society." Whestmorel's voice started to tremble with anger. "And we will survive you and the Brotherhood—"

"Nobody's coming after any of you. But if you're looking to change that, keep knocking on my door with bullshit accusations. I'll answer it, I promise you."

On that note, the meeting was over. As Whestmorel wheeled away and headed for the door, V and Qhuinn stepped out with him, and Tohr shut himself in with Wrath and the dog.

When he looked at the King, he found himself

surprised. Instead of the out-of-control fury of the past, Wrath remained deadly calm. Hell, he didn't even seem surprised.

"In the last thirty years," Wrath murmured, "have they organized at any other time?"

"No, not that we were aware. They were just re-adjusting their standards from bloodlines to bank accounts."

Wrath nodded as he sat back down. "So now they've got a critical mass. That's why they're coming forward."

"I know we didn't kill Broadius." Tohr paced back and forth. "And it doesn't take a genius to figure out that people who deal with people who deal in guns can wake up dead in their own bed at any minute."

"You got that right." Wrath leaned to the side and stroked his dog's head. "We need to find that killer. Fast."

"Yes, my Lord." Tohr bowed to his King. "We're doing everything we can. We're going to find the supplier of those guns, and when we do, I have a feeling we'll be looking the murderer in the face."

"Maybe. Or maybe not. Whestmorel and his group could have killed him themselves—or, even more likely, had someone do it." Wrath shook his head and eased back. "These new *glymera*-types are just bound and determined to follow in the footsteps of their predecessors, aren't they. Right into their own fucking graves."

The great Blind King smiled coldly. "But like I said, if they want a try at the throne? I welcome the challenge."

CHAPTER THIRTY-ONE

Apex held Callum until the flames in the hearth were so low, there was nothing to them, just a glow under all the ash. The wolven had fallen still a while ago, but he hadn't retreated. They'd just stretched out together on the floor, the other male lying on Apex's chest with his head tucked in.

It was nice not to have to talk.

In words.

Feeling someone else's body heat against your own was a kind of conversation, an exchange that amplified the warmth and kept you cozy even after the real fire had died down. And, yes, he had to go back to the big house and make sure Mayhem was doing what he was supposed to. But he wasn't leaving. Not quite yet.

He wished it was not ever—

Callum shifted his shoulders so they could look into each other's eyes. And when the gaze of the wolven moved down to Apex's mouth, it was clear what was coming. Or at least what was being considered.

"Whatever you want," Apex whispered. "And it can be nothing at all."

The wolven sat up and hovered his hand over Apex's pecs—in a way that reminded him of what he himself had done outside with the other half of the male.

When that palm finally lowered, it landed on his sternum, right over his heart. Apex's breath caught— and stayed in his throat—as the hand slowly moved down onto his belly. There it stayed, going up and down, as he started to pant.

Of course he hardened; there was no hiding the thick length that made a bulge in the front of his leathers.

Abruptly, Callum leaned forward, and though Apex got himself ready to be kissed, that was not where those lips went. He felt them on the side of his throat, just a soft brush. And then another. And then . . . the caress of that mouth went lower, to the V formed by his fleece and the t-shirt under it.

Meanwhile, the wolven's touch was drifting around, going to Apex's hip, to his upper thigh . . . to his inner thigh.

When he moaned, there was no keeping that on the DL, either. He did try, though. He didn't want this spell to be broken—and not just because he was so fucking turned on. If he could help Callum heal? And this was part of it so the male could move on?

Well, wasn't he a Good-goddamn-Samaritan, even though this was going to kill him in the long run—

"*Fuck*," he groaned as Callum made a pass across his lower abdomen.

At least he knew better than to reach for the male: He planted both his palms on the floor, making sure they stayed put even as his hips rolled with anticipation.

Tug. Tug. Tug . . .

His fleece was pushed up, and the t-shirt, too— and then it was skin on skin, the wolven's palm sliding across his bare flesh, just under his waistband. And now Callum was moving in between his legs.

He was more than happy to make room.

Especially as there were two hands on him, running up the insides of his legs. Yet the spot where he needed contact the most was avoided. Biting his lower lip to keep the protest in—

Tug. Tug. Tug . . .

Oh, fuck yes, on his button fly this time.

As shit went nuclear in his veins, and his cock developed its own heart rate, he wanted to stay connected to the higher purpose of this, namely that whatever was happening was part of some kind of vital healing for a male who dearly deserved it. Unfortunately, that clarity was hard to keep front and center as the subtle pulling and pushing while those buttons were freed just about had him busting his nut—

He didn't wear boxers. No briefs, either.

Certainly not a thong.

So there was a moment, just a moment, when those fingers touched his erection. And right after that, there was a cool sensation on his hot shaft.

Apex glanced down his chest. The sight of the wolven bending over his partially exposed arousal nearly had him coming.

So he squeezed his eyes shut.

"This is you," Callum said roughly. "This is your body."

"Yes, *fuck*, yes . . ."

Tug. Tug. Tug . . .

Always three. And this time, it was his pants getting pulled down. To be obliging, he lifted his pelvis—and away they went, to his knees.

He risked a glance. His erection lay, thick and hard and ready, up his belly, and Callum seemed transfixed, those gleaming eyes locked on the sex that had come alive for him, and him alone.

"You're . . . what's that word in your language?" Callum murmured. "*Phearsom?*"

Good thing the male came up with the answer. Apex wasn't sure of his own name at this point—

The wolven's tongue licked his lips. And then came the bend: Callum lowered his head and leaned forward—

"I'm gonna fucking come," Apex moaned.

"That's the plan."

―――――

Don't think too much about any of this, Callum told himself.

The warning was necessary because he didn't trust his mind not to cough up something awful and ruin the moment. And he had waited a long time for this reconnection. He'd done this with the vampire once before, back in the past, prior to all his trauma. That hookup had been meant to be a beginning. Instead, it had been a farewell.

With a lingering awe, and no small amount of fear, he slipped a grip around the thick shaft, and Apex threw his head back while the stroking began, his upper lip cranking off his beautiful, long fangs, his black eyes shut so hard, his brows crashing together. The vampire's breath was pumping hard, inhale, exhale, inhale, exhale—

And then it happened.

The release that Callum somehow felt, too, even though it was not his own: As hot jets came out and marked that six-pack, and those heels kicked into the floor, and that torso arched up ... it was the first thing that had happened, in so very long, that was any good.

That was uncomplicated.

That was simple and real and powerful.

And *good*.

Callum blinked away tears, but he still managed to see everything. And it was beautiful. It was raw, and sexual ... and clean.

As soon as it was over, the orgasm done with, that

powerful, heavily muscled body still, Callum had an instinct that was not to be denied.

He stood that still-hard cock up and opened wide.

When he swallowed the length right down, he was vaguely aware of Apex barking out loud, and the sound was made again as the sucking started. Opening his throat, Callum took all he could, all there was, and it was too much—and he loved the choking.

More importantly, there was no being trapped. He was free to move, unrestrained. He was *choosing* this.

He . . . wanted *this*.

He thought about the *symphath*. And redecorating.

And the way fresh memories about people who had lived through suffering with you could be the new furnishings for old rooms.

A change that resurrected everyone, a restart to . . . everything.

Keeping a hold on the base of the erection that was filling him up, he splayed his hand wide over the ridges of Apex's stomach muscles. He knew when the vampire was getting close again—he could tell by the way his breath was getting so harsh once more. And when it was time, when those hips were jerking up and down, and the male was on the verge of crying out, Callum knew he had a decision to make.

Stop because this was too much. And stay in the past.

Or keep going because this was too much.

And rejoin the living.

CHAPTER THIRTY–TWO

On the whole, the job was not that complicated. From an IT perspective, that was.

All Mayhem had to do was take both
the images being generated from the thirty-two
cameras, and the sound feeds from the microphones,
and channel them into a sorting and storage platform
whereby the users—whoever they might be—could
sift through them, isolate them into permanent files,
and transfer or store the data depending on what was
needed. It was standard security monitoring stuff.

Any idiot could fucking do it.

Okay, fine, any idiot who—like his good self—
knew the program being used, and how to link up each

of the units, and what was a problem that could be troubleshooted—troubleshot?—and what was going to require a rebooting if things were only momentarily brain-dead or a replacement if a component was defective.

A good two hours into the shit, and Mayhem was very aware that Apex, for however smart the guy was, did not have the disposition necessary to perform this job. Patience was required, a real go-with-the-flow kind of problem-solving: On the second unit failure, the guy would have taken out his gun and started aiming for the ceiling.

And it was hard to pinpoint exactly what was the trigger for the catch-on, but when light dawned on proverbial Marblehead . . . Mayhem was seriously under-impressed with himself.

He was at the top of the cellar stairs when the realization occurred to him, standing under a unit they'd placed directly above the entrance to the lower level, the laptop balanced on his palm, his neck getting a strain as he looked up to confirm the fucking little red light was turning green—

When all of a sudden, he straightened his head, looked back over his shoulder, and started counting.

One . . . two . . . three . . .

There was a total of five units down the hall and in what he could see of the great room with the hearth and the animal heads.

The math continued. Each of the bedrooms down below had a sensor. And also the rooms upstairs that were unlikely to be slept in by vampires, even with all the daylight shutters in place. All the bathrooms. The kitchen, too. The whole house, wired for image and sound.

Like it wasn't so much about security . . . but rather, eavesdropping.

And the back end was interesting, too. The feeds were consolidated and sent to three places—

"Hi."

Mayhem jerked to attention. "Oh, hey. I didn't see you."

"Sorry," Mahrci said softly.

Frowning, he glanced around. "You okay? Is there someone here?"

"Can I ask you something?" she continued at a whisper.

He nodded. "Sure."

"I don't mean to put you in an awkward position. But . . . Apex said we all had to leave because some kind of timeline has been moved up. Can you tell me what this is about?"

When he shook his head, he discovered that however frustrated he'd been by the blackout on information, he was now glad Apex hadn't told him much—because it meant he could be honest, here and now.

"I don't know anything." He shrugged. "And I asked Apex a hundred times. I'm just supposed to sync up everything and supply the feeds to a couple of sources. That's all he would say."

She crossed her arms over her chest. "Well, I'm packed up. Not that I brought much."

Don't come on too strong, he told himself. *Be cool, be cool—*

"You can leave with us, if you want. And if you need a place to stay, you can stay with me—or Apex would take you in, if you want—"

"No, I wouldn't ask anybody to do that," she murmured. "Especially Apex, given that he works for my father."

"Well, I'm still an option. Just sayin'. No pressure."

Mahrci's flush lit her cheeks, in a way that made him realize how pale she'd gotten. "Oh, thank you, but I have somewhere to go. And no one will find me."

So it's like that, he thought with a pang in his chest.

As he locked his molars, he told himself he needed to put his zip code where his mouth was: He'd told her he was fine being used. He needed to back that shit up and not be a little bitch about being left behind—

"Are you safe?" she asked. "In your home?"

"It'll do." He didn't bother to inform her he had more booby-traps in his one-bedroom apartment than there were snowbanks around them. "Don't worry about me."

When the laptop made a chirping noise, she said, "Are you finished?"

"No, not even close. I still have to do the upper and lower levels." He looked around again—and saw nothing but her. "I'm making good progress, though."

And what do you know, he decided to work even faster. If he could get this wrapped up soon enough, he might just ghost out before dawn and not have to stay over day.

Drawing out this goodbye with Mahrci seemed harder than getting it over with.

"You mind if I take care of your room now?" he asked. "I can get it done and then you're free to— whatever."

"Oh yes, of course."

Together, they descended to the lower level. Her bedroom was the first on the left, and the door was partially open. He wondered if it was still from him dragging her ex out of there. Good times, good times.

Stepping aside, he waited for her to go in first—and, oh, man, she'd just had a shower. He could smell the shampoo and conditioner, the soap, too, and not just in the air, but on her.

He might have noticed upstairs, but he'd been distracted by a choking sense of dread . . . that he probably was never going to see her again after this—

He stopped his sad sacking and frowned once more. "Are you sure you're okay?"

Mahrci stared up at him, her hands worrying at the sleeves of her sweater, pushing them up, pulling them down.

"You can tell me what's really going on," he heard himself say. Then he motioned to the security unit on the ceiling. "That isn't connected to the system yet."

"You already know . . . everything."

"All right."

He gave her a chance to continue. When she didn't, he walked under the pod he'd screwed in earlier and fired up the laptop. Waited for its light to change.

Double-checked that it was entered in the manifest right.

"Bedroom one, I'm calling this," he murmured.

"Can I help you?"

"No, I got it." He eyed the Vuitton duffle that had been set just outside the bathroom. "Are you leaving before dawn, too—"

"Will you come with me?"

Mayhem stopped breathing. Then he slowly lowered the laptop. "What . . . are you saying?"

———

Across the way, in the garage quarters, Apex was out of his mind and totally grounded at the same time, especially as he looked down his body again and saw his arousal stretching Callum's mouth, going in and out of those lips, being slicked from the sucking. And then at his base, that fist that was gripping him. And there was also a cup around his balls—

"I'm coming," he growled as he tried to hold it in. "Callum—"

The wolven just went all the way down, and big surprise, that caused the ejaculations to explode out of him.

Whereupon they were promptly swallowed.

Arching into the pleasure, giving himself up, Apex was exactly where he wanted to be—he just wasn't sure about the other male.

Except then Callum retracted until things popped out, literally. After that, the two of them just stayed where they were, Apex loose-limbed and on his back, the wolven perched over the cock he had just sucked off.

"Are you all right," Apex asked hoarsely.

There was a heartbeat of pause. And then the male answered—by extending his tongue, lowering his head, and licking his way around Apex's stomach. Which he'd come all over the first time.

"Oh . . . fucking hell . . ."

The sensations of that warm, slick tongue lapping over his abs was enough to bring the good times back for a third time—and he was never, ever going to forget the sight of Callum bent down to him, the wolven's arms bowed out, his icy blue eyes gleaming from under his lowered lids, the heat and the sex making everything razor sharp and totally buffered at the same time.

"Sorry," Apex mumbled as he got hard all over again. "It's been—"

He stopped himself.

Callum paused, too. "It's been . . . what?"

"A really long time. Since I've done anything like this."

"How long?"

"I don't want to freak you out," Apex muttered.

When all he got was a whole lot of no-more-tongue-action and an arched brow, he groaned, "I haven't been with anyone in person in decades."

This got him rewarded with another lick, right over his belly button. "And what about by yourself."

"I'd rather not answer that."

"Why?" More with the licking. Thank fuck. "Why don't you want to—"

"Not often, okay. It wasn't often."

And when it happened, you were all I was thinking of, he thought—

Callum froze again. "I was?"

Fuck, guess he'd said that out loud. "Yes, you were."

In the silence that followed, Apex looked over at the ashes in the hearth. Then at the suitcase that was still sitting there with its top blown off, like it was a shooting victim. And finally, he returned to the wolven's beautiful, masculine face . . . specifically those lips, those eyes, that flush.

"What did you think of," Callum said softly, "when I came to your mind?"

"It wasn't anything bad—"

"What did you picture?"

Apex lowered his lids. "That I was about to kiss you."

"About to?"

"That was all . . . it ever took."

Callum licked his lips. "Are you thinking about kissing me right now?"

"Yeah. I am."

With the prowl of the wolf he was, Callum stalked his way up Apex's chest. Then he hovered his lips just two inches away.

"Was I this close?"

Apex started to breathe heavy again. "Yes."

The wolven lowered himself a little. "How about . . . this close?"

"Yes," Apex whispered.

Down a little more. "What about this close?"

All Apex could do was nod—because suddenly he was coming once more, his cock kicking as he groaned, his chest pumping as his hips did the same.

And that was when Callum sealed their lips— and went even farther. He laid his body down, all his contours fitting Apex's like they'd been made together. The kissing just kept on going, but Apex was careful. His arms stayed by his sides.

He wanted Callum to know that he was free to leave at any moment.

Even as he prayed the male would not go.

———

The kissing . . . was waking up parts of Callum that he hadn't accessed for years. Decades. Not since before he'd been—

No, he wasn't going there, to that female and her guards. He was staying right *here*, on top of his vampire, in front of the fucking ashes of the past.

Callum felt Apex's orgasm once again, the wetness, the heat, fusing their stomachs together. And the mouth-to-mouth was incredible. Apex was a harsh male, a killer with a prison record, a remote mystery in so many ways. But fucking hell, he had the softest lips, and the sounds he made? It was a purring, a groaning, a panting—

And that was when it happened.

Callum started to find his own release.

He'd been so focused on Apex that he hadn't paid attention to his own body: the fact that he was hard, that he was straining for a release, that his balls were getting tight. And his hips just took over as he began to work his erection against Apex's.

Even though his combats were a barrier, he felt enough.

He felt so much.

Breaking off the kiss, he dropped his face into Apex's neck and shuddered and bucked and grabbed on to whatever there was—the vampire's arms, his shoulders. Then he locked ahold of the other male's hands.

It was so good, it was so right.

It was like being cleaned from the inside out. And when he finally stilled, he exhaled and went limp.

"Are you okay?" Apex asked roughly.

Dimly, through his wonderful float of relaxation, Callum thought . . . that was the third time the vampire had posed him that question.

Callum lifted his head. "I'm trying to be."

Apex closed his black eyes. "You shouldn't force it."

"I think . . . I might be," Callum whispered.

He had to believe it was possible.

He just *had* to.

CHAPTER THIRTY-THREE

C ome with you?" Mayhem repeated. "Where?"
Even though, duh, the answer was yes.
Disney World? Sure. Off the lip of the
fucking Grand Canyon? Fine. Edge of the world? All
she had to do was—

"I know asking you is a little forward." Mahrci
reached out. "And it's not because I think you can't
handle yourself."

Oh, so this was about Remis and his band of
Brooks-Brothers-wearing thugs? Hey, at least the bastard's name fit, 'cuz Mayhem sure as shit would like to
ream—

"I'm not worried about him." He smiled. "And

you can be as forward as you like with me. I'm just curious where we're going."

An answering grin teased her mouth. "We're? So you'll—"

"I told you." He memorized the way she looked at him. "I go with the flow. And you're . . . my kind of flow."

"That's just . . . thank you."

There was a long moment. Then he couldn't help himself. He stepped into her and touched her face.

"You're welcome. Although I feel like I should be the one with the gratitude. And you still haven't answered me, but it's good. You just let me know where to go and I'll be there. I trust you."

"Let's leave as soon as you're done, okay?" That worried look came back to her eyes. "Please?"

"Sure." Even though he really didn't want to get back to work. He had . . . other things . . . on his mind. "I've got about—well, let's say another couple hours? And I'm going to need to do some final testing with Apex."

He wasn't exactly sure where the guy was, but he had a feeling it was across the yard in that garage. That wolven had always been a thing for Apex. Maybe *the* thing.

What a road, though. With that kind of past?

"Oh, and listen, I didn't bring much," Mayhem tacked on. "As long as Apex is good with taking the SUV back to Caldie? I'm free as a bird to ghost out."

Mahrci's smile returned and he couldn't help it. He dropped down and brushed her lips with his own. As she gasped, he eased back.

"I maybe shouldn't have done that. Not the time or place—and don't worry, I'm not making any assumptions."

Well, he was making one: She still wasn't being completely truthful with him. Yes, she was worried about that ex of hers—he just had the sixth sense there was more to it than that. But hey, whatever it was had given him an in he was more than happy to enjoy: He'd been wrestling with the fucking rank-ass idea he was never going to see her again, and what do you know, for a go-with-the-flow male like him?

That had *not* been the right flow for him.

"No . . . it's all right," she murmured. "I want to do a lot more of that. The . . . kissing, I mean."

Well, wasn't that a hi-how're-ya to his hey-nannies. "Me, too."

"Good." She laughed in a little awkward rush, and started to head for the door. "Well, I guess I'll leave you to it—"

"Mahrci." As she paused, he lowered his voice to a growl. "I'm not scared of your father, either. Just so we're clear."

As she put her hand to the base of her throat, it was as if she were feeling someone squeezing the life out of her.

"I am," she said roughly. "I'm terrified of him."

———

All that mattered, Mahrci told herself, was that Hemmy had agreed to join her at her safe house.

The one she had bought in secret, and furnished herself, and kept quiet about.

The rest could be sorted out from there, once they were both safe: Their relationship. Her father. The future in all its forms. Which, if they could just get free of her situation, she was suddenly looking forward to for the first time in . . . well, maybe ever.

Abruptly, she nodded as if she were in a conversation, instead of talking to herself. Then she blurted, "I'll just need you to take my vein before we go—"

As she spoke up, Hemmy's head jerked to attention. Then he dropped the laptop and lost his balance, all at the same time—and when he tried to catch himself before he fell, they both calculated where his boot was going to land at the same time: The computer. With all his work on it.

He did what he could to correct the lurch, but he went too far, his heavy weight veering off-kilter wildly. So she did the only thing she could. She launched herself at him, pushing him backward onto the bed, landing on top of him in a tangle as they both hit the mattress. While they bounced, she had to laugh and so did he.

"I guess that was a little bit of a surprise," she said as she went to roll off him.

Hemmy put his hands on her hips, stilling her. "Where are you going so fast, female—if you're comfortable, I am."

Looking into his eyes, she flushed. Underneath her body, his muscles and heavy bones were a landscape that she fit herself into with a precision that seemed like destiny. She also couldn't ignore the way her breasts pressed into his pecs or how the hardening length at the front of his hips made her want to straddle him properly.

Need, hot and hungry, bloomed in her veins.

"I'm okay here . . ." she said in a guttural voice. "If you are?"

In an equally low tone, he replied, "I'm *very* okay."

Think, Mahrci. Think—*what were you saying?*

"Oh, the vein thing." She shook herself back into focus. "Right. Well, I don't want to give you an address or anything—that way, if someone asks you, you can be truthful. You don't know where I am. But if you take my blood, you'll always be able to find me—and where we'll be staying."

Reaching up, he traced her face with his fingertips. "That's a brilliant idea. There's just one thing."

"What's that?"

"It has to be your wrist." His touch drifted down to her jugular. "Not here."

Mahrci's breath caught. "Why not . . . there."

"Too much for me." He shook his head ruefully. "I have self-control, but there are limits, and until we—or *if* we . . ." He stroked her vein with his forefinger. ". . . get all the way there, I need to take from the wrist."

A sudden image of him baring his fangs and bringing the twin, sharp points to her throat flooded her with even more heat—and it shouldn't have been a surprise, but wow, what a relief to think of something that came with pleasure, instead of stress and worry.

She stared at his lips. "There will be time for that. Later. When we are away from here."

The soft growl that came out of him was the kind of thing she felt in her marrow. And even though it was folly, she wanted a hint of what was to come.

She moved her wrist up to his mouth. "Take my vein. Now."

Hemmy closed his eyes and arched up, his hips rolling against her, his long, hard erection pushing into her upper thighs. With a moan, she split her legs around his lower body—

They both groaned in need. And yet his hand was gentle as he took her forearm and held it steady. "Are you sure you want to do this?"

As she didn't trust her voice, all she could do was nod.

The next thing she knew was the brush of his lips, soft and warm, against the center of her palm. And then at the heel. And finally . . . right over her vein as he kissed her there.

"Do it," she commanded.

There was a hiss as he bared his fangs, and then—

The bite came with a sweet sting of pain and she threw her head back and exhaled his name. The sensation of the sucking, warm and slick, went through her entire body, until her brain melded things and she felt it . . . on her sex. Letting herself fall limp, all she wanted to concentrate on was what she was feeling—and she threw gasoline on the fire by imagining them naked, skin on skin, him between her legs, penetrating her as he—

Hemmy broke the contact and slipped out from under her, hopping off the bed. As he stumbled, he caught himself on the wall, stopping his forward pitch with his palm on the doorjamb into the bathroom.

The sound of his breath sawing in and out of him was the sexiest thing she had ever heard.

As the puncture wounds on her wrist weren't sealed, she licked them closed. And then had some paranoia that maybe he'd leapt away because he hadn't liked her taste—

"I just need a minute." He pushed into the loo and stood over the sink, still in that bend. "*Fuck.*"

"Hemmy?"

"I'm just trying not to . . ."

"Throw up?" she said as she sat forward with horror. "Is there something wrong with my—"

On a quick pivot, he put his hands on his hips and stared out at her with a wry expression on his face.

The enormous erection straining the front of his pants was especially obvious because of the overhead fixture he was standing beneath.

Talk about your mood lighting.

"I don't know how I'm going to work with *this*"—
he pointed at the thing—"in the way."

Mahrci licked her lips. "So why don't you . . . take
care of it. And show me what you like while you're at it."

That groan came back again. "Yeah?"

Mahrci nodded. "I want to watch."

With a low curse, Hemmy cupped himself through
his jeans, and as he did, his head fell back, the ropes of
muscles that ran up the sides of his throat flexing. As
she felt an answering pleasure in her core, she squeezed
her thighs together.

"Let me see you," she whispered breathlessly.

At her urging, his fingers worked the button and
the zipper with a facility she admired. And then he
pulled the two sides back—

His sex broke out, thick and hard and proud, and
slipping a grip around the shaft, he didn't wait.
Hemmy began stroking himself, the corded strength
running down his forearm and into his hand flexing
and releasing with the movement.

Desperate for some friction herself, she rubbed
her legs together, her body hungry for what seemed so
far away, and yet was so tantalizingly close. And as her
breasts grew heavy and her breath got short, he quick-

ened his rhythm, his hips thrusting and pulling back as his fist went up and down—

"Do you feel me," he said in a guttural voice. "Inside of you ..."

"Yes," she gasped. "Oh, God—"

Later she would replay the electric moment, over and over, when he grabbed a towel off the counter and put it over the head of his erection. Meanwhile, her eyes squeezed shut as she orgasmed at the same time he did—who was first? Did that matter?

Hell, no, it didn't.

All she cared about was them getting to her safe house, and having some proper alone time—so they could do this a couple more times, fully naked, in bed.

When she finally returned to herself, her lids lifted. She was in a different position altogether on the mattress, her feet tucked under, her knees locked together, one hand pushing into the juncture of her thighs. Across the way, Hemmy was collapsed back against the bathroom sink, that towel still held in place.

His hooded eyes sought hers. "I am going to work faster than I have in my entire life."

Mahrci flushed and smiled. "Good."

CHAPTER THIRTY-FOUR

Hours passed. Apex knew this because his back was getting stiff, and his feet were cold. But he didn't care. He and Callum had stayed where they were as the fire had died out, and he had been the one to mentally dim the lights when the wolven had fallen asleep. He'd even risked a hand on the male's shoulder, the closest he was going to get to giving in and wrapping his arms around the body that lay so solidly against his own.

Fucking hell, he was back on the rocky shore of "Maybe They Had A Chance After All."

Even though he knew better than to believe the optimism would last.

Just because you wanted something didn't mean it

was yours. And he still believed the male had a much better shot without him—

His phone went off with a *bing*.

Instantly, he stiffened. The last thing he wanted was this moment to be interrupted by—

Bing! came another text.

Locking his molars, he willed the cell to STFU. Why the hell hadn't he turned the ringer off? It wasn't like he wanted to talk to anybody—

Bing!

Callum's head lifted and the wolven's half-mast, husky-eyes were the most beautiful thing Apex had ever seen.

"You should get that?"

"FYI, no one ever calls or texts me. Unless I'm with you, evi-fucking-dently."

Whatever it was, he didn't want it. But because he needed to keep what peace there was for twenty-four more hours, he shifted his hips, shoved a hand into his ass pocket, and took out the cell.

"It's just Mayhem," he said with relief. "He can wait—"

Bing!

Cursing under his breath, he put in his code with one hand—because he'd never trusted facial ID; someone could just kill you and put the screen in front of your dead puss—and then navigated to the text section.

When he started reading, he frowned—which caused Callum to sit up. And it was amazing—the separation was, in terms of inches, so minor, but the center of his chest locked down like a vise. But really, did he think the wolven was going to run off, never to be seen or heard from again?

As if Callum was answering that question, his eyes went to the cold hearth and his face tightened.

"Hey," Apex said, to derail himself from a mental spiral that was likely inevitable, "how about I make us something to eat?"

Not that he was hungry.

"I'm good. But help yourself."

"Okay."

"What was the text?" Callum said, even though it was unclear whether he was aware that he was speaking. He was still staring off into space.

"Mayhem wants to leave."

"Oh? You better go see him off."

That stinging sense the wolven was about to pull another disappearing act tightened every muscle in Apex's body. And just to prove—to himself—that he was not completely entangled, he nodded even though he was looking at the profile of the male and had no intention of going anywhere.

Unless he was getting kicked out.

When there was only silence, Apex glanced down at himself and realized his pants were still open. He hadn't even fucking noticed.

"So yeah . . ." Getting to his feet, Apex put himself back together. "I think I am going to head over to the big house—"

"I'm leaving, too."

"Oh?" Apex felt himself go still. "Really?"

"About an hour ago, I sent my resignation in to the owner. I was going to tell you that when I came looking for you—but then . . . I saw you through the window, and . . ."

"Things happened."

Actually, the wolven's departure was good, Apex told himself. Safer, considering what would be arriving at Ghreylke soon. And better for Callum.

Yet the mourning returned, a load that had been put down for a moment—and was now twice as heavy for the brief respite.

"Where are you going to go?" he heard himself ask.

"I don't know. I just know . . . not here. I think I'm looking for a fresh start."

"Fair enough." What the hell was he saying? "I mean, good for you. Yeah, that's really healthy. Ah, anyway, I think I'll head over and chat to Mayhem—"

Callum looked up. Finally. "Will you come back here? This feels . . . rushed. It's not how I want to leave things between us. I did it wrong once already."

"I know. I was there." Glancing at the cold hearth, Apex found himself blinking quickly to clear his vision. "But, yeah, sure. I'll be back."

Callum got up, but it wasn't for some kind of hug. He went over to lie down on his bed. As he stared up at the ceiling, Apex sensed the departure had already happened, even though they were still technically in the same room.

As he hesitated, he learned a truth about himself that he could have done without: This awkwardness was proving that everything he'd said to the wolf had been right, yet there was another layer to it all.

He was waiting to see if Callum was going to change his mind.

Not about leaving the estate, but about needing Apex to stay, right now.

Mayhem didn't matter. The job didn't count. The big house could have been on fire and he would still be standing here, waiting to be called into service.

The reality was . . . there was still nothing he wouldn't do for the wolven. Even if letting Callum go remained the way this was all going to end.

Fresh start, indeed.

"I won't be long," he muttered as he headed for the door.

He got some kind of indistinct response, and there was no reason to ask for a repeat of it as it had just been a sound, made in the back of the throat. A dismissal.

Apex closed the door quietly behind himself and descended the stairs. Halfway to the big house, he glanced back at the garage. Callum had gotten up and turned the lights all the way off, the windows dark as the night.

Goddamn, this was like being back at that bedside, in the prison, reading tea leaves for improvement, and ultimately being disappointed—

The door of the big house opened, and Mayhem leaned out. "You coming or going?"

Wasn't that the question of the hour.

Apex got his walk on, and as he came up to the other male, he didn't want to think about things he couldn't control anymore.

He didn't want to think about anything.

"You done?" Even though one of the guy's texts had already said that. "We good?"

"You're all set. But I figured you'd want to try things out first."

Closing the door as he entered, Apex wasn't surprised to find Mahrci with her LV duffle right next to Mayhem's black nylon bag from Dick's. Cabela's. Wherever.

Beauty and the Generic.

Except as the two looked at each other and their eyes lingered, Apex didn't have the heart to be cynical about their future. Who was he to doom-and-gloom on their parade?

"So you're leaving, too," he said to the female.

In reply, he got a nod and some conversation he didn't bother tracking. While all kinds of syllables were thrown around, he stared at the pair. Like the luggage, they were standing side by side, and the ease between them was obvious. No shadows thrown by dark emotions. No past clawing its way into the present and fucking things up. Just two people who were attracted to each other and ready to see where it all goes—

"You're lucky," he heard himself say.

That stopped both of them.

Which was his clue to step in and offer his hand for a shake. "Thanks, Mayhem."

The male glanced at what was clearly his female. Then he shook what was offered. "Um, okay. So how about we go through the program before I go?"

"Nah, it's okay. I know how to reach you if something doesn't work."

Mayhem's brows popped. "Um, yeah, you can always call me. But are you sure? I mean, everything is functioning—"

"I trust you."

"I tested and retested the feeds—"

"I know you did." Turning, he put his palm out to Mahrci. "Something tells me I'm not going to see you again."

The female ducked her eyes. "You never know."

"Yeah, I do. What do you want me to tell your father?"

"Nothing. That's my problem, not yours."

Finally, someone who got it, he thought.

"I always did like you."

Just as the female went to take his hand in her own, he saw the bite mark on the inside of her wrist. Well, things had progressed, hadn't they. And he was willing to bet that it wasn't the only vein on her that had been taken—although with her wearing that turtleneck, he couldn't tell.

Not that it was his business.

"You okay taking the SUV back?" Mayhem asked. "I was just gonna, you know, dematerialize with her."

"No problem. I'm thinking of leaving the vehicle here, anyway. It's Whestmorel's."

His job with that male was done, and not just with this installation.

Guess everyone was disappearing.

As they both stared at him, like they were worried about his mental health or something, he marched over to the door.

"Take care of yourselves," he said as he indicated the way out.

"You, too," Mayhem said as he picked up both bags with one hand, then slipped an arm around Mahrci's shoulders. "Call me if you need me—"

"You already said that."

The happy couple walked out and then Mayhem glanced over his shoulder one last time. At which point, Apex was certain he wasn't going to see the male again, either.

After he lifted a hand in goodbye, he watched them disappear into the night.

Then he just stood there, running up Whestmorel's heat bill with the door wide open. It was just impossible not to keep doing a compare/contrast with that couple to his and Callum's situation—but that was the thief of joy, right?

As he glanced back over at the dark windows of the garage's second story, he thought, *Yup, sure the hell is.*

"I better double-check the system," he said into the cold breeze that was coming at him.

Right? Work was why he was here, after all.

Not this . . . heartbreaking other stuff.

CHAPTER THIRTY-FIVE

After Whestmorel took off, Tohr stayed for the next three audiences, all of which were the kind of wholesome palate cleansers a male appreciated when the great Blind King had already used up all his restraint tokens: Two births, and a mating blessing. Perfect.

And now Tohr was out in the bracingly cold air.

As he walked away from the Audience House's rear door, he followed the shoveled path to Vishous's FT Headquarters. The converted barn was named after the brother's old computer setup, back at the Pit. He'd called his towers and their monitors and keyboards his Four Toys, so when they'd decided his security think tank of IT uber geniuses had to go on the property, V had christened the outbuilding right from the planning stages.

The second Tohr approached the entrance, the doors unlocked for him, and as he stepped inside, he looked down the lineup of workstations to the glass box at the end. V's private office had its frosted privacy panels disengaged so the brother, who'd left earlier, and the other male in there were fully visible—and as Vishous turned and looked out, all kinds of hurry-up got motioned.

Tohr made quick work of the center aisle, which was not hard to do considering that all of the males and females were totally into their work, monitoring the properties that the Brotherhood owned or rented out, doing identity verifications, researching whatever . . . needed researching.

It was quite the operation—

"Tell him," V commanded as Tohr opened the glass door. "G'on, son."

The younger male in the all-glass room seemed to retract into himself. But Allhan was like that. The kid was lightning brilliant, with the kind of smarts that made V seem like someone who could just do a little math in their head well. But the social anxiety was real.

Tohr sat down in the chair by the desk to make

himself seem smaller. In a deliberately quiet voice, he said, "Tell me what?"

V handed over the pages that had been bugging Tohr ever since they'd been left behind in the frickin' waiting room.

"Allhan?" Tohr held up the documents. "Did you figure out something about this? Because if you did, it might be important."

The young, who was almost as tall as a mature male, but built like a soda straw, was nearing his transition—and V was telling everybody that it was because of this, and only because of this, that the kid lived with him and Doc Jane: It was just so they could help him through the change. Because Jane was a doctor. And because Al was an orphan.

Yeah, it had absolutely nothing to do with the fact that, intellectually, the kid was V's mini-me, and V, for all his razor-sharp exterior and ice-cold moods, cared about the people in his circle.

His tiny, teeny circle.

Which now included this kid who was his son in everything but name.

"It's the last page," Allhan said. "I concur that the tables reflect recurring charges in some kind of currency, and note that there are sixteen different entries, which suggest once-a-month and then four quarterly payments. But the final page isn't about money at all. It's a message."

Tohr turned to the last sheet. And as he looked at all the numbers, he thought . . . Christ, to him, it was just a fruit salad of sums and totals.

"It's a code," Allhan added.

Popping a brow, Tohr glanced at V. The pride on the brother's face was so obvious, the guy and his goatee were positively beaming.

"What does it say?" Tohr couldn't even fathom how anyone could tell—

"It's a name." The kid came around and pointed with a long, thin finger. "You see all this? It's just filler, it doesn't mean anything. Here, in the center. You see how these sums add up along this same line? Every fifth numeral is the sum of what preceded it, and corresponds to the alphabet numbered sequentially."

"Yeah, sure." Um . . . not at all. "But I'm not certain I see anything."

"It's a very basic alphanumeric code."

"Oh, okay." Still nothing. Nope. "Can you translate the message for me?"

"A name." Allhan glanced back at his adoptive dad. "One name."

"Tell him, son," V prompted.

"Whestmorel."

Going still, Tohr stared at the pair. Looked down at the alphanumerical whatever. Looked up again. "You're certain?"

Allhan nodded. "It's obvious."

As Tohr let his brain run, Vishous lit up a handrolled and nodded at his son. "You did a great job, I'm super proud of you."

"I can go?"

"Yup." As the kid headed for the door, V said, "I want you to go have something to eat. You skipped First Meal, 'kay?"

"Yes, sir."

After the glass panel eased shut, V glanced over. "He needs to put on some weight. That change is coming like a freight train. Not that he has a big appetite to begin with—anyway, surprise surprise, our little friend with the fucking ascot and the shiny shoes."

Tohr flipped back through the pages. "You're analyzing all the tables, of course. Or having Allhan do it."

"Yeah, but without any routing or account numbers? We're not going to get far when it comes to whose money it is or what it's being used for. All we can be sure of is that payments have been sent and received.

And clearly the message that was intended to be conveyed to us is that Whestmorel is in charge."

"Broadius's gun collection."

"That's what I'm thinking."

So the two events were connected, after all.

"He really is organizing, then," Tohr murmured, "not that I'd doubted it after his performance tonight."

There was a period of silence, broken only by the soft, hypnotic sounds of V smoking.

"You want to know what I think?" Easing back in the chair, Tohr stared out the glass wall at all the brains. "I think those sixteen entries are people giving money to buy arms because they're getting ready to try a violent overthrow. Broadius was the middleman, and he made the deal, but maybe he pocketed some of the funds, or he got ahead of himself and tried to do a double cross."

"I agree."

"As for Whestmorel, I think the sonofabitch was posturing to Wrath. He knows we didn't have shit to do with Broadius, and he's closing his ranks. It was a flex, plain and simple, to come here like that." Tohr frowned. "The question is . . . how the hell can we prove it."

Vishous tapped his hand-rolled over a glass ashtray. "We could always ride up to his house, throw a bag over his head, and work on him a little." When Tohr shot a level stare across the desk, V shrugged. "That is an option."

"But not the one we're going to take." Tohr looked at the pages and thought about the guy's attitude. "More's the pity, though. I do think a cordial visit to his abode . . . might not be out of place, however."

V exhaled and popped his palm in the air, the stub of his hand-rolled letting out a little stream of smoke from its tip. "I volunteer."

Tohr narrowed his stare. "No burlap bags. I find any burlap, anywhere, and you're off the assignment. That also means no duct tape."

"My way is faster."

Getting to his feet, Tohr checked his watch. "We're already inching up to a civil war. Let's not rush that conflict, shall we?"

CHAPTER THIRTY-SIX

As Mahrci re-formed, her heart was pounding. All things considered, it was kind of a miracle she'd managed to dematerialize without a trazodone on board. But she'd been so determined to get Hemmy off her father's property—

The male became corporeal beside her, and as he turned to the house, his eyes went wide. "Oh . . . wow."

Taking a deep breath, she, too, pivoted to the old converted barn. "So this is . . . my home. Where I really live."

Not that she came very often, although that was going to change now.

"Come on," she said as she took his hand. "I want you to meet the female who raised me."

For some stupid reason, she was all aflutter as she pulled him up the walkway. Then again, she had been delighted by this place since the moment she'd bought it. The barn was painted, well, barn red, and had white piping at all its corners, along its roofline, and around its windows. Set in its snowy field, the structure, with its attached grain silo that had also been converted, made her heart sing.

And maybe a little part of that cardiac a cappella was the male who was with her—

The arched-top door—which had always reminded her of what a hobbit entry might look like—swung wide.

As the older female appeared, Mahrci felt tears flood her eyes. "Crawlyn!"

She skipped ahead, and the instant she felt those familiar arms come around her, she nearly lost it. After everything that had happened, this was the only place she could go. The only person she trusted.

Pulling back, she glanced at Hemmy. Well . . . there was another one now.

"I'd like you to meet . . ."

While she trailed off, Hemmy stepped forward. "Ma'am, it's a pleasure. My name is Mayhem—but that's not a descriptor, I promise."

As he put out his palm and met Crawlyn right in the eyes, Mahrci knew he'd won the older female over. Hell, he'd had her at "ma'am."

"Well, I am most pleased to meet you." Crawie wiped her hands on her granny apron and smoothed her graying hair. "I am Miss Mahricelle's nanny."

Hemmy's bow was so courtly, so respectful, Mahrci had to blink her eyes quick. Or maybe that was from the sense that they were both safe out here: She'd done it. She'd gotten free of not just Remis, but her sire.

"Come, come." Crawie stepped back and motioned into the homey living room. "I prepared the spare guest room for your friend, as you requested."

Although given the twinkle in her eye, she knew that "friend" was a loose term of art.

"Thank you, ma'am," he said as he squeezed through the door with the two bags.

Walking in the main living area, Mahrci looked around with fresh eyes, and hoped that Hemmy liked the cottage style. She and Crawie had decorated the whole place together over the last year, picking up comfy sofas and chairs, folksy art and rugs, and hand-made furniture from some humans who still lived as they had centuries ago.

As Mahrci entered the kitchen, she frowned at the purse and coat that were on the table.

"Oh, that's right," she said. "It's bingo night."

"It is. I shall be back in about three hours." Crawie pulled on her red-and-cream wool coat. "I left plenty of food in the refrigerator. Do help yourselves—and, Mayhem, I must say, I've heard only good things about you. I look forward to sharing Last Meal and learning more firsthand."

He bowed at the waist again. "Ma'am, I can't wait."

"And you know, it's nice to have a male in the house—it makes one feel safer, and I shall not apologize for my old-fashioned beliefs." Crawie gave Mahrci another hug—and this one lingered. "Are you well enough?"

"Yes, *mahmen.*"

As the older female pulled back, there was a gloss of tears on her eyes, too. Then she put her hand on Mahrci's cheek. "It's going to be fine."

Is it, she wondered. She wasn't totally sure, although this was an important first step.

On the way to the exit, Crawie paused. "Oh, and I taped all your game shows. I wasn't sure whether or not you'd had a chance to watch them."

"Oh, I haven't! Thank you."

The older female raised a hand, and then departed. After which . . .

Mahrci looked at Hemmy. "She is everything to me. *Everything.*"

"I can see that, and it makes me happy. You need someone like her in your life." He frowned. "But— taping shows? Does anybody do that anymore?"

"Oh, she takes that job very seriously. She has backup VCRs for parts, and a closet full of blank tapes she got off eBay. She doesn't want to learn any new technology. Says there's no room in her brain for it—and when you have her chicken pot pie, you won't want any of her memory replaced with how to work streaming services."

Hemmy laughed. "Sounds good. And you like game shows?"

"Oh, I do! I love a good puzzle, especially the word-search kinds like *Wheel of Fortune.* Come on, let me show you to our"—she winked at him—"*your* room."

The door to the basement stairs was not far— because nothing was far in the little barn. And at the bottom, there were three bedrooms: a primary suite, which Crawie had always refused to sleep in, and then on the far side of the living area two others that shared a bathroom.

Mahrci hesitated in front of the door to the suite.

Then she looked up at Hemmy.

That was all it took.

No telling who kissed who first. But they squeezed through the narrow doorway together, the duffle bags grabbing on to the jamb until Hemmy dropped them both. The next thing she knew, he was dragging the luggage in with his foot and then bumping the door closed with his hip.

Over to the bed. On the bed. He was on top.

She went for his pants. He went for hers.

And then came The Great Shoewear Debacle.

The entanglements were epic because of their impatience, and they were both laughing as they tried to get each other's laces undone.

Screw what they were wearing on top. When the pants were off on both sides, with his boots and her trail shoes kicked all over the floor, she pulled him back onto her. Arching up, she split her legs and reached down—but he was already there with his touch.

As she met him in the eyes, it came out, even though it probably would have been better to keep it to herself, given how early it was.

But at least he also said the words:

"I think I love you—"

"I know I love you—"

They both laughed as she got a little teary. And then he became very serious. "I know this is spur-of-the-moment, Mahrci. I know . . . I know all the reasons I should hold back. But I go with the flow—and you are who and what I want."

Mahrci stroked his face, a brilliant flare of happiness making her feel incandescent. Except then everything that was really going on nearly wrecked her.

"We need to talk," she said gravely. "Before you—"

"If you think there is anything that will change my mind about you, you're wrong. I'm here, I'm down for whatever, and I'm serious about staying. I can handle myself, I'm not scared of anyone or anything . . . and I've spent a lifetime looking for you, even though I didn't know your name or your face."

"B-but—but—"

"No buts. If you feel differently, fine. That's okay. But there's nothing you need to tell me on my side."

With sadness, she exhaled. "You don't know what you're saying."

"Yeah, I do. I've lived through prison. For fifty years." He assumed a wry expression. "Although honestly, that's just because I had nothing else to do and I thought it would be a fun challenge to see if I could survive it."

Now she blinked for a different reason. "I'm sorry—you just . . . went to prison?"

"Yeah, the bakery was getting a little boring. I figured I'd spice things up, so I just walked on in. Think of it as adventure tourism at its best. That's how I met Apex."

"You . . . well, I'm a little bit surprised. But better than you being a criminal."

"You know, that's what everybody says. And it's the God's honest. Just ask Apex."

"I suppose you have seen a lot of . . . things."

"When I tell you I can handle myself, I'm quite serious." He shook his head. "But we can stop talking about that. Let's stick with four-letter words that start with *L*."

She took a deep breath. "I won't hold you to this. You know, if you wake up tomorrow night and we've had sex twelve different ways—"

"Made love." He slipped his hand under her shirt and kept it on her stomach. "This is not sex, at least not for me."

"Me, neither."

"And I accept your doubts, but I'm a bonded

male—it happened quick, just like they always said it would. So I'm just going to hold us together until you find the faith in who we are. Take your time. I'm good."

"I really think I love you," she whispered.

"And we're going to keep talking—afterward."

"Afterward, yes," she said as he started to kiss her again.

There was more unclothing, and then he was running his lips down the side of her throat, and onto her breasts. Arching up into his mouth, she moved her hands into the long hair at his nape.

"Now . . . I know . . ." she gasped, "what mullets are for—"

As she gripped those blond waves, the joining was everything she had ever wanted, deep and complete. And as they started moving together, she did what he had taught her worked best. She went with the flow.

Which in their case, was another word . . .

For true love.

CHAPTER THIRTY–SEVEN

Of course everything was done right.

As soon as Apex had fired up the security system, all feeds were a go—and the images and sound were routed to the three places he'd requested. No problems, no delays. No malfunctions.

Which was why he'd brought Mayhem on to the project, he thought as he left the big house an hour later.

The male could drive a person up a wall, but his tech skills were unparalleled.

Although fine, maybe Apex himself was a little on the touchy side.

As he followed the footsteps he'd made before, he was aware of a heavy weight on him. The windows were still dark on the second floor of the garage, and he imagined that Callum had already left when his proverbial back was turned.

Just like before.

Would it be another thirty years before their paths crossed again? He couldn't say he had a lot of hope.

Going around the truck and the disengaged plow, he opened the garage's side door, and the motion-activated light in the stairwell came on. He stared up the steps. Before he'd come over here, he'd put his duffle by the front door of the big house. Repacking hadn't been hard. He'd never unpacked. No sleeping, either.

He had brushed his teeth.

Maybe he should be the one who just left? It was a good theory to try out, but come on. He didn't have it in him—

The muffled shout was the kind of thing he wasn't sure whether he heard in real time or imagined because he was, as usual, back in a past that had become his own because of who he loved, not because he'd lived through the trauma himself.

When the sound was repeated, he was hit with a cold wash of panic. Taking the stairs up two at a time, he burst through the door—

The hoarse moan of pain was coming from the bed, and with the door open, there was just enough light to see the wolven thrashing in the sheets: He was naked now, and for a split second, Apex was convinced that *symphath* had come over to give some more "advice."

God, Callum's body was beautiful—

But the ragged curse that rose up was *not* about pleasure.

"*Callum*," he said as he rushed over. "Wake up, wake up—"

Another hoarse shout hit the air, and then Callum jacked upright on his hips, his white-rimmed, terrified eyes fixating over Apex's shoulder, his chest pumping up and down, his arms straining as he held on to the covers.

"Callum." Apex stroked the wolven's shoulder. "It's okay, you're safe—"

"Apex?"

He moved his face into the light flowing in from the stairwell. "Yes, it's me. Look at me—that's right. That's good. You're not back there. You're with me and we're safe, at your place."

"Oh, God . . ." Callum closed his eyes. "I can't do this anymore. I can't live like this any—"

"Just take a deep breath. Breathe with—"

"*Fuck me.*" The wolven grabbed on to Apex's arms. "I need you to fuck me—*fuck me!*"

It was the last thing he expected, and Apex split in half in that moment: One part of him was an absolute no. He was not having sex with the male he loved for the first time like this, in this desperate, frantic confusion.

The other part of him, who had waited so long, instantly hardened.

And then Callum started kissing him, that mouth seeking Apex's and plying, begging, talking even as his tongue licked out.

"Fuck me, I need you to fuck me . . ."

Over and over, he repeated the hoarse plea against Apex's lips—until he broke the contact, undid Apex's pants, and then rolled over so he was facedown. Looking around his shoulder, he was babbling while he arched his back and offered his ass.

"Fuck me," he begged through tears. "You've got to fuck her out of me. Please—just fuck me—"

He reached back and pulled Apex forward. On top of him.

As soon as the weight seemed to register, the moan sounded different. Or Apex told himself it did. Who knew—

Callum opened his legs, and Apex's cock fell in between like it knew what it needed to do. What its job was. What it was being used for, born for.

Licking his hand, Apex reached in between their bodies, and then he was finding—

The groan that came out of the wolven was ragged. "*Fuck me.*"

Something snapped as the penetration happened. In both of them.

Instantly, the rhythm was unhinged, Apex letting his hips loose to the point where he had to hold on to the iron slats of the headboard for leverage. With the bed banging, and Callum grunting, and their bodies moving together, Apex stared at the wall.

In the midst of all the passion, he died inside.

Even as they both orgasmed at the same time.

CHAPTER THIRTY-EIGHT

No, you can't bring a clawhammer, either," Tohr muttered as he went to Vishous's glass door to leave. "You have to fucking chill if you're coming to Whestmorel's."

"Fine. And as long as he behaves himself, I'll behave myself, true?" V's diamond eyes shifted over to his monitors. "Let me just sign out of—"

As the brother frowned and went silent, Tohr gave him a minute. Like . . . a whole frickin' minute. "V? What's going on?"

When there was no response, he raised his voice at the brother: "What's happening?"

Okay, see, here was the problem with V. After all these centuries together, fighting in the war, keeping

Wrath alive, getting through disasters and deaths that could not be borne, Tohr had seen this expression on the guy before—and it had never, *ever* been associated with good things.

"Vishous, son of the Bloodletter," he snapped, "my nerves are fucking shot after the last two nights—"

"I don't know what I'm looking at."

Going around behind the desk, Tohr frowned. Then leaned forward—like that was going to do anything.

"What the hell is that?" he murmured.

On one of the massive screens, there was a composite image of . . . two-inch-by-two-inch tiles. And each one of them appeared to be a snapshot of a different part of a house that was—

"Jesus, could they use any more bark on shit," V remarked. "And what's with all the frickin' animal heads."

"Have you ever seen this before? This house?"

"Nope. I mean, it kind of looks like Rehv's place up on Lake George. Same era, but . . . not it." Vishous highlighted one of the little images and enlarged it, a study with a desk and shelves of books coming into better view. "What's with all the duffle bags? And I think there's sound—"

From out of the speakers, there was the subtle *whirr* of a heater.

"Why are you seeing this?" Tohr asked.

"Don't know. It's a pirate feed, routed through an external source that appears to be syncing with my cell phone number and getting forwarded here. Sophisticated stuff. I'm kind of impressed."

Moving his mouse around, V clicked on random views, and each time, they got new rooms and different background noise.

"Nice kitchen," Tohr murmured. Then he reached over the brother's shoulder and pointed to an image in the center. "Try that one—I mean, can you make it bigger—"

On cue, the view of a bedroom took up almost all of the screen.

V kept clicking around, more close-ups called to the fore. "Yeah, this is some kind of storage platform for security feeds, but I don't know why I have permission—"

"Hey, click down there. Someone's coming in—"

V was already on it. As he called up that tile, the tone coming through the speakers changed, but there wasn't any clear conversation. The males who were entering the home were speaking so softly, not much carried.

"Nice hoodies," V muttered. "That hide their fucking faces."

"Are we watching a robbery here?"

"It's not a burglary. No B&E."

Four of the intruders were in those black sweatshirts with the hoods, but there was also a guy in a suit, who seemed to know his way around.

"I don't recognize him, do you?" Tohr asked.

"Nope. But I'm screenshotting the close-up as we speak."

V continued to follow the group's progress through the house, clicking on tiles.

"They're not there to rob the place," Tohr said.

"No, they're on the premises to do some damage to someone, and they're looking for whoever it is."

As the group came together again in the front hall, the guy in the suit started pointing all around. One by one, the males took cover, sheltering themselves . . . and waiting.

Rubbing his eyes, Tohr braced a hip on the desk edge and felt sorry for whoever was going to walk into the attack.

"Fucking hell," V said as he lit a hand-rolled. "This is Big Brother, in a bad way . . ."

CHAPTER THIRTY-NINE

As Callum lay under Apex's too-still body, he turned his face to the side and tried to catch his breath. Deep inside of him, the vampire's cock was twitching in the aftermath of a violent orgasm. It had been the same for Callum. He'd come so hard, he'd thought his skull was going to explode. And now that the storm was over . . . he knew it had been wrong.

In the silence, he was very aware that a line had been crossed. It was obvious even before Apex stiffly retracted himself, got off the end of the bed, and did up his pants. While saying absolutely nothing.

It was the first time Apex didn't ask him if he was okay.

Because Apex wasn't okay.

Looking over his shoulder, Callum felt a piercing pain in the center of his chest. Especially as Apex stared at the open door to the stairway with the kind of haunted expression Callum had seen in his own mirror every night.

"I'm sorry," Callum said in a voice that cracked. "I shouldn't have done that."

"It's okay," came the dead response.

No, it wasn't. It was as if he'd infected the other male with his . . . everything.

"I'm going to go now." Apex finally glanced over. "I just . . . need to go now."

Rolling onto his back, Callum pulled the duvet across to cover his nakedness and sat up. "Thank you."

Apex closed his eyes. "Don't say that. Not after . . . whatever that was."

"Not for the sex. For . . . everything else."

The vampire just walked over to the door. Hell, he'd already left, and who could blame him. Callum had used him like an exorcist, to banish a demon it was up to himself to get rid of. Damned if he knew how, though—and in his lost, fumbling way, he was very aware, deep down in his soul, that he had ruined something beautiful.

Apex said something that didn't carry, and then the male was disappearing down the steps.

"I'm sorry," Callum repeated loudly.

There was no response to that.

As the door shut below, he closed his eyes. For once, the darkness didn't bring that female to his mind. Instead, he saw those fragile flowers his vampire had brought him, all those years ago.

He'd managed to kill it all. He really had.

Getting out of bed, he stubbed his toe on the open suitcase, and all he could do was just stand there and think about what he was going to put in it. There wasn't much because he didn't have much. Just a couple of shirts, some pants and socks. No underwear. Two pairs of boots.

He had nothing of real value. Maybe he should just ditch it all, and leave it for the next groundskeeper to pick through.

In a sad daze, he descended the stairwell naked. He could still smell Apex's sexual arousal—it was on his own skin, inside of him, in between his legs. When he got to the narrow footer at the bottom, he started his change as he opened the side door.

So that as he emerged, he was on all fours.

Letting his wolf go, he watched from the back of their combined consciousness as his animal side took him away, far, far away. It was a relief to just give up—

even though he knew where his wolf was taking him because they'd always communicated on a base level. It was how the beast had known to protect Mahrci, to make sure those coyotes got good and gone. And how it had not hurt Apex or Mayhem.

And why it had been aware that it was important to stay with Apex when the male had been talking out on the front porch. About the life the male had imagined for them.

Yes, he even liked Wheaties, Callum thought.

Why had he lied about hearing all that?

Probably because at the time it had been too much closeness.

Oh, God, what had he done.

At least his wolf was taking him away so he could do no more damage: They were going back to where he had begun, where he had been born and raised. Back to Deer Mountain, and the cave with the hot spring that had at one point been his home.

Far, far away, from the vampire who had loved him more than he deserved.

Never to return.

CHAPTER FORTY

Oh, great. The douchebag was back.

As Apex passed the bumper of that gray BMW, the last person on the planet he wanted to deal with was Mahrci's ex. But hey, the night was determined to be god-awful, so why not?

Pyrocant, he believed was the right word. Someone or something that was bound to destroy you.

Every time he thought he'd reached another low with the wolven? There was something even shittier revealed. And now? There was just fuck all left of him. He was utterly hollow as he went up the steps to the porch, and entered the big house. Kicking the door shut, he looked past the duffle bag he'd left by the exit, to the empty ones still in the study. Quite a collection, but as Mayhem would have said, at least they were in order.

The idea of taking all of them back to Caldwell in that SUV required way more energy than he had. Like the vehicle, he was just going to leave them.

Whestmorel could deal with it all when he came up here the night after next.

On that note, Apex glanced up at the security unit mounted on the ceiling.

Yup, he was quitting, too. He'd done what he'd set out to do, and now it was time for the chips to fall where they did. At least he could have the satisfaction of knowing that he'd—

"Where is he?"

At the sound of the male voice, Apex looked over to the hearth. Remis was standing by the thing, one foot up on the ledge where people sat to warm themselves, his gray suit jacket unbuttoned, the bruising on his face starting to swell already.

"Where's who," Apex asked.

"Your friend." The aristocrat put his foot down. "The one who assaulted me."

"He's not here." Man, he was so bored of all this shit. "He left."

"Where did he go?"

"He left, that's all I know. He's a drifter, so no, I don't know where he lives, but I have his phone number, and you're welcome to it. Whatever the hell went on between the two of you has nothing to do with me."

"That's where you're wrong."

Apex picked up his duffle. "We don't need to have a problem, you and me."

"It's a little late for that—"

"Let me stop you, before you hurt yourself." He pointed around the ceiling. "You know how much your boss, Whestmorel, hates distractions—and you ending up on life support because you do something stupid with me right now is the worst kind. It's expensive, and carries a long recovery, so it comes with a delay."

Not that that aristocrat's nights weren't numbered already.

Remis sauntered over, putting one loafer in front of the other in an S-curve, like he was a supermodel. Man, that left eye was bloodshot. Maybe because the doorknob got him in the socket.

"Tell me where your friend is, and you're free to go."

"I'm free to go anyway."

"No, you're not."

Well, maybe it wouldn't be that bad to use this fuck-

ing idiot for a punching bag, Apex thought as he put the bag down again.

Or he could just put a cap in the idiot's brain right here and now and be on his w—

The blow to the back of his head came from out of nowhere.

As the floor rushed up to meet him, he thought, *Sonofabitch. This is going to hurt . . .*

And the last thing he saw were all those animal heads, the glass eyes staring at him as if they were welcoming him to the club of dead things in the house.

"Callum," he said hoarsely as he passed out.

CHAPTER FORTY-ONE

It was just after dawn when Mayhem pushed his chair back from the kitchen table so he could cross his legs and drum a beat on his thigh. Between him and Mahrci, there was a half-eaten pecan pie, three plates smeared with pie streaks and melted vanilla ice cream, and three cups with a quarter of an inch of cold coffee in the bottom of them.

Crawie, who he'd totally fallen in love with, had gone to bed about twenty minutes ago.

And yes, it had been the best chicken pot pie he'd ever had.

Too bad his stomach was grinding like everything had been spoiled.

"So you see," Mahrci concluded, "this is very messy. The whole thing."

Mayhem stopped tapping his fingertips and rubbed his eyes. He never got headaches. He had one now. A real humdinger.

"Let me get this straight," he heard himself say. "Your sire is about to declare war on both the Black Dagger Brotherhood and Wrath, the great Blind King. He, ah, he has a consortium of aristocrats behind him, and you think—you think they're arming themselves and preparing for an insurrection that will topple the throne and elect your father as some kind of president?"

"Yes." She took a deep breath. "I started to get suspicious about a year ago, when he began pushing me to be with Remis and get mated. He'd never particularly cared one way or the other about me or who I was with—and I've always known why."

"Why," he prompted.

"I think my *mahmen* was already pregnant with me, by someone else, when they got mated. She was very beautiful, a perfect status symbol for a male who was on the rise, and if I'd been a boy, maybe things might have been different. Her later dying on the birthing bed with their blooded son had not been part of Whestmorel's plan, and I think he only kept me as potential leverage for later. On my side, I knew I didn't belong anywhere in the world, and I had no one but Crawie, so I always tried to stay in his good graces. One night, about a month ago . . . I overheard him and Remis talking about buying guns? And then this male named Broadius started coming around our house."

She shook her head. "My father knew if Remis mated me, the male was locked in. He does this to people. That's why he had Apex install all those cameras. He's pulling the aristocrats together for a meeting at the Adirondack house, and he's going to record everything so he can make sure there are no cracks in the consortium. If he has these males on tape prepared to commit treason? He's got them for life. They try to get out and all he has to do is threaten to expose them."

Mayhem frowned. "Is Apex . . . involved in all this shit?"

"I don't know. You'd have to ask him. He's been my father's head of security for about two years now. I mean, I'm on the periphery and I found out about it. I'd find it hard to believe that male doesn't know and isn't working on all of it."

His first thought was that that wasn't the Apex he

knew. Overthrowing the fucking King? Come on. But it had been a long time since he'd seen the guy. Maybe things had changed.

Also, how close had they been anyway?

"Apex does the legitimate security," she tacked on. "Remis is the other side, in spite of how he tries to make himself look like a gentlemale. That's why I worry about you."

"Yeah, he's still not a problem." Mayhem sat back again because he didn't know what the hell to do with himself. "And you tried to tip off the Brotherhood?"

"Yes. I asked Crawie—and I probably shouldn't have—to sneak these papers to them. I had her go to the Audience House on a pretense and leave them behind." The female looked down at the pie. "My father's forgotten about her. He has no idea I've been supporting her all these years or that I bought this house. He has no clue where I am now—and he's not going to care. The idea that somebody like me could take down somebody like him? Unfathomable."

"What are the papers you turned in?"

"I found them in the trash. They were supposed to have been shredded. I think they're contributions for weapons, but my father isn't dumb. The data is blinded—so I don't know who the people are, and really I'm just guessing it all has something to do with the payments for guns that they were talking about." She drew her dark hair back. Let it fall down on her shoulders. "And I just wanted to signal the Brotherhood about my sire somehow so I made up this page of numbers. As I told you, I've always liked puzzles and stuff—it's the *Wheel of Fortune*, right? Anyway, I figured someone over there would be smart enough to decode the name."

A sudden surge of aggression had his fangs tingling. "And Remis and your father don't suspect you?"

There was a long silence, and he knew she was trying to keep her emotions in check. So he reached out and took her hand.

"No, I've never mattered enough to be considered a threat to them," she said roughly. "I broke up with Remis and then told Crawie to take the papers to the Audience House. I went up to Camp Ghreylke just long enough to make sure she was okay, that nothing came of her going to the Brotherhood. I figured I could call my father and Remis to me if something went wrong. If I'm in trouble, fine. Her, I will always protect."

"Then Apex and I arrived."

"And into the belly of the beast we all went."

"Jesus," he said, not for the first time. "So that was

why Apex didn't tell me shit about the job. It's a fucking treason plot."

With a feeling of dread, he put a hand into his ass pocket and took out the burner phone he used. But what kind of conversation could he have with the guy?

"You're calling Apex?" she said.

"I need to know." He held up the phone. "I gotta see what he says—and then I'm going to the Brotherhood. I'm not going to be involved in this kind of shady shit, no fucking way. And I ultimately control those security feeds. I can give them access."

"You can't tell Apex—or even the Brotherhood— where you are. I'm sorry, but I don't know who to trust."

"Oh, I'll keep my location a secret." He cleared his throat. "I'm not sure I can trust him, either."

As he hit send on the male's number, he got a series of rings. And then the anonymous voicemail. He ended the call.

"He didn't pick up."

Mahrci shook her head. "I'm sorry. Maybe he's . . ."

"All along he refused to tell me anything about what we were doing—"

His phone started ringing, and he immediately answered. "What the fuck is going on."

There was a chuckle. "Mayhem? Is that your name?"

Rising to his feet, he said, "Remis? What the fuck are you doing?"

"Looking for you. I mean, I found someone. But he's not you—although he is remarkably loyal to you. You can't believe what I've been doing to him, and he still won't tell me where you are—"

Mayhem pegged Mahrci with hard eyes and put his forefinger to his lips, all *shhhh.*

"—no matter what I do to him."

"You want me." Mayhem stalked around the kitchen, his fangs fully descending. "You can have me. Leave Apex alone."

"Well, at this point, there isn't much left of him, soooooo—"

"I'll come to you. At nightfall. But if he's dead—"

"What are you going to do," the male cut in with a bored tone.

"I'm going to disappear on you. And where's the fun in that? Don't hurt him anymore or you don't get me."

Mayhem ended the call and collapsed back down into his chair.

"Oh, my God," Mahrci said. "What's—"

Hopping back up to his feet, he ran down into the basement, where their duffle bags were. Rummaging through his own, he found his personal laptop, the one that he'd encrypted so completely that it might as well be in outer fucking space.

Signing in, he accessed the program controlling all those security units he and Apex had installed. The other male's instructions had been clear: The feeds were supposed to go to three different places, Apex's number and two others he hadn't recognized, at least one of which had to be Whestmorel's.

But thanks to a back door he'd created, he'd added a secret fourth, his own. Because . . . well, maybe his sniff test had been a little whiffy—

"Oh, fuck," he breathed as he looked at the live feed from the great room.

"What is it," Mahrci said as she came around the corner.

"Stop," he ordered in a voice that cracked. "I don't want you to see this—"

She fucked him right off and looked over his shoulder at the screen . . . at the picture of Apex tied to a chair, his face so bloody, the only way he could be ID'd was from his clothes.

"Oh, God," she moaned as she wrenched away.

Mayhem slapped the laptop closed. "I'm going to fucking kill Remis. I'm going to fucking kill him at nightfall."

"I'm coming with you—"

"The fuck you are—"

"I know the secret way in." She crossed her arms over her chest. "And you're going to want the element of surprise. There were four males in the background, and the last thing you need is for them to kill him because they know you're in the house."

Tragically, she was right.

And between one blink and the next, all Mayhem could see were those animal heads, staring down at his old friend.

With their vacant glass eyes.

CHAPTER FORTY-TWO

At some point, pain wore out its receptors.

If you had enough of it, either your brain or your body itself just hit the dimmer switch and things receded. The reprieve was never permanent, but when it happened, you were so damned glad, you didn't care.

Apex had learned this over the last thirty years. When he'd been mourning Callum.

Unfortunately, his current respite was over: He could tell because it was dawning on him that his neck hurt. Kind of silly, really. His face and his upper torso had taken the brunt of the beatings. Then again, his head had been lolling on his shoulder for how long now?

When he went to open his eyes, he was careful not

to move much because he didn't know whether he was alone. No doubt Remis had tucked himself in downstairs so he could get his beauty sleep for the day—

Whrrrrrrrrrrrrrrr.

What the hell was that sound—oh. The shutters. It must be nightfall.

Back to the eyeball-opening thing. Fantastic, one was so swollen shut, he couldn't budge it.

"—tonight. No, tomorrow is better. I'm making sure everything is prepared—yes, I know you want to meet as soon as possible, but we need to clean up loose ends—"

Remis's voice. Like he was on the phone.

"—and do this the right way. I need one more night. I'm sorry. You don't want complications? Well, I'm making sure we don't have any of them. They both did work on the security system so it's best we cut those risks." Footsteps. Coming closer. "You always told me, patience wins the battle and the war. So let me do what we agreed needed to be done." The male stopped right in front of him. "Yes. Of course. No, there won't be anything left. The sun is the best cleanup we have. Yes. Right. Yes, I will. Goodbye."

Apex was careful to keep breathing slowly, in and out.

"I know you're awake."

A moment later, Apex's head was repositioned and Remis was right there, eye to eye. "I have to say, you're impressive. Fortunately, your friend Mayhem called your phone—I'm pretty sure you don't remember giving me your code. It was the only piece of information you did give up. Anyway. I'm just keeping you alive until he arrives—"

"Leave him . . ." Holy fuck, was that his voice? ". . . alone."

"Sorry, he picked on me first. Isn't that the way the young say it? And I'm going to finish it."

"Leave—"

The slap came from the left and there was good follow-through with it, a spool of blood releasing from Apex's mouth. And hey, now his head was lying on his other shoulder, so all those tense muscles were stretching out. Bonus.

Meanwhile, he just let himself float off on the pain cloud. In the background, he was vaguely aware of Remis posturing and the four brass-knucklers he'd brought with him standing around, like a rugby team getting coached.

Apex was pretty sure he was hit again. A couple of

times. Until he was just drooling blood on his fleece. Again.

It was okay. He wasn't making it out of this alive, and that was all right. He'd been done as of last night anyway. The only thing he was really worried about was Mayhem, and dear God, he hoped like hell that that female didn't insist on coming with him.

Mostly, he hoped that the Black Dagger Brother Vishous got the feed from this house.

He was going to die in this chair, but if the Brotherhood could just get here in time to save the other two—

Wait, there was one more thing he had to do.

"Remis," he croaked.

"Oh, you're back." The male got down on his level again. "You know, that eye doesn't look very good—"

"I killed your boy."

One brow lifted in arrogance. "Excuse me?"

Apex took a deep breath. "Broadius . . ." The name came out as barely more than a hiss, so he put more into the name. "Broadius. I killed him."

Forcing his head to level, he looked up at the camera that he'd mounted to the right of the hearth. Little could he have known what it would be filming. But hey, if they were going to kill him, he needed to make sure the aristocrats didn't do something jinky and pin that hit on someone else. Apex knew firsthand the *glymera* had a long history of making up shit to engineer results. The whole prison camp had been stocked with the victims of their agendas.

"Go . . . get my duffle." He stared at the camera. As if he could will the Brothers to come. "By the front door. I'll . . . prove it."

Remis barked a command. A moment later, one of the guys in the hoodies brought the bag over.

"Open . . ."

"Well, fucking unzip it," Remis demanded to his goon. "Do it—"

Hoodie did the duty—and pulled out the white parka and snow pants Apex had been wearing the night he'd broken into Broadius's tacky fucking McMansion, disarmed the security system with the code he himself had set when he'd installed it, and snuck up the stairs, finding the bitch in his dressing room.

"Stripe of . . . blood on the sleeve."

Apex had deliberately laid the bastard out on his bed. 'Cuz you sleep where you lie. And in doing so, had got himself messed.

"Scent the blood . . . and there's also a gold cufflink and his phone. In the bottom."

Apex looked up at his camera with the eye that was working—and waited for the inevitable question.

"What the . . . hell are you thinking? Why are you fucking with us like this?" Remis breathed.

"I owe the Black Dagger Brotherhood," Apex said to the camera. "And I know what you're doing. Whestmorel and you are plotting against . . . the King. The Brothers liberated the prison camp . . . so I owe them and couldn't let you destroy them—"

Remis put his head in front of Apex's and then trained his sight at the same angle, right up at the monitoring unit.

Apex started laughing, even though it made him spit up even more blood. "Say . . . cheese, motherfucker. You're on *Candid Camera*—"

Remis yelled like someone had stabbed him in the back. Because . . . someone had.

And out came the gun.

As everything went slo-mo, that muzzle swinging around toward Apex's head, there was a sudden crashing, a splintering of glass—

As a great white wolf broke through the triple-paned window, took two tremendous leaps, and bit Remis in the face. The force of the attack was so vicious, it knocked the male over.

Unfortunately, the hoodies were also all armed. And they were somewhat trained.

Three aimed at the wolf.

One aimed at Apex.

"Callum!" he screamed. "Watch out!"

CHAPTER FORTY-THREE

With grim purpose, and a full complement of weapons, Tohr dematerialized to a historic Adirondack great camp that was bigger than the one Rehvenge had, and not on a lake. V had figured out which estate had been featured on the security feeds by doing image matching searches on the rooms during the day.

While the entire Brotherhood had watched Apex get tortured for information.

And what do you know, Whestmorel had bought the estate and all its acreage two years before.

As Tohr waited for his brothers to join him for the infiltration, he surveyed the house. The place was rambling and sided with a forest's worth of cedar shingles, and lights streamed from out of countless diamond-paned windows. Parked up close to the front porch, there was a gray BMW and a black Suburban—

Tohr was the first to see the wolf off to the left; it was coming in low and fast over the snow—but the predator wasn't focused on them. It was gunning for the house in a purposeful way that was not like a wild animal's at all.

A wolven? Like Lucan?

Something's going down, Tohr thought as another appeared. And another. And—

That first wolf threw itself at one of the front windows like it didn't know glass was a thing. And just as the crash sounded out, the shooting started—

"Are we too late," V said as he became corporeal, still staring at his phone screen. "Are—"

"We gotta get in there!" Tohr barked. "Now—"

As other brothers arrived, the two of them were already crossing the distance, while wolf after wolf threw themselves at the windows on the first floor. It was a Pella-nightmare, and he took advantage of the attack, jumping through one of the lupine-created apertures.

He landed with his forties up, and he picked off the male in the hoodie who was about to shoot Apex in the face, putting a bullet right through the side of the male's skull. While all that gray matter vaporized out of the exit wound, V aimed at another male, who was about to shoot the first wolf. The brother's weapon just discharged into thin air, though, because a second wolf got there before he did, the predator tackling the hooded assailant to the floor.

Two more left. Tohr pulled a quick pivot, squared his sight at the one taking cover behind half a bear that had been mounted like it was coming out of the wall. The first shot hit the grizzly.

The second entered the shooter's shoulder. As the male brought his gun around and aimed at Tohr, they had a moment of their eyes meeting. Then Tohr pulled his trigger a nanosecond before his foe did—

His gun jammed, the malfunction freezing the mechanism inside his autoloader, causing the next bullet in his chamber to stay right where it fucking was. Which meant a clean shot, from out of that muzzle pointed at his own high thoracic region, was taken.

Pop!

Tohr jerked and put his hands to his throat by reflex, bracing for the pain, knowing his bulletproof vest was too low to save him—

The shooter was the one who went down to his knees.

Behind the guy, Mayhem jumped out of a hidden compartment in the wall on the far side of the bear, a female right on his heels. They both had guns—and given the way the male looked over his shoulder in complete shock, it was clear she had been the one with the dead right aim.

After that, there was only silence, except for the heaving breathing and the dripping of blood.

And the chewing.

Like all skirmishes, it was over before it began, and there was a split second where Tohr and his brothers swept their gun muzzles around, in case there were more attackers coming. And the fact that he was able to recover his senses so fast from an almost-mortal event was the only benefit you got from having been shot at so many times: His brain was used to close calls.

But he knew he wasn't going to sleep right for a couple of days.

Meanwhile, across the way, Mayhem and the female lowered their weapons to the floor and put their hands up—

"You're fine," Tohr barked. "At ease."

Justlikethat, the wolves retreated, the predators ghosting out of the broken windows, disappearing into the wintery night. Except for one. The white predator who had made a meal out of Remis was still inside, standing over his prey.

"Clear the rest of the house," Tohr ordered Rhage as he took out his phone and headed grimly for Apex. Hitting send on a number he called all too often, the ring was answered immediately. "Jane, we need you—"

V bent over and picked up a suit of white snow clothes. Then he reached into a duffle and brought out something that gleamed gold in the light.

Apex, the male who by all rights should be dead, said, "I did it. I killed Broadius . . ."

"We know," V said as he unsheathed a black dagger and started cutting all kinds of zip ties. "I heard it all, on the feed you sent me."

And then Apex seemed to pass out—or maybe that was his death confession.

Meanwhile, that white wolf wheeled around and leaped over two dead bodies to get to the male.

The great predator whimpered and nudged at Apex's arm. Then he lay down, and a set of ice-blue eyes looked over at Tohr, begging for help.

"It's on the way," he told the animal. "We're going to take care of him."

If he lives, Tohr tacked on to himself.

CHAPTER FORTY–FOUR

The first thing Apex smelled was a flower.

In the dense darkness of all his wounds, he couldn't identify what kind of rose it was, or even where it was around him. But he knew that someone had brought him . . . a rose.

Opening his lids was like lifting a car, but he was so compelled to answer the mystery of where he was and why—

"It's . . . you," he croaked.

Callum was sitting at whatever bedside this was, right beside him. And as the wolven came to attention, those gleaming, husky eyes were luminous with un-shed tears as they locked on his own.

Or rather, the one that he was able to see out of.

"You're awake." As Callum took his hand, that touch, that connection, did more for him than any drug ever could. "You're back."

Apex tried to nod, but holy hell, his neck hurt. So he just said, "You brought me a rose?"

Callum moved to the side so that the bloom, in its slender vase, could be properly seen. It was not white. It was red. The color of . . .

"You remembered that I liked white flowers," the wolven said roughly. "So when I went to the florist's for you, I thought . . . what would he like. What flower would he choose, this vampire . . . of mine."

That was when he saw the others. There were yellow daffodils, and blue something-or-others, and pink sprays. All in little slender vases.

"Beautiful," Apex wheezed. Although he wasn't sure whether he was talking about the buds . . . or the male. "Where am I?"

"The Brotherhood's training center. The clinic there."

Apex looked around, seeing all kinds of medical equipment surrounding a hospital bed. Very nice sheets, smooth and soft, had been folded over his bare chest, and the pillows under his head registered as quite luxurious.

"How long . . ."

"Three nights." Callum ran his thumb back and forth over Apex's inner wrist. "And it's going to be a while before you can be safely released."

"Were you here—"

"The whole time." Callum stifled a sob. "And I'm not leaving unless you tell me to—"

"Never."

"You don't have to say that."

"I know." Apex tried to sit up, and couldn't manage it, so he just slumped back down on all the very nice bedding. "Why did you come back to the big house? How did you . . . know?"

He was never going to forget the sight of that wolf crashing through that window at just the right time— and going after Remis like the male was a meal he'd ordered for takeout.

Callum sniffled and wiped his eyes. "Are you sure you want to go through all this now—"

"I need to know. It was . . . too close. It was almost . . . over for me."

There was a moment as the wolven seemed to

gather himself. "Well, Mayhem got in touch with Lucan—it took him almost all that day to reach my cousin, and Lucan happened to be in my cave when they finally connected. When I left after you and I . . . after I made that unforgivable mistake, I found my cousin . . . and we talked. All day long. I just . . . kept talking about it all, and getting things more sorted in my head. It wasn't until the sun had set that Lucan finally checked his phone and got the message you were in serious trouble. We arrived there right as the Brotherhood did."

"You came for me . . ."

"You've always been there for me. Always. Even when I didn't deserve it. How could I not do the same for you?"

Apex had to look away. Pain that had nothing to do with the physical, and everything to do with the soul, racked him, even through all the drugs that were being pumped in through his IV.

Leaning forward, Callum brushed Apex's face. "I'm so sorry. For what happened. I was desperate, floundering . . . I'm learning that this healing business is nearly as violent as the trauma itself."

It would have been nice to take a deep breath. But

that was a no go. Even with his healing capabilities, which were so much better than, say, a human's, Apex knew he was in critical condition.

And that was before you added a broken heart—

"I didn't want our first time to be . . . that," Callum whispered. "And I'm going to regret that for the rest of my life. But what I'm not going to do is stop trying to get free of what was done to me. I realized, as I sat up on that mountain and stared out at the valley far, far below, that if I don't fight for me . . ."

His voice caught and he cleared his throat. "If I don't fight for me, I can't fight . . . for *us*."

Apex's eyes shot back to the wolven. Callum's expression was grim, but intense, his inner conviction such that he appeared to glow with some kind of aura.

"I'm going to sort myself out. I'm not letting her win. This is going to be an ugly fight, Apex, and it's not going to be linear. But you've given me the will to want *me* back."

All at once, the world got wavy, and as Apex felt a hot tear sear his cheek, Callum reached out and brushed the wetness away.

"She's cost me all those years," the wolven said roughly. "I can't get them back . . . but if by some miracle, you'll give me another chance, one last chance—

I want to eat Wheaties with you. Every sunset of every night, for however long we live."

Apex exhaled. "You . . . did hear me."

"Yes, I did." Those beautiful husky eyes lowered. "It was too much for me to take in. I'm so fucking broken, Apex. And I'm saying that not for your pity, but because it's the truth. I'm not a good bet, I know, and this is going to be a long, hard walk back to the land of the living. I really am going to try, though—"

"I love you."

The wolven went utterly still. That stare lifted. "You don't have to say that."

Using all the strength he had, Apex moved his hand over and took the other male's. "You're the bravest person I know. And besides . . . I've hung on for this long. Why the hell would I get off . . . just before the dawn comes. I'm tougher than that—just like you're tougher than the past."

"I love you, too," Callum said hoarsely as he leaned over the bed. "And I'm going to win this, just so you know."

Apex smiled a little, even though it made his broken jaw hum. "Of course you will. And yes, I want to watch you eat Wheaties for the rest of my life. But I need you to know that I'm . . . more of a Cap'n Crunch guy."

They started laughing, at least until Apex groaned and had to stop.

And then came ... what Apex would forever after consider their first kiss.

It was far, far from their last.

The Brotherhood had cleared the whole mansion first, of course.

A week later, as Mahrci stood at the front door of the vast brick house she had grown up in, she looked through the grand entrance as if it were a place she had never been before: Even though she recognized the black-and-white marble floor, and the grandfather clock, and the oil painting of her mother through the arch into the parlor . . . the composite didn't resonate.

Then again, so much of everything had been a lie.

"You don't have to go in."

She glanced up at Mayhem. He was by her side, a silent, intense presence that was unwavering—even though she knew he didn't want her to be here. But she'd had to come. She needed to see this all for herself.

"Yes, I do," she whispered. "I have to go inside one last time—"

Down at the far end of the corridor, the flap door into the pantry opened, and the Black Dagger Brother Tohrment, the one with the navy blue eyes and the military haircut with the white stripe in front, emerged. His appearance was a welcome one. Though she had all she needed with Mayhem, the idea there were other people around made her a little less paranoid.

"Thanks for letting me come," she said as the warrior came up to them.

"Always. You're always welcome."

As the males greeted each other by clapping palms, she wandered into the dining room, remembering the meals she had eaten there with her father. And then there was the library, and his study, and . . . the parlor. When she came back to the base of the formal staircase, she looked toward the second floor.

"You can go up there, too," Tohrment said. "And take anything you want."

"Where is he," she whispered. Even though she knew the answer to that.

Her father, Whestmorel, had disappeared.

After the horrible scene at Camp Ghreylke had been stabilized, a group of Brothers had come here—and found the mansion, the guest house, and the garage uninhabited.

The male had taken the staff with him. And, from what she understood, all the computers in the house.

"We'll get him," the Brother said.

He didn't go any further than that. Then again, what was going to happen to her father after the Brotherhood took him into custody was going to be too grim to put into words.

Mayhem put a hand on her shoulder. "I'll go up with you?"

It was a while before she shook her head. And then she looked into his eyes. "I don't want anything from my room. I just . . . maybe it can all be given away, or something."

"Absolutely," Tohrment said. "Safe Place will take the clothing and shoes and provide them to females in need."

"Good. That's . . . good."

As a result of his treason, all of her father's possessions had been seized by the King, part of the provisions of the Old Laws. But she was quite sure the bank accounts had been emptied before he'd left—Whestmorel had been prepared for this, had no doubt been working for the moment when his plans became public and the Brotherhood went after him.

Her sire was now an enemy of the great Blind King. And though she felt no love for him, there was all kinds of dread for what he had brought upon himself.

With a shiver, she stepped into Mayhem's body and wrapped an arm around his waist. As she tilted her head, it came up against his pec, right on the spot that felt like home to her now.

He didn't tell her everything was going to be okay—because he never lied, and his rock-solid integrity, after all the falsities and schemes of her father, was among the traits she valued most in him. He just stood by her, strong and tall, steady as a mountain.

She trusted him completely. And that, along with Crawie's safety, was all she needed in life.

"Let's go." Mahrci took a deep breath. "Apex and Callum are due at our house in a half hour, and you wanted to help with setting the table."

As he nodded and brushed her mouth with a kiss, she felt a renewed sense of well-being. Focusing on the present was the way to deal with a past you otherwise couldn't live with. And Lassiter knew, it helped to have a mate who supported you with all their heart and soul.

"Keep in touch," Tohrment said. "Anything either of you need, we're here."

Mayhem smiled in a wry way. "Vishous has made the dubious decision to offer me a job. Guess he was impressed with my tinkering."

The Brother smiled. "I heard he was going to do that. You thinking it over?"

"Oh, I'm in." Hemmy glanced down at her. "Nothing we'd rather do than help the King."

"Yes," she echoed. "We're both committed to Wrath. One hundred percent."

Tohrment bowed at the waist, an honor that was not lost on her.

Funny, for however pretentious her father had been, he had never received such respect. And now, as a result of his quest for power, he was begging for the kind of attention that was going to guarantee him a cold grave.

But the consequences of treason were not the kind of fate you could get out of. Not when the Black Dagger Brotherhood was in charge.

Not when you went after Wrath, son of Wrath, sire of Wrath, the great Blind King.

"Let's go home, my love," she whispered.

"Anything you say," Hemmy responded. "And anywhere you want to go."

Way upstate, a good two-hundred-plus miles north of Caldwell, Apex re-formed before a storefront that, against all odds, was just as he'd remembered it to be. Thirty years later? What were the chances.

But, yup, the Bloomin' Buds Flower Shop was still in business.

The rest of the Connelly town square was pretty much the same, too. Couple of new businesses, but still the Christmas-card-perfect little town. There were even strands of lights and wreaths linking up the sidewalk lamps, and a big pine tree by the gazebo in the center of the public park was as yet still lit red and green and gold—

Next to him, Callum re-formed, and the second the wolven became corporeal, the two linked hands and tilted in for a kiss.

"So this is the place?" Callum asked as they eased back.

"Yes. Every night, I came here."

"Can we go inside?"

"Did you like all those white flowers?" the other one asked the wolven.

Callum spoke up. "Yes, ma'am. Yes, I did. White roses are my favorite. He prefers the red ones."

The woman glanced at her business partner. Then she doubled back, and drew one perfect bloom out of the bouquet.

She approached with the rose outstretched. "Here. Give this to him. On the house."

Callum accepted the gift, and stared at the old woman with soft eyes. "That is very kind of you." Then he turned to Apex. "For you, my love."

Apex took a deep breath, and thought . . .

Who knew reality could be better than the life he'd had to make up for them?

Because there was no way he could have cooked up this strangely perfect reunion in his own mind, back in the days when he had been playing pretend with the way they'd lived. In fact, everything that they were doing together now, the sex, the sleeping, the conversations—this moment right here—was just so much more than what he'd tried to create in his mind.

"Thank you," he said as he took the bloom, put it to his nose, and inhaled. "Oh, wow. That's beautiful."

Apex checked his watch. "Right before closing. Why not?"

They walked forward and Apex opened the door, a little bell ringing. The shop was twice the size it had once been and arranged differently, only the refrigerator unit in the same place. Now there were all kinds of cards, teacups, photo frames, and stuffed animals for sale . . . as well as snow globes, ornaments, baskets, and baby blankets . . . and of course, flowers.

"How can I help—"

As the female voice cut off, Apex looked toward the checkout. No cash register anymore, but a laptop. No more paper receipts. No more clutter.

But the woman standing next to a halfway-made arrangement of red roses was the same.

Well, almost the same. She had aged thirty years, her hair a white cap, her face lined, her hands craggy with veins and bones.

"It's . . . you," she whispered.

Apex glanced down at his black clothes, and thought of all the weapons on him. After everything that had happened at Camp Ghreylke, he wasn't about to be this far north without being armed—fuck it, he wasn't going unarmed anywhere. Not that he had ever really done that, at any rate.

"Yes," he replied. "It is."

Lifting his eyes back to the woman, he thought about how the noninterference rule between vampires and all the rats without tails was still very much in place. But he'd had to bring his love back here. It was part of them reclaiming their collective past.

They'd enjoyed a very nice Last Meal with that *symphath* the night before, for example. And were going back next week for another round of dinner and desensitization, as they called it.

So, yes, they'd had to come here—

Bing!

As the bell went off, the three of them looked over to the door. And as a woman stepped in, with a man behind her, it was another case of well-there-you-are: It was the other half of the "buds" part of the business, and Apex remembered how the woman had been so afraid of him last time. How she'd moved her purse closer to her, and had looked like she was about to hop on the phone to call the police.

"Hi," he said. Like he knew her.

"Hello . . ." she breathed as she looked him over.

She, too, had aged, her face wrinkled, her hair white as well. The man who was with her was the same, older and wizened, and Apex approved of the way he stepped

in close and put his arm around her: The protective impulse might have been made by an old man, but it was testament to the fact that though the exterior may have aged, the spirit remained alive.

"This is . . ." Apex stepped back and indicated Callum. "Who I was buying those flowers for."

The woman behind the counter came out, her expression shifting from shock to wonder. "All these years. I wondered what happened to you."

"Me, too," the other one said. "We always talked about you."

Apex nodded as he relinked his hand with Callum's. "It's been a long time. But I found him again. We just had to come here."

"You gonna introduce us?" the old man said.

The woman next to him nodded. "This is my husband, Ernie. And this is . . ."

"An old customer of the shop's," Apex supplied.

From what he remembered, she had been full of sorrow when he'd seen her. The sadness had been palpable.

But it wasn't there anymore.

"Guess fate was kind to both of us," he said roughly.

Tilting her head to the side, she reached for her mate's hand as well. "Yes, it was."

Just like his wolven was.

Just like ... their future was. For no matter what happened next, be it highs or lows, trials or triumphs, here or wherever they went ... they were together.

And that was all he had ever wanted.

ACKNOWLEDGMENTS

With so many thanks to the readers of the Black Dagger Brotherhood books! This has been a long, marvelous, exciting journey, and I can't wait to see what happens next in this world we all love. I'd also like to thank Meg Ruley, Rebecca Scherer and everyone at JRA, and Hannah Braaten, Carrie F@#*^ Feron, Jamie Selzer, Sarah Schlick, Jennifer Bergstrom, Jennifer Long, and the entire family at Gallery Books and Simon & Schuster.

To Team Waud, I love you all. Truly. And as always, everything I do is with love to and adoration for both my family of origin and of adoption.

Oh, and thank you to Naamah, my Writer Dog II, and Obie, Writer Dog-in-Training, and Bar-bar, who all work as hard as I do on my books!